KILL OR BE KILLED

I drew two beads from Marines on the roof of a three-story bank. I ran at them, launched into a *gozt*, and blasted the first woman off her perch. She tumbled to the ground, rebounding several times before her skin faded. In the meantime, the second woman spun and leveled her rifle on me as I rose and started for her.

"I don't have to kill you," she said.

"That's your job."

"Don't come any closer."

I did.

She fired.

The bead struck my skin, rebounded, and I was on her, knocking the rifle from her grip and withdrawing my Ka-Bar.

"You should have killed me," I said, then closed my eyes and punched her with the blade . . .

Also by Ben Weaver

BROTHERS IN ARMS

REBELS IN ARMS

BEN WEAVER

An Imprint of HarperCollinsPublishers

For Kendall and Lauren
Who remind me that we are all children . . .

EOS
An Imprint of HarperCollins*Publishers*
10 East 53rd Street
New York, New York 10022-5299

Copyright © 2002 by Ben Weaver
Excerpt from *Hammerfall* copyright © 2001 by C. J. Cherryh
Excerpt from *Rebels in Arms* copyright © 2002 by Ben Weaver
Excerpt from *Trapped* copyright © 2002 by James Alan Gardner
Excerpt from *Acorna's Search* copyright © 2001 by Hollywood.Com, Inc.
Excerpt from *The Mystic Rose* copyright © 2001 by Stephen R. Lawhead
ISBN: 0-06-000625-0
www.eosbooks.com

First Eos paperback printing: September 2002

Eos Trademark Reg. U.S. Pat. Off. And in Other Countries, Marca Registrada, Hecho en U.S.A.
HarperCollins® is a trademark of Harper Collins Publishers Inc.

Printed in the U.S.A

10 9 8 7 6 5 4 3 2 1

Acknowledgments

I'm indebted to Jennifer Brehl and Diana Gill at Eos for their support and encouragement. Without them, Captain Scott St. Andrew would have seen early retirement at the end of book one!

My agent, John Talbot, continues to inspire me with his keen wit and pragmatic advice regarding the publishing industry.

Finally, both Robert Drake and Caitlin Blasdell helped me create this series, and I know they're very proud of what we've accomplished.

The Seventeen System Guard Corps
Articles of the Code of Conduct
Revised 2301
(adopted from old United States Marine Corps Articles)

ARTICLE I

I will always remember that I am a Colonial citizen, fighting in the forces that preserve my world and our way of life. I have resigned to give my life in their defense.

ARTICLE II

I will never surrender of my own volition. If in command, I will never surrender the members of my command while they still have the will and/or the means to resist.

ARTICLE III

If I am captured, I will continue to resist by any and all means available. I will make every effort to escape and to aid others to escape. I will accept neither parole nor special favors from the enemy.

ARTICLE IV

If I become a prisoner of war, I will keep faith with my fellow prisoners. I will give no information nor take part in any action which might be harmful to fellow Colonial citizens. If I am senior, I will take command. If not, I will obey the lawful orders of those appointed over me and will uphold them in every way.

ARTICLE V

Should I become a prisoner of war, I am required to give name, rank, and willingly submit to retinal and DNA analysis. I will evade answering further questions to the utmost of my ability and will not consciously submit to cerebral scans of any kind. I will make no oral, written, or electronic statements disloyal to the colonies or harmful to their cause.

ARTICLE VI

I will never forget that I am fighting for freedom, that I am responsible for my actions, and that I am dedicated to the principles that make my world free. I will trust in my god or gods and in the Colonial Alliance forever.

PART 1

◀ ▶

Campaign Exeter

From my seat on the dais, I looked over the crowd of cadets about to graduate from South Point Academy. Could they really listen to a middle-aged soldier like me drone on about the challenges of being an officer? After all, the commandant, a war vet himself, was already at the lectern and boring them to death with that speech. In fact, when the commandant had asked me to speak, I had panicked because I knew those kids needed something more than elevated diction and fancy turns of phrase. But what?

The commandant glanced over his shoulder and nodded at me. "And now ladies and gentlemen, at this time I'd like to introduce a man whose Special Ops Tactical Manual is required reading here at the academy, a man whose treatise on Racinian conditioning transformed that entire program. Ladies and gentlemen, I give you Colonel Scott St. Andrew, chief of the Alliance Security Council."

Applause I had expected, but a standing ovation? Or maybe those cadets were just overjoyed that the commandant was leaving the podium. I dragged myself up, wincing over all the metal surgeons had jammed into me after the nanotech regeneration had failed. Unless you were really looking for it, you wouldn't notice my limp. I tugged at the hems of my dress tunic, raised my shoulders, and took a deep breath before starting forward. The kids continued with their applause, their eyes wide and brimming with naïveté.

"Thank you. Please . . ." I gestured for them to sit, then waited for the rumble to subside. "First, let me extend my gratitude to the commandant for allowing me to be here today." I tipped my head toward the man, who winked. "As all of you know, we are living in some very turbulent times. The treaties we signed at the end of the war are now being violated. Rumors of yet another civil war persist. But let me assure you that we at the security council are doing everything we can to resolve these conflicts. Now then. I didn't come here to talk about current events. I came here to tell you what you want to hear—a war story—not because it's entertaining, but because it's something you need to hear . . ."

I lay in my quarters aboard the SSGC *Auspex*, cushioned tightly in my gelrack and in the middle of a disturbing dream. My name wasn't Scott St. Andrew; I wasn't an eighteen-year-old captain and company commander in the Seventeen System Guard Corps, in charge of one hundred and sixty-two lives; and my cheek no longer bore the cross-shaped birthmark that revealed I had a genetic defect and came from poor colonial stock.

In the dream I was a real Terran, born in New York, and about to download my entire college education through a cerebro. I sat in a classroom with about fifty other privileged young people who would never need to join the military as a way to escape from their stratified society. I looked down at the C-shaped device sitting on the desk in front of me. I need only slide it onto my head and learn.

But I couldn't. I was afraid I might forget who I was, forget that my father, an overworked, underpaid company geologist, had tried his best to raise me and my brother Jarrett, since my mother had left us when we were small. Jarrett and I had entered South Point Academy just when the war had begun, and Jarrett had died in an accident during a "conditioning process" developed by an ancient alien race we called the Racinians. The conditioning, which involved the introduction into our brains of mnemosyne—a species of eidetic parasite found aboard Racinian spacecraft—enhanced our physical and mental capabilities . . . *and* aged us at an accelerated rate.

No, I couldn't forget. I needed to remember what I had become, because I sensed even then that if just one person could learn something from my story, from my mistakes, then the universe might forgive me my sins.

They were many.

So I sat there, watching the others put on their cerebroes and flinch as the datalock took hold. Some grinned as they were "enlightened." All that cerebroed data became a part of them, while I would rather my life, all that I had done, become a part of it. Still, I wonder if anyone will really care about the war between the alliances and the seventeen colonial systems a thousand years from now. Future generations might never understand that in the year 2301, hundreds of thousands died in the name of what United States president Abraham Lincoln had once called "a just and lasting peace." They died for a cause, and for those untouched by war, that is too often incomprehensible. I knew that even the young people in that room had no true concept of war. I wished I could teach them, but all I could do was sit there until the shipboard alarm yanked me out of the dream.

I sprang from my rack, expecting the captain's voice to boom over the shipwide comm. Nothing. The alarm droned on and drove me to the hatchcomm. I dialed up Lieutenant Colonel Jeffery Disque, Twenty-second Battalion Commander, a middle-aged man with buttery brown skin and a striking shock of gray at just one temple. He eyed me with disgust, then spoke in a voice hoarse from screaming at insubordinates. "What is it, Captain?"

"Sorry, sir. Thought maybe you knew why the Klaxon sounded."

Disque yawned, his lip beginning to quiver. There I was, some antsy kid who had beeped him out of slumber. The first time I had met him, I had an immediate sense of just how ill proportioned his ego had become. You could fit planets, star systems, entire nebulae inside the thing. Then again, having a battalion commander who thought he could live forever wasn't always a bad thing, especially when the rounds were flying. He would never order another company to turn tail on yours, and you might even find him outside his command tent, pumping off rounds himself . . .

I cleared my throat, grew more tense as he just looked at me, failing to answer. "Do you know why the Klaxon sounded, sir?"

He screwed his sour puss into a tighter knot. "'Course I know why that goddamned alarm is going. You think I'm a brainwipe, Captain?"

"Sir, no, sir."

"That's a nav alarm. We're changing course."

"Sir?"

"We just got new orders, Captain."

"We're not going to Kennedy-Centauri?"

"Nope."

"Then who is? Those people in Plymouth Colony need us. You saw the holos. Civvies are getting shot in the streets."

"Then whoever's left better hide, 'cause the Twenty-second Battalion ain't going there."

"We have to send somebody." Disque could not have known that my own life depended upon us reaching Kennedy-Centauri, not that he would have cared.

"Bandage your bleeding heart, Captain. I'm sure they'll dispatch another element. We got a more interesting op. I know you're going to like it. The briefing alert will hit your tablets in a couple of minutes."

"Aye-aye, sir."

"Anything else, Captain?"

"Uh, no, sir. Thank you, sir."

He flashed an ugly grin and nodded.

Even as I switched off the hatchcomm, it rang again. Someone was at my door: Rooslin Halitov. I let him in. He steered himself directly to the chair at my desk and sat, scratching nervously at his jaw.

A year prior, I would never have imagined that a cadet who had tried to take my life, a cadet who had despised me more than anyone else in his world, would eventually turn down his own shot at company commander to become my executive officer. One look at the guy—blocky jaw, blond hair, barrel chest, flaming blue eyes—made you think, yeah, he was the neighborhood bully. And Rooslin had grown up to become academy bully. Then, after we had both seen and had doled out more death than the Corps could have ever warned us about, we had become uneasy friends. His transformation had not come without a price.

"Know what that alarm's saying to me?" Halitov asked. "It's saying: you're fucked."

"We both are—'cause we're not going to Kennedy-Centauri."

"Shit . . ." He rubbed eyes full of sleep grit, eyes that had looked years younger only a few months prior. "You talk to Breckinridge?"

"Just found out myself." I crossed to my gelrack, dropped heavily onto the mattress. "She can't change this." I sighed out my frustration. "Anyway, Disque says we'll get the decrypted poop in about twenty minutes."

"Fuck Disque. I hate that prick. He's going to get us all killed, then stand on the big pile of bodies and give his victory speech: 'These young men and women have given their lives so that the seventeen systems might one day be freed from Alliance tyranny . . .' Yeah, they gave their lives so you'd have a soap box to stand on, you asshole."

"Next time we're out drinking, I'm going to pay you to do that. Of course the old man will show up behind you."

"This ain't funny . . ." His sober expression dampened my smile. Thankfully, the hatchcomm beeped again, distracting us from feeling any more sorry for ourselves. I checked the monitor. It was our Accelerated Assimilation Trainer, Captain Kristi Breckinridge, who, with short, dark hair gelled back and a body conditioned to machinelike precision, could steal some officers' breaths with a salacious glance or a chokehold, depending upon her mood or how obviously they had gawked at her. I opened the hatch.

"Captain," she said, then didn't wait for an invitation and pushed past me. "Shut the door." She regarded Halitov with a curt nod, turned her clandestine expression back on me. "He has to leave."

"He stays."

A dangerous realization lit her gaze. "You haven't told him, have you? You understand that information is highly classified . . ."

"Told me what?" said Halitov, feigning ignorance.

"Sit down, shut up," I said, then faced Breckinridge, trembling with the realization that I would stand up to her, be honest with her—even reveal that I had done some research on her past and discovered things that made me distrust her even more. If she wanted me to play her game, I'd play—but by my rules. "He knows everything. And you're going to help him, too."

She swore under her breath, closed her eyes. "Scott, that wasn't the deal. He hasn't been invited to become a Warden."

I looked at her, grew rigid. "You came in here, said the Colonial Wardens—the most powerful and elite group in the Seventeen System Guard Corps—wants to recruit me. Turns out you guys are running a little coup to motivate the new government and want me to help. Then you tell me you know something about my brother, get me thinking that maybe he's not dead, and finally, you promise me that I can meet a woman on Kennedy-Centauri who has epineuropathy just like me, only her conditioning process is perfect, and she's got three times the strength and endurance of the average conditioned soldier. You say you can fix me, make me like her, 'cause the Wardens have found a second conditioning facility on Aire Wu, when everyone thinks there's just one, on Exeter, currently occupied by Alliance troops. If I ever do get reconditioned, if there is a cure to this rapid aging, then I'm *not* going to keep that information classified. Every conditioned solider deserves to know about and receive that cure, and the first one in line is going to be him." I pointed at Halitov.

"You'll do what we tell you—or you'll get nothing," she snapped.

"I'm not sure I want anything from people like you. I know what happened at the academy, the hazing and the cheating—"

She snickered. "Don't you have better things to do than pry into my life?"

"Not when mine's on the line. They cleared you, but you were guilty, I bet. Then you graduate, try to get into the Wardens, but the request is denied five times—until the CO who's been denying the request suddenly changes his mind. I talked to an old buddy of yours, Grimwald. He told me just how you got that CO to change his mind."

Her cheeks flushed. "If I were you, I wouldn't say another word."

"But I'm not done. We haven't even gotten to your brother. Yeah, I know about him, too. Disabled and abandoned. Your parents are gone. He's all you have in the world. So why is he still there, rotting away in that hospital?"

She eyed me for a moment, then, in the next second, she reached out with her mind into the quantum bond between particles and crawled across the bulkhead behind me, shifting like some arachnid unimpeded by gravity. She slipped in and got me in her patented chokehold. Her voice came low and harsh, directly into my ear: "You . . . don't . . . know . . . anything."

"I know you're an opportunist. You have no honor, no loyalty."

"What I have . . . is your life in my hands."

Out of the corner of my eye, I saw Halitov jab a pistol into Breckinridge's head. "Let him go," he said.

She thought a moment, then ripped her arm away, shoved me aside. "You want to push my buttons? I can push yours. Should we talk about your mother?"

I massaged my neck, felt a sudden tightness in my chest.

"Oh, spare me this bullshit," groaned Halitov, his expression turning emphatic. "We're dying. We need to be reconditioned."

"That's right," I said, then glared at Breckinridge. "He gets reconditioned—or I don't even meet with your people—whenever that's going to happen, because we're no longer en route to Kennedy-Centauri."

"I knew that before the nav alarm sounded. We'll reschedule. I sent word to my people on a chip tawted out just five minutes ago."

"I hope this little meeting will be soon," said Halitov.

Breckinridge's stare turned menacing. "It will be." She took a deep breath, sighed heavily. "Got more news for you. We've done some studies on the aging side effects. In one month you might age a standard year. In the next month, you might age only three, four months, in the following month, you might age naturally. We haven't found a pattern or a way to predict the effects yet."

"Oh, that makes me feel all warm and tingly," sang Halitov. "Tomorrow I wake up, and my bones are cracking and my hair's falling out and I can't even remember that I had a sex drive, which, by that time, won't be driving me anywhere, anymore."

"Shut up," I told him, then gestured that Breckinridge go on.

"We have learned that as the aging progresses, there's a long-term memory imbalance that interferes with the short-term. You can't remember if you shut off the vid, and you can't stop reciting some obscure data cerebroed into the deepest parts of your mind."

"I've seen that effect," I said, recalling an old woman from the Minsalo Caves, a recently young old woman who had become a misfiring human computer, confused and ultimately suicidal.

"Finally, I do have some good news," Breckinridge said, brightening slightly.

Halitov rolled his eyes. "This I have to hear."

"I know where you're headed."

I raised my brows. "Really?"

Within an hour of our conversation with Breckinridge we were tawting out seventy-five light-years from Earth to the moon Exeter. Halitov and I had met there at South Point Academy, but our training to become officers had been interrupted by the war. I never thought I'd return to the place where my career had begun, but I later learned that Halitov and I were shipped there because our friend Mary Brooks, chief of the Colonial Security Council, had orchestrated our transfer to the Exeter Campaign: #345EX7-B. We would, she hoped, take back control of the academy and the damaged conditioning facility from Alliance occupation troops. She also knew we would satisfy our curiosity regarding our friends Paul Beauregard and Dina Anne Forrest. During a black Op, Dina had been killed, and in love with her, Paul had gone AWOL to take her to the Minsalo Caves on Exeter, where he thought she might be revived because a strange healing process occurred there, one I had experienced firsthand. The idea that a cave could raise the dead seemed ludicrous, but there were alien artifacts within those caverns, and history is woven with stories of places that heal the body and the soul.

Thus, Paul Beauregard, son of the famous Colonel Beauregard, head of the Colonial Wardens, thought he could save the woman he loved, and the last we had heard, Alliance Marines had found his ship but not him or Dina. More than ever, I hoped that he had succeeded, and I already burned to abandon my

mission and head out to the caves to find out for myself. My own heart ached for Dina, though somewhere deep inside I had already begun to accept her
death.

We reached the Jovian-like gas giant of 70 Virginis
b, and Halitov and I took in the view through a narrow porthole.

"Weird coming back, huh?" he asked.

"Yeah."

"You think Beauregard really got her into the
caves?"

"Who knows."

He nudged my shoulder. "Hey, that was some
smooth negotiating with Breckinridge. I really liked
the part where you brought up her disabled brother.
Real smooth."

I gave him a dirty look. "She's scum."

"No, she's hot."

"If you had a disabled brother, wouldn't you want
to be there for him, care for him? Would you leave
him to rot away with strangers?"

"I don't know . . ."

"Well, I do."

We stayed there for a few minutes, neither saying a
word until the order to drop came in.

The insertion went off well, with the loss of only one
troop ship. Within an hour we stood outside my command tent, watching artillery fire stitch across the
night sky above the academy. Relentless enemy gunners played connect the dots with the constellations,
or so it appeared.

In the valley below, our three platoons stealthily

advanced toward the admin building, that great assemblage of isosceles triangles glowing in the tracer light and framed by the distant mesas.

"I don't get it. We blanketed this place with EMP bombs," said Halitov.

"Which knocked out all localized weaponry and electronics," I said. "They've obviously resupplied. Pulse wave's a singular event. Doesn't affect new weapons brought into the area."

"Then I want to know how they rearmed themselves so quickly . . ."

"They must be making drops on the other side of the moon, maybe out where Beauregard took us when we stole that shuttle the last time we were here."

"Then how come our eyes in the sky haven't picked up those crab carriers making drops?"

"I don't know."

"I say they got a cache already here, maybe underground. Maybe out in the Minsalo Caves."

"Maybe—"

A tremendous boom just meters away cut off my thought. From the corner of my eye, I saw that my command tent had exploded in an upheaval of sparks and sharp-edged debris.

"Son of a bitch!" cried Halitov.

Even as the shrapnel rained down, he and I dropped to our bellies, reached for our wrists, and tapped buttons on our tacs, activating our combat skins. The phosphorescent membranes of energy enveloped us, and the Heads Up Viewers rippled to life, superimposing themselves at an arm's length from our faces and giving us reports of our own vital signs and skin status, as well as troop movements and a half dozen other options visible only to us. Once skinned, you could always tell when someone else's life force was drained just by examining how brightly they glowed in the standard green night-vision setting.

As usual Halitov wasn't glowing very brightly, not because his life force was drained but because the mere act of skinning always triggered his claustrophobia, and that fear, born of a childhood trauma in which he had been locked in a box for days by neighborhood bullies, took a heavy toll.

"Rooslin! You're okay, man! You're okay!" I shouted over our command frequency.

His reply resonated in the combat skin shimmering over my ears. "Yeah, yeah, but look at Javelin's platoon. He's only got one squad holding back. Javelin? Report!"

Before the second lieutenant could reply, I ordered my skin's computer to bring up a digitized image of Mr. James Javelin and his people as they advanced toward the administration building. But the three squads in his platoon weren't supposed to be advancing; they supposed to remain on the perimeter and sweep for snipers or take out any bunkers containing artillery troops who might aim their big guns at mobile command bases—like my own—set up in the foothills. All right, Javelin had left one squad back, but those raw recruits were pinned down by fire from not only the administration building, but also from a rear attack by Alliance Marines positioned on the barracks' rooftops. I watched one recruit get his head blown off, followed by a second, who aimed his QQ90 particle rifle at some distant muzzle flash that became all too bright as he took a scintillating, accelerated round to the right eye. His head whipped back, and down he went—a man whose life I was responsible for, a man who had died because I had failed to recognize that one of my platoon leaders was not obeying orders, dammit.

The second lieutenant's tinny voice finally broke over the channel. "The Fourteenth and the Fifteenth have breached the admin building, Captain."

"All three of your squads were supposed to fall back," screamed Halitov.

"In theory, yeah, Captain. But you ain't down here looking at this defensive fire. The Fifty-first Platoon needed our help making the breach. And I didn't have no time to call back and wait for your okay. I gave it to them. If you got a problem with that, you come down and have a look for yourself—*sir.*"

Halitov's reply came heated and fast over my private channel. "I'm payin' that motherfucker a visit."

"Wait—"

He charged off, his combat skin swarming with dark blotches as he switched the setting to camouflage. I watched him wind a tortuous path down the foothills for a few seconds, then vanish.

I lay there on my gut, monitoring the blips in my HUV, each representing one of my combatants. I zoomed in our now-popular second lieutenant, saw an image of him piped down from one of our satellites. He crouched behind a stone knee wall abutting one of the walkways. "Javelin? Copy?" I called.

"Yes, sir?"

"The XO's on his way. Before he gets there, I want you to pull your people out of admin and resume your supporting positions."

"I do that, sir, and we'll lose the Fifty-first."

"You don't know that. Pull your people out. That's a direct order."

"Communication terminated," said my onboard computer.

The bastard had cut the link.

My job as company commander, though sometimes complex, was pretty damned simple at the moment: monitor the actions of my three platoons to ensure that our objective of seizing the administration building was achieved. I was supposed to direct troops as needed and react accordingly to the defenses we encountered. I was not supposed to go down there and fight myself—

Which is exactly what I did.

As I charged down the hill, switching my skin to camouflage and feeling that familiar surge of adrenaline, one memory flashed repeatedly, as though locked inside a shard of tumbling glass. I saw my old instructor, Major Yokito Yakata, standing in our classroom and telling us about our newly conditioned bodies: *"Other forces of nature—the strong and weak nuclear forces, gravity, electromagnetism—we're all of these, and we're only beginning to discover the potential power here. One day, we'll abandon our TAWT drives and will ourselves across the galaxy."*

Willing myself to another location was something I had tried successfully already, but only for short distances, and the feat had left me weak and dazed. I had no desire to appear instantly at Javelin's side but be so spent by the journey that I could not effectively reprimand him.

Consequently, I was a ripe target as I raced across

the open field between the foothills and the admin building, reaching out into the quantum bond, believing I could accelerate my pace. But, as had frequently happened in the past, I didn't feel a damned thing.

A large formation of boulders adorned with plaques commemorating some of South Point's most prestigious graduates stood about twenty meters ahead—my only cover.

With particle fire digging ragged trenches within a meter or two of my path, I made the "difficult" decision to get the hell out of there. Even as I hauled ass, my computer issued the warning: "Particle fire locked on." In my HUV, a representation of my body appeared in a data bar, my skin glowing red in a region near my shoulder. I cocked my head, and yes, a stream of fire split the air, coming right at me. If that Marine held his bead for a little longer, it would eventually wear down and penetrate my skin.

"Come on, you son of a bitch," I muttered to myself, then leapt forward, reached out, found the bond between me, the air, the ground, and the boulders ahead.

Gozt is the bullet thrust, one of the quitunutul fighting arts that, in low G, turns you into a deadly projectile. At that moment, though, I was more interested in presenting the smallest possible target to the Marine behind me, and with me in the *gozt*, all he looked at was a pair of boots dematerializing into the night.

I reached the boulders, then broke forward out of the move, letting myself tumble once before landing hard, way too hard, on my feet. I staggered as the impact reverberated up my legs. Sensing the bond as a viscous gel I could mold, I prepared to dart from my cover, toward a pair of rear doors set within an alcove where I knew Javelin had positioned himself. More particle fire began chewing into the boulders, blasting away slabs of stone that sent me scurrying sideways, toward a deeper crevice near my knees.

The Marine who had first targeted me was now closing the gap. Knowing he had me pinned down, he would leap over the boulder and rack up his point-blank kill at any second.

I had to move. Looked to the rear doors. Saw a gauntlet of fire crisscrossing the way. Then, behind me, the firing suddenly stopped. I edged around the boulder, stole a look across the field. Nothing.

A pebble struck my shoulder. I looked up.

The Marine issued a hysterical cry as he dropped down from the rock, his skin fluctuating between green, black, and ocher.

My own particle rifle had been disintegrated in my tent, but I still had my blades, a pair of old-fashioned Ka-Bars kept in sheaths stitched onto my boots. I reached for them—

But he was on me, knocking me back with his boot and jabbing the muzzle of his particle rifle into my neck. Our skins crackled with reflected energy, though he had his setting low enough so that he wouldn't rebound violently.

Particle fire belched from his weapon, and a harsh, white light suddenly grew from the skin protecting my neck.

I caught a glimpse of the Marine's face. He was a kid like me, maybe eighteen, nineteen, so scared that he had whipped himself into a frenzy to get the job done. He wanted no guilt, no fear; he was merely neutralizing an enemy troop. Nothing personal.

His boot pressed harder. I reached up, tried to grab his leg, but all that reflected fire kicked my hands back. I probed for the bond. Gone again.

And that's when the fear, the real, unadulterated fear that wrenches you from a nightmare and keeps you up into the wee hours staring at the shadows, pinned me more effectively than the Marine ever could. I just lay there, watching the Reaper wave.

2 ❯ **Over twenty years** have passed since the night I was lying behind that boulder. I remember that moment as though it had happened only seconds ago. In fact, I can remember each and every soldier who has tried to take my life and every one whose life I have taken. This is the curse of having a memory so keen, so enhanced by alien technology that it is impossible to forget. And I wish I could forget how someone, I'm not sure who, perhaps myself, shouted in my ear, "Get up!" Those words, that feeling of urgency, penetrated the fear. I rolled out of that Marine's bead. He continued tracking me with his fire.

I shivered with relief as the bond returned, shy though it had been, and the Marine's water-slow movements confirmed that. As I came out of the roll, I reached up, seized the barrel of his rifle, and hauled myself up with it, despite his firing.

Shards of rock torn free by his rounds tumbled around us. Artillery continued booming overhead, along with the smaller arms fire slicing up the field around us, and it was difficult to hear him scream as I ripped the rifle out of his grip, then reached for his wrist, locking my grip around his tac. With fingers strengthened by the bond, I tore off the tac, taking his hand with it. His combat skin trickled away, dissolving down to his ankles as he clutched his ragged stump, his mouth working to form something that wouldn't come out. He spotted his severed appendage lying on the ground. "My hand," he finally cried. "My hand."

I had about three or four breaths to make a decision. I could kill him or just let him go. He seemed too shocked to pose a threat. I thought back to the last time I had been to Exeter and been faced with an identical situation. My decision then? The wrong one.

"It's okay," I told the Marine. "Just be quiet. It's okay." I shifted up to him, slid my arm around his back as I lifted my leg, fishing out my Ka-Bar. "It won't hurt anymore."

For a second, he looked down, saw my Ka-Bar coming toward his gray-and-azure utilities, and said, "Tell my mom I'm sorry . . ."

Before he finished, I buried the knife in his heart. He looked at me, eyes going vague as he slumped in my arms. I let him fall, shuddered, withdrew my knife. Stood there. Swallowed.

I had just robbed a mother of her son. I hated myself as the tug and pull of war made me shudder once more. I hated myself, but I refused to become a victim of my own guilt. Sergeant Judiah Pope, my old squad leader, had been killed by a Marine whom I had shown mercy. So I killed that Marine behind the boulder with extreme prejudice, and there are those who still hate me for this, call my actions brutal and unnecessary. They were brutal. Unnecessary? It was war.

I took off and found Javelin, a husky kid with dark, curly hair and the face of an angry St. Bernard, along with his platoon sergeant, a lanky blond woman named Fanjeaux. They huddled in the alcove, their gazes far away as they monitored images in their HUVs.

"Lieutenant Javelin," I barked as I scrambled into the alcove. Then it dawned on me. Only two of them were there. "Where's Captain Halitov?"

It took a moment for Javelin to pry himself from his screens. "Sir?"

"Where's Captain Halitov?"

"Sir, I don't know, sir. And with all due respect, I'm busy right now." His gaze went distant. "Tao, Rumi, Jackson? Fall back to that second corridor. Now!"

"Hey, Mandella, Rickover? What're you doing?" asked Fanjeaux incredulously. "Move out!"

I activated my HUV, ordered the computer to show me Halitov's location.

"Unable to locate Captain Halitov."

"What do you mean?"

The computer repeated stoically, "Unable to locate Captain Halitov."

"Has his tac been removed?"

"Unknown."

I opened the command channel. "Rooslin? Copy?"

Particle fire drummed along the wall behind us.

"Captain? We have to move," cried Javelin.

"Rooslin? Do you copy?"

If he did, I couldn't tell.

A standard artillery shell whirred in, dropping no more than ten meters beside us, then exploded in a blue lightning storm whose bolts reached out, tore a gaping hole in the alloy wall, and sent shock waves rumbling through the ground as we dropped for cover.

"Rooslin? Copy?" I repeated. "Rooslin?"

Javelin clambered in front of me. "Sir! We're locked. We have to move!"

I swore, hustled my way to the wall, with Javelin and Fanjeaux falling in behind, particle rifles at the ready. We reached the southeast corner of the building, and I hazarded a glance around that corner. Clear.

"I wouldn't be here if you had followed orders," I told Javelin, my voice low and steely. "I'd be up at my tent, which wouldn't have been blown up. And now I can't reach the XO."

"Sir, I'd be happy to debate this after we obtain our objective."

"Oh, we'll be talking. And you won't be happy." I cleared the skin near my face so he could see my blackest look. "Let's go!"

We stole our way along the east side of the building, darting between walkways, knee walls, and low-lying shrubs until we neared another entrance where four Marines had set up a bunker using lightweight alloy blast plates to create a silvery carapace behind which they had manned their big guns. Artillery fire from one of our guns had blown apart the shield, and "smart schrap" from the shell had ignited to repeatedly poke at the Marines' combat skins like a billion tiny, sharp-edged jackhammers making one hundred thrusts per second. Their remains, covered by pale, wet viscera, lay across the shattered blast plates.

I waved Javelin ahead of me. "Good," he said. "We'll coordinate from here."

"Get the Fourteenth and the Fifteenth out of there," I said. "Get them back to their original positions."

"Sir, I say again. The Fifty-first is getting its ass kicked in there."

"Not for long. Just get your squads. Cover us when we come out."

I started for the doors, one of them hanging half off from the blast.

"Sir, you're not going in there?" Fanjeaux asked.

"Just wait for my signal."

Javelin smiled, probably glad I wanted to take off on what he deemed a suicide run. "Yes, sir."

I stepped over the dead Marines, ducked, and forced my way past the shattered door as I heard Javelin give the order over the general frequency for the Fourteenth and Fifteenth Squads to fall back and reinforce the Sixteenth outside. With the Fiftieth Platoon back in line, all I had to worry about now were the Fifty-first and Fifty-second, whose mission was to enter admin and neutralize the enemy while attempting to cause minimal damage to the structure, no small feat to be sure.

Even as I left the door and turned right, down a corridor that would take me past a long bank of offices, I heard the muffled booming of microcharges and the closer rat-a-tat of particle fire. With the light sticks mounted on the wall either shattered or flickering, I paused, brought up a thermal view in my HUV, then reached for a Ka-Bar. The sickly sweet odor of something burning made me grimace and search for its source.

Perhaps twenty bodies lay along the corridor, some Alliance Marines, others green recruits from my own company. The computer zoomed in on each of the casualties, identified the victim, then noted the loss in our central database. Familiar names flashed again and again, the computer now a beacon of death holding me in its light. Nearly every member of the Seventeenth Squad lay in the hall, incinerated by the Western Alliance's latest toy: a silent laser rifle that dismembered you with surgical precision. For nearly all of my people, this had been their first and last combat experience. As the centuries-old superstition dictated, you died either at the beginning of your service or at the very end . . .

I found my mouth opening, words coming in a gasp, "Oh my God . . ." In all the chaos, I had failed to keep close tabs on the number of troops I was losing.

Someone rounded the corner ahead. I tensed, shrinking to my knees. My HUV zoomed in, IDed the soldier as Aaron Cavalier, whose surname befit him. Though he, too, was about as green as his people, he had taken on the responsibility of commanding three squads with a chilly detachment that had infuriated me. Recently, I had become nervous when a rumor reached my desk about his using "jaca," a synthetic narcotic that hides itself from detection. I had offered him a subtle warning about "medications," and he had simply yessed me to death. Young Mr. Cavalier had no idea of what he would face, and the fact that he seemed to breeze through his life, numbed perhaps by drug use, made me believe all the more that his rude awakening would strike a much harder blow than it did to the average guardsman.

Cavalier staggered down the hall, his skin down, his particle rifle hanging limply from his side. As he drew closer, I saw a burn on the side of his head—a near miss from one of those lasers. He drew closer, tripped over a corpse that had once answered to him, then fell to his knees.

"Cavalier," I called, de-skinning so he could see me better.

"Who's that?" he asked, oblivious to my approach, though I came directly toward him.

"Lieutenant, it's me." I reached him, grabbed his wrist, helped him to his feet, dragged him toward the wall.

He furrowed his brow, spoke in a weird lilt. "Oh, yeah. The captain. The big man. Got the Racinian conditioning. Got the superhuman alien parasites in your head. Trying to save the galaxy before you become an old man, so they say. Got the big command going. Trying to stay alive so you can make sure they spell your name right in the history logs but lookin' kinda depressed and makin' me think that maybe, just maybe, who knows, maybe you want to die."

I grabbed him by the neck. "Lieutenant, where's the rest of your platoon?"

He returned a zombie's stare. I shoved him away, took off running down the corridor. "Computer? Can you locate Captain Halitov yet?"

"Negative."

It took me about five minutes to get down two levels to the offices of South Point's Honors College, where, according to my tactical computer, the rest of Cavalier's platoon had become pinned down by roughly three squads of Marines. I crouched before a pair of glass doors, chanced a quick look:

A maze of corridors and offices inside made for an urban combat environment that even the most experienced troops would dread. By the time your computer told you a Marine was hidden behind a desk, that Marine would already be dodging from cover and firing.

Tight quarters or not, I was responsible for every soldier crouching within that maze, and the fact that the Marines were tightening their perimeter, getting ready to flush them out, turned that sense of responsibility into a deafening roar to help them.

I got on Cavalier's command frequency. "Sergeant Canada? Copy?"

"Copy, sir," said the young woman whom I imagined poised behind some piece of furniture, her short, brown hair damp with sweat, her narrow green eyes pleading. "I don't know what's wrong with the LT. But he just . . . he just walked away."

"Copy, Sergeant. You got command."

"Sir?"

"In about ten seconds, you're going to be surrounded. I want you to push all three squads back, toward the main entrance, north side. Get them into the stairwell and get them out of here."

"We're falling back, sir?"

"Affirmative. Now go!"

"Aye-aye, sir!"

Even as she barked the orders to her people, particle fire from the Marines cut loose with an echoing report that would've driven any de-skinned combatant to his knees, clutching his ears.

Knife in hand, I opened the door, ran forward, reached an intersection in the corridor, glanced right, left, locked gazes with a Marine kneeling against the wall, not more than two meters away.

Even as he fired, I ran to the wall, up it, tipping sideways on my own volition and coming over him. I

doubted he had ever seen a conditioned soldier because my maneuver so stunned him that he broke
fire, turned, and gaped up at me as I dropped on him,
driving my Ka-Bar past his combat skin and into his
gut. The fact that I was able to penetrate his skin with
a mere blade further surprised him, and that was
probably his last thought, accompanied by a horrible
sting I knew all too well.

To describe the next thirty minutes in gut-
wrenching detail would, some argue, be cathartic.
Not for me. Suffice it to say that all but three of my
people got out while I summarily and unceremoni-
ously killed all twenty-two enemy Marines. Were it
not for my combat skin, my hands, arms, chest, and
legs would've been soaked in blood. How many parents, brothers, sisters, husbands, wives, and children
would cry because of what I had done?

When I was finished, I hit the stairwell, taking the
steps two at a time. I reached the first floor landing,
seized the door, swung it toward me.

A Marine guarding that door from the other side
whirled, brought his rifle to bear on me while jamming his boot into the door.

I groped for the bond, believing I could find the
particles between me, the air, and the rounds soon to
explode from his muzzle. I would apply force to those
rounds, to that bead, bend the stream back toward
him like a garden hose that would spray into his face.
I had seen Major Yakata perform a similar feat, and I
had employed the same technique on Gatewood-
Callista. Before the Marine would realize what was
happening, his own rounds would have gnawed into
his combat skin, then his flesh and bone and brain.

The rounds came, all right, striking my combat skin squarely in the chest and driving back toward the opposite wall. I dodged right, reached the wall. Dodged left, hit another wall. I started for the staircase.

Then a sudden boom reverberated through the well. The Marine's skin sparked, veins of energy fingered their way across his shoulders, then the skin darkened and sloughed off. A strange look came over his face as the rifle fell from his hand, and he collapsed a second later, revealing Battalion Commander Disque, clutching a smart schrap grenade launcher, smoke rising from its muzzle.

"Captain, I want you topside. I want what's left of Zodiac Company stationed along the perimeter. Grid points should already be uploaded. We'll talk about this fuck up later."

"Yeah, Yankee Company'll mop up your mess," said Derick Kohrana, Yankee's captain and company commander. He slipped in behind Disque, clearing his skin to reveal girlish lips and a face that looked pretty, even while twisted in disgust. I barely knew Kohrana, heard he was quite a womanizer with those big eyelashes and smooth line of bullshit. I hated him. He went on: "I don't know why everybody thinks these conditioned guys are the way to go. I really don't."

"You can stow that and get your platoons in here," Disque told him. "Now!" Kohrana left, then Disque faced me, gaze still flaming. "What the fuck are you waiting for?"

"Sir!" I hustled around him, into the hall, and jogged by a long line of guardsmen from Yankee Company double-timing in the opposite direction. "Computer? Location of Captain Halitov?"

"Unknown."

"Set alert if his tac comes back on-line."

"Alert set."

I had no idea what the hell had happened to my friend, and his absence made me realize just how much I had come to depend on him, not just as a fiercely loyal XO, but as the last vestige of my old life, of my early days at the academy, of a time when both of us had been blithely unaware of what was to come. I remember the night my brother Jarrett had told me he was dropping out of the academy. He represented home to me, and his leaving meant that I would no longer be safe.

As I ran down that hall, I felt just as vulnerable as I had that night at the academy. Rooslin was gone. After Jarrett, Rooslin had been my home. Now I was the only one left.

Much to my chagrin, Yankee Company managed to neutralize the Marines inside the admin building. In fact, within six hours, our battalion, along with two others, took control of the academy grounds. Thankfully, Disque was so busy with logistical concerns that he had, thus far, not had the time to tear me a new orifice for my company's failure.

With our atmoattack jets streaking overhead in a clear display that we also controlled the skies, I sat on a collapsible chair outside my new command tent, waiting for my second lieutenants to report, waiting for my computer to tell me something, anything, about Halitov.

Javelin came loping over, stood at attention. "Sir, reporting for debriefing, sir!"

"At ease. Get two more chairs out of the tent. Bring them out here."

Not thrilled by the errand boy task, Javelin groaned, "Aye-aye, sir."

He disappeared into the dusty brown hemisphere that blended into the landscape. Second Lieutenants Aaron Cavalier and Grace Thomason arrived, Cavalier still appearing only half-present, Thomason brooding over something that seemed to turn her dark skin even darker. Her nostrils flared as she met my gaze, snapped off a salute, gave the standard acknowledgment, then turned her big brown eyes away.

Javelin returned with the chairs, and I gestured that the three take seats. Javelin and Thomason were clearly bewildered by my informality, which was, of course, lost on Cavalier.

"So we fucked up today," I began.

"And you want to sit around and chat about it, sir?" asked Javelin.

"As a matter of fact I do."

Javelin nodded, decided to press another button: "Sir, have they located Captain Halitov's body yet?"

"Captain Halitov is still MIA. Presumed alive."

"That the official word?"

"That's *my* word."

"Sir, permission to speak off the record, sir?" asked Thomason.

"Go ahead."

"Halitov's probably dead. I lost nearly half my platoon. Cavalier lost even more. And for what, sir?"

"Not glory," said Javelin as he widened his gaze on me. " 'Cause like you said, we fucked up. Sir."

"I got drafted into this, made an officer just 'cause I

got a college degree," Thomason said. "You know, at first, I really thought we were doing something noble. Fighting for what you said—a just and lasting peace. The alliances have been exploiting the colonies for far too long. But sir, Scott . . . it's all bullshit, man. It's just about money. And land. Our side is as corrupt as theirs, but at least they're going to win. They have more resources, more personnel. Period. I watched so many of my people die today, and I'm just . . . I don't know if I can do this. It's more than just morally and ethically wrong. It's suicide."

There I sat, looking at them, my command staff: a pain in my ass know-it-all, an unconfirmed junkie, and a conscientious objector. For a second, I wished I were back on Gatewood-Callista, in charge of my platoon. I actually wished that Sergeant Mai Lan, mutinous bitch though she had been, was working with me. She hated my guts and thought I was wrong about everything, but she had been far more capable than any of these people. Javelin was a noncommissioned officer who had cashed in on the war's demand for personnel by lobbying hard for his commission. Cavalier, like Thomason, came from the farms of Tau Ceti XI, where he had earned his degree in agriculture, then had received the word: you're drafted. Dodging the draft was punishable by a long prison sentence, even death in extreme cases. I should have sympathized more with those two, but they weren't like me, soldiers who wanted to find out what duty, honor, and courage really mean. Thomason had once told me that she was not supposed to be shouting at troops. She was supposed to be teaching high school science to a class of bright-eyed young colos. Cavalier just wanted to be out in the fields, with his crops, figuring out new ways to yield even more food. Perhaps the violence of war, standing in such sharp relief to a field of corn nodding in the breeze, had driven Cavalier to find an escape through hallucinogens. I vowed that before we left Exeter, he would come clean with me, or I would do everything in my power to get him discharged. I had already debriefed him privately, had stripped away his command and given it to his platoon sergeant, but that hadn't seemed to faze him.

"Sir, did you hear what I said?" Thomason asked.

"Yeah. And sorry, Lieutenant, but I'm not in the mood to change your mind."

That hoisted her brows.

"You three think Halitov and I don't have enough experience for this command. Yeah, maybe you heard about what we pulled on Gatewood-Callista, how many Marines we took out, but I know you still don't think we're capable. Truth is, none of us is ready for this. And I'm not sure there's any amount of training that can prepare you for what we've seen. But here we are, in the shit. And we will make the best of it because *I'm* in command. No other reason. We won't decide on our own who needs help and who doesn't. We won't reinterpret orders to suit ourselves. We won't suddenly decide in the middle of combat that our political biases and agenda have changed and that maybe it's not right to kill these people anymore. Finally, we won't numb ourselves to the world. We're going to keep our minds clear and do our jobs. You fucked up inside because you didn't trust in me. I'm making the decisions. I'm not going to hesitate. I'm not going to steer you wrong. And if I ever do, I'm going to pay for it with my life. You can count on that. Now that's the end of my little heart-to-heart. Comments?"

Cavalier's chin slowly lifted. "When are we gonna eat?"

I was about to lean over, grab him by the ear, and shake him until all that garbage in his head oozed out and allowed him to return to us, but Lieutenant Colonel Disque came marching up the hill, toward our powwow.

Javelin glanced at the lieutenant colonel. "Shit. Are we dismissed, sir?"

"Dismissed."

"Captain St. Andrew," Disque called, singing my name in a tune that might as well be my funeral hymn. "Finished debriefing your three losers?"

I rose, snapped to, and issued my salute, as my people practically ran off. "Sir, my platoon leaders have been debriefed, sir."

"At ease, Captain," he said, then dropped heavily into one of the chairs Javelin had failed to pack away. "You know on my way up here, I passed this long line of glad bags, and I have to tell you, most of the bodies stuffed in them were from your company. You dropped in here with a hundred and sixty-two. What do you got left, son?"

I sat, cleared my throat. "Sir, roll stands tall at eighty-nine, sir."

"Stands tall? Are you kidding me? They condition a fuckin' gennyboy, somehow he gets ahold of a company, loses his XO, loses nearly half his people. Jesus Christ!"

My brother's words haunted me once more: *You'll*

always be a gennyboy first, an officer second. The only way you'll get respect is by earning it through what you do— and even then they'll talk behind your back. I'm telling you this because you're my brother. You have to hear it.

Every muscle in my body tightened, and I imagined myself throttling the lieutenant colonel right there. He had called me gennyboy, and I could report him for that. But he knew I wouldn't start that fire between us.

"Sir, I have a morale problem, and I am—"

"Of course you got a morale problem. We all got one. These kids have been ripped away from their homes. We've shoved weapons into their hands and told them to fight. But you got it even worse because they don't relate to you."

"Because I'm a gennyboy."

"Being a mining kid is one thing, but between the epi and the conditioning, you're not quite human to them. What're you going to do about that?"

"Sir, I don't know, sir."

Disque leaned back in his chair, cradled his head in his hands. "Well, you better think about it. And let me tell you something: you can't run around playing fuckin' Superman every time your company screws up. You have to teach them right, stand back, and let them do their jobs. What you did, going in there, taking out all those troops . . . yeah, you got your people out, but you didn't learn a goddamned thing about being a commander. You cheated your way out of the situation."

"But sir—"

"You hate me, but I'm willing to bet that I'm one of the only guys you're going to meet who actually gives

a crap about your character as an officer. You got it
hard, St. Andrew. No doubt about it. Brother killed.
Birthmark on your face. Getting a little gray there
in the temples because of your fucked-up conditioning . . . I don't envy you. Not at all. I do, however,
envy the fact that you got a friend in a high place. I
just received a communiqué from the office of Mary
Brooks. We're setting up a Hunter-Killer Platoon,
sending them into the Minsalo Caves to weed out any
Alliance presence still there. They want you to lead it.
Maybe you've been in those caves before, but I still
don't think you're ready."

"Sir, I am ready."

"You calling me a liar?"

"Sir, no, sir. Just offering a different opinion, sir."

"We'll see." He stood, accidentally knocked over
his chair, then picked it up. "Fuckin' military issue."

I stood, found it hard to meet his scrutinizing gaze.
"Sir, would you like me to put together a command
team?"

"You know, if I had any say in this, you wouldn't be
going."

"I understand, sir."

"I'll put together your team, throw in your three
platoon commanders, whom I know you get along
with so well. And I'll make Kohrana your XO. He'll
keep you honest."

My shoulders slumped a little. "Yes, sir."

"One more thing. Off the record. What do you
think happened to Halitov? He's MIA, but . . . think
he went AWOL?"

"Sir, no, sir."

"Every corpse but his has been accounted for. Air search has nothing. What do you think?"

"Sir, Captain Halitov would not go AWOL."

He studied me. "Then he'd best be dead, because no one deserts on my watch. No one."

3 ❯ **Disque had been** trying to teach me something in that meeting, but I hadn't been listening. I would earn the respect of my people if I listened to them carefully, then allowed them to find creative solutions to problems. I needed to let them do their jobs and not rush in to save the day. I had failed because I had wanted too badly to win. And I still didn't know how to accept and learn from my failures. I kept wanting to win because, well, that was easy . . .

The strange disappearance of Captain Rooslin Halitov became a popular topic of conversation, second only to war news tawted in from Kennedy-Centauri. While the remainder of my company rotated on watch duty but otherwise enjoyed some much needed R&R, I lay on a thin gelrack in my command tent, listening to the familiar *ta-ta-ta* of the insects we had nicknamed "triplets" when I had been a South Point cadet. In the distance, an occasional round of particle fire echoed off the mesas. That would be troops warding off the *shraxi*, those toothy nocturnal carnivores that emerged from their burrows and traveled in threes. Though less than a meter tall when standing on their hind legs, *shraxi* could take down a man in just a few moments. They were nasty creatures, but I didn't mind them as much as I could have. Their presence, the cool, dry air, and the music of the triplets swept me away from all the stress. I needed to relax. In just a few hours I'd be traveling via Armored Troop Carrier out to the caves. I imagined I was just a first year again, having only to worry about my studies and physical training.

My tac beeped. I swore, sat up, activated my HUV, and took the incoming call, which originated from the SSGC *Auspex*, in orbit with six other troop transports as well as nine capital ships and their support vessels. It was odd that the caller was not identified, but when I saw who it was shimmering ghostlike in the display, I knew why.

"Hello, again," said Captain Kristi Breckinridge, wearing her unflappable game face. "I understand you're heading out to the Minsalo Caves in the morning."

"That's classified."

"I have a message for you from Colonel Beauregard. He asks that you do everything possible to find his son."

I wondered what was really going on with the brass: I already felt like a pawn, and Beauregard's message only confirmed that. "Disque told me he got orders from Ms. Brooks. Is that true? Did the colonel twist some arms to get me in there?"

"I can't say. And you do, of course, have another mission to accomplish. I understand X-Ray Company's going out there to secure the conditioning facility."

"That's correct."

"You know they're wasting their time, right? The alliances never got the facility back on-line. According to our intel, that quake caused irreparable damage."

"If that's true, then you and the rest of the Wardens

just sat around watching the Seventeen waste resources."

"If I'm the colonel, wasting the Seventeen's resources
is not a huge sacrifice—if I can retrieve my son."

"Does he know how many people died here? And
for what? It's not like there's anything of real value,
now that you're saying the conditioning facility can't
be repaired."

"What about the caves themselves?"

"What about them?"

"If the colonel's son is there, and Dina is with
him . . . I mean, if she's alive . . ."

"You don't believe those caves can bring people
back from the dead, do you?"

"You told me you'd been healed by them yourself."

"Healed, yeah. Resurrected? No."

"Well, I hope you find out in the morning. Last
thing: the colonel will honor your request to have
Halitov reconditioned, with the understanding that
once he is, he becomes a Colonial Warden."

"Oh, he understands how blackmail works. He understands it as clearly as you do."

She rolled her eyes. "I'm offering both of you *life*.
Have you checked the news lately? All of the original
Sol colonies have fallen. Forget Mars. Forget all of Sol.
The alliances are beginning a major push outward.
They're going to leapfrog from system to system, se-
curing each as they go along. Rumor has it they're
getting ready to stage a major offensive at Kennedy-
Centauri. The colonial capital will fall if the Wardens
don't intervene. Like it or not, that is the way it is."

"Are we done?"

"Not yet. Why are you lying to me about Halitov?"

"Lying?"

"You think I don't have access? He's listed MIA."

"I never said he wasn't."

"Scott, as much as you don't like me, I'm here to help you. I'm a resource. We have several people down there who are looking for him right now."

My tone softened a little. "Really?"

"Alive or dead, we'll find him."

"Thank you."

"Sounds like you still don't trust me."

"Say hi to your brother for me." I cut the link, imagining the fire in her eyes. Then I sat there, thinking about my friend. *Rooslin, what happened to you?*

"Sir?" cried Platoon Sergeant Canada from just outside my tent. "Sorry to disturb you, sir. But we got a problem!"

I came out of the tent, saw her standing there, face illumined by the light stick in her fist. "What is it, Sergeant?"

"It's Lieutenant Cavalier, sir." She turned, pointed outward. "There."

Out in the distance, atop one of the smaller cliffs within Virginis Canyon, stood Second Lieutenant Cavalier. I immediately skinned up, zoomed in on him for a better look. He was naked, arms outstretched against the great silhouettes of rock and the dusty curtain of stars. His head lolled back, his eyes closed, and his mouth fell open, as though in ecstasy. He stood mere inches from the sheer drop-off, the canyon floor a dizzying three hundred meters below. I de-skinned. "Airjeep! Now!"

"They're on patrol. It's going to take a few minutes, sir."

"How the hell did he get up there?" I said, breaking into a jog toward the canyon.

"I don't know. Maybe he bribed an MP to drop him off."

Privates from Yankee Company positioned along the barracks' perimeter began fanning out from their posts, drawing closer to the cliff for a better look.

As I neared the canyon, I still couldn't believe that one of my officers stood atop a wall of mottled strata that we cadets had called Whore Face, because of her good hand- and footholds. It appeared one of my officers was going to commit suicide on my old training ground.

"How long on that airjeep, Sergeant?" I hollered.

"Couple minutes."

We reached the canyon floor directly below Cavalier, and I had to skin up to see his face. "Cavalier!" His name echoed off into the night. He didn't react.

I swept my gaze down, across the rock, all the way to the floor. Three hundred meters. If the quantum bond remained true, I could scale that in a few heartbeats, make it up top, maybe talk him down. But if the bond failed, even my skin wouldn't save me. I'd rebound until most of my bones were broken. Was his life worth the risk?

Trembling with indecision, I stared once more at him, actually smiled as I thought, *It's just a dream. After that call from Breckinridge, I fell back asleep, and this is just a dream. I don't have to feel guilty about not trying to save this guy* . . .

"I think he's going to jump, sir," said Canada, as

Cavalier wormed a little closer to the edge, dirt dropping off from his toes, now hanging in the air.

"Jesus God, what do we got now?" boomed Disque as he marched up beside me. My bad luck placed the lieutenant-colonel's command tent only a hundred meters away.

"I think he's hallucinating, sir," Canada said.

"Oh, really? Thought he was just taking the family jewels for a walk," Disque retorted, then he skinned up, set the volume on his voice way up to mimic an old-fashioned bullhorn. "Lieutenant, what in God's name are you doing on my cliff?"

It was all I could do to remain there and listen to Lieutenant-colonel Jesus work his "subtle persuasion" on Cavalier.

"Son, I asked you a question," Disque shouted, now even more incensed.

Without another thought, I just did it, ran like I was on fire, found the bond, exploited the hell out of it, and began sprinting up the canyon wall as though it were the floor.

"Holy shit," Disque cried. I wanted to believe he'd seen other conditioned officers in action, but a feat of this magnitude had probably never reached his eyes.

All right, so I did trip over a few pitons jutting from the rock. Those little metal spikes had been left over from all our training exercises, but they didn't stop me from reaching the top and rounding the corner about four meters away from Cavalier, who still hadn't opened his eyes.

Tentatively, I stepped toward him. "Aaron. Hey, man. I'm right over here."

"You think I want to die?" he asked, then began

chuckling to himself. "That why you think I'm up here?"

"One of my officers strips naked, stands at the edge of a cliff, and I'm thinking he wants to jump. Call me crazy."

"St. Andrew, get that idiot away from the edge right now!" ordered Disque.

"Sir, yes, sir!" I boomed halfheartedly.

"I love it," said Cavalier. "All this attention, me right here on the edge, surrounded by nature. I love it. This place, this moon, Exeter . . . it's alive. It knows I'm here. It's aware of me. And I *mean* something to it, just like right now, I mean something to all of you. My life matters."

Blinding lights wiped past me, shone in my eyes a second as an airjeep rose from the canyon, hovered a few meters away from us. An MP rose from the passenger's seat, aimed a CZX Forty antigrav rifle at Cavalier. "Lieutenant, stand down!"

"Hey, I got this," I shouted to the MP.

"It's a security problem now, Captain," barked the MP.

"Aaron, they're going to hit you with the CZX to make sure you don't jump. You know what that's going to feel like. Just move back from the edge."

"No, I'm going to stay here, and I'm going to be important, and my life's going to really matter, and people are going to remember me. That's what I'm going to do. That's what's going to happen."

A quick hiss, and the MP fired—but the weapon's beam did not lock on to and encase Cavalier in its energy. The MP had misadjusted the power setting, and the beam blasted Cavalier over the edge.

I gasped, slid out toward the drop-off, saw him dropping away, heard his cry . . .

And one, two, three, I leapt over the side, after him.

In those days, I considered myself pretty damned foolish because only a fool would throw himself off a cliff knowing that the bond, his only safety net was, at best, unreliable.

Then again, that wasn't the first time I had literally jumped off a cliff. Before I was conditioned, I had fallen from that very wall and been saved by Sergeant Pope. Clearly, the universe was toying with me, amusing itself through my angst and its repetition of time and place.

About halfway down, I knew I'd be all right. The bond surged within me. But about halfway down, I also realized that I would not reach Cavalier in time, and no one below had a CZX to save him. He hit the ground, back first, and his entire body snapped like a twig and went limp. I hit the deck, bent my knees, and my skin tapered off as I willed myself away from the bond.

A handful of grunts gaped at me, finding more interest in my jump than in Cavalier's death. I rushed to my lieutenant, checked his neck for a carotid pulse. No pulse. No chance.

"All right, everyone, back to your posts," ordered Disque. "Louis, get a detail in here to"—he made a face at Cavalier's broken body—"take care of this."

Louis, a sergeant from Yankee Company, saluted and activated his tac.

Disque came over, and, surprisingly, put a hand on my shoulder. "Son," he began quietly, almost sympathetically, "your people . . . they're dropping like flies."

"Bad joke, sir," I said, my gaze not straying from Cavalier.

"Yeah," Disque said. "Bad joke."

At 0600 local time, X-Ray, Yankee, and Zodiac Companies piled into admin's war-torn primary assembly hall for a nondenominational memorial service in honor of our fallen comrades. The regimental commander, Vivian Hurly, read a little speech from the screen of a palm-sized tablet, while we stood in formation. I noted that we had heard the quote-laden speech at least twice before. There was nothing personal, nothing uniquely passionate about words she would continue to recycle. Disque, of course, also went through the motions, though he did shock some of us and his superiors, when, at the close of his brief remarks, he said, "A lot of people died here—but we still kicked fuckin' ass. Remember that!"

Those not shocked included the back row of grunts, most from Yankee Company, who cheered and repeated his message at the tops of their lungs until squad corporals evil-eyed them into silence.

After the service, we ate, though I couldn't stomach much more than a piece of toast and some lukewarm coffee. I met up with Canada, who now officially assumed Cavalier's spot, and we headed out to the airfield. Javelin and Thomason had already gone off to fetch our gear from the supply sergeant.

We took a path overlooking the academy grounds from about a hundred meters up. I had taken the route many times during my cadet days. Thin columns of smoke still rose from the barracks where X-Ray Company had taken on Marines dug in between the buildings. Still more smoke rose from the library and classroom buildings, both of which had sustained major damage from artillery fire. The longer I looked out at the academy, the more depressed I felt. The training ground of my cadet days— a place where we had all been wonderfully naive and untouched by war—was vanishing before my eyes.

"Sir, I, uh, I wanted to, now that we have a moment, I wanted to talk you about . . ." Canada sighed against her stammering.

"What is it, Sergeant?"

"So I'm officially in charge of the Fifty-first now."

"I'll have your star in hand right after this Op."

"So I really get the star, all ten points, just like that?"

"Are you kidding me? Yesterday, I was a cadet. After this place got invaded, and we made it out, they gave me my commission, a platoon, and sent me home to Gatewood-Callista. My first platoon mutinied on me. So they made me a captain and gave me Zodiac Company." I grinned over the irony. "I love the Seventeen."

"Sir, I'm not ready."

"You think I was? You think I am? They can dump all the information they want into your brain, but data can never replace real experience happening in real time. The tech guys will argue with me there, tell me that data contains experiences, memories that will seem as real as any others. But there's always a little voice in my head that tells me you never did this, you never learned that. It's just the cerebro. They can't erase your doubt without erasing you."

"Which is why I'm not ready."

"Which is the reason why you're perfect for the job.

You're a clean slate, ready to be molded into a powerful and decisive officer based on very real combat experiences. You'll be okay."

"Thanks for the vote of confidence, but I know you're desperate for personnel."

"We're all desperate, and the shortage will get worse if we don't have good leaders."

"You think I'll be a good leader?"

"You're from Aire-Wu."

"What's that supposed to mean?"

"The narrative in your folder says that four generations of your family have worked in the timber industry there. Butanee was it?"

"Yeah, but lumberjacks don't make for good leaders. Trust me. We're all bush people, like to be alone, and we do not want anyone micromanaging us."

"I grew up in a mine. We traded in ore. Miners and lumberjacks are cut from the same cloth. And you'd be surprised how well we adapt to leading and being led."

"I would be. Because right now I feel pretty lost. I mean, everyone knows Cavalier was taking something. How am I supposed to get my people past that? What if Cavalier wasn't the only junkie? What then?"

"You'll deal with it. We both will."

"How can you be so confident?"

"Because this is my company. And no one, I mean no one, is going to let me down. If it makes you feel better, just keep telling yourself you *are* ready. It's a pretty good lie. It works for me. Most of the time."

"Aye-aye, sir."

"And Canada? One last bit of advice. I'm sharing all my fears and doubts with you, and to be honest, that's not the way to play it with your people. If they see you're afraid, if they see you're indecisive, they will not follow. Everybody hates Disque. But most of us would follow him to our deaths. I'm not saying you have to be a prick. Just calm. Always assessing the situation and reacting like that." I snapped my fingers. She nodded.

We walked a few more moments in silence, me thinking about the fact that she came from Aire-Wu and remembering that the second conditioning facility was supposedly there. Eventually I asked, "Sergeant, in all the time you were home before you got drafted, and believe me, I know Aire-Wu's a big planet, but just out of curiosity, did you ever see any military presence there that seemed, I don't know, unusual?"

I paused to read her expression, and, strangely enough, she looked a little nervous. "What do you mean? The Seventeen's always had a base in Butanee."

"Never mind. Forget it."

"Wait. So everybody thinks the Racinians terraformed my world, and there are always research projects going on to learn the truth. We even had guys digging in the middle of one of our tree farms, not too far from a few of the mills. I remember those lab coat guys were escorted by military people. Is that what you're talking about?"

"Maybe. Did they ever find anything?"

"I don't know. If they did, they never told us about it. They paid my dad a lot for the okay to dig, though. Stayed there a few months, filled in the holes, and pulled out. Why do you ask?"

"Just following up on something. Thanks."

"And thank you, sir. I mean for the advice."

"Anytime."

"Oh, I almost forgot to ask. Any word about the XO?"

I shook my head.

"It's like someone just plucked him off the battle-field."

My voice grew thin. "Yeah, it is."

We neared the tarmac, and abruptly the solitude of the path and stillness of the morning yielded sharply to the whine of warming turbines, the faint howl of the wind sweeping down from the mesas, and the hollering of squad corporals. About fifty yards ahead, Javelin, Thomason, and Kohrana loaded backpacks into the cargo hold of a G21 Endosector Armored Troop Carrier, one of two quad-winged birds of prey that would carry our three squads to the caves. Since it was a special operation, officers were supposed to pitch in as much as the grunts, and I was glad to see my command team pulling their weight. I had figured that Javelin and Kohrana would dole out the grunt work to, well, the grunts. Still, they had not taken the entire burden of loading upon themselves. A half dozen privates stocked the other ATC while the rest shifted in single file into the hold.

"Captain," Kohrana said, looking up from an underwing cargo bay and backhanding sweat from his brow. "Thanks for dropping by."

"Is our gear stowed, XO?" I asked, all business and denying him a reaction to his remark.

"Yes, sir. The gear is stowed. Almost finished boarding."

"Very well. Alert the pilots. Dust off at their discretion."

Canada and I left him and headed up the gangway, into the hold. I took a jumpseat between her and Javelin. Opposite us sat privates zippered into black combat utilities that hardened the appearance of even the prettiest young women. A shudder broke through me as, for a moment, I spotted a grunt who looked a little like Dina. I closed my eyes.

"Sir, all present and accounted for," said Kohrana. I jolted as he took a seat opposite me and lowered the big safety bars over his shoulders. He clipped the stock of his QQ90 particle rifle into the deck mount between his legs. "Dust off in thirty seconds," he reported.

The turbines cycled up, and all that raw power rumbled through the hold for a full half minute until we rose in a vertical takeoff. I switched on my tac and let Disque know that we were en route and would issue status reports as necessary. He gave me the unwelcome news that several Western Alliance capital ships had just tawted into orbit and were squaring off with our fleet. His advice was as crude as it was curt: "Haul major fucking ass. Read me, Captain?"

"Loud and clear, sir!"

The first Racinian ruins on Exeter had been discovered inside the Minsalo Caves, and I knew more about them than most of my colleagues. My dad was a geologist, and maybe it was in my genes, but most of my life I've had a special interest in rock formations, sedimentary layers, and, well, dirt. Not the most interesting stuff, but I like the idea that rocks are like history books, though their stories rarely lie and are not influenced by personal agendas. There may not be any more pure form of history.

The caves' colossal entrance hung on a cliff wall nearly six hundred meters above Virginis Canyon's dry riverbed. The first time I had come to the place, we had been forced to rappel down the cliff, then pendulum ourselves inside the cave. Our entry via the ATCs would be far less dangerous and dramatic. I watched from a small window as the first ship hovered near that great open mouth of stone, turned tail, and backed up toward the cave. The gangway came down, and even as it made contact with the cave floor, my guardsmen flooded out, their skins set to a fluctuating camouflage of red, brown, and alabaster-white that mirrored the colors of the cave walls. I skinned up myself, called on my HUV, and watched a digitized image of them dispersing.

"Captain, First and Second Squads are in," reported Squad Sergeant Hurley, one of Kohrana's people from Yankee Company.

"Copy that, Sergeant. Establish your perimeter points down to the Great Hall. Copy?"

"Copy, sir."

"You meet any resistance, you take them out."

"Yes, sir."

"So, Captain, rumor has it you've been here before," said Kohrana, as the ATC banked hard, then began lining up its tail with the entrance.

"That's no rumor. And here's a tip: most of this place isn't on the map. Somebody gets lost, all that rock could interfere with GPS signals and transponders. So let's keep everyone buddied up and tight."

"Does it ever bother you?" he asked suddenly, fingering his own cheek and staring at the birthmark on mine. "I mean, does it itch or anything?"

Before I could answer, the hold's gangway began yawning open, and our safety bars automatically whined up and away.

"All right," cried Mazamo, a stocky blond woman and Third Squad's sergeant. "Ready on the line. By the numbers. Just like the drill."

The troops formed a neat line, with the first poised at the red mark near the gangway's edge.

At that moment, I couldn't help but launch into one of Sergeant Pope's old morale boosters. "Squad, are you ready?"

"Yes, sir!" they boomed.

"Very well. Go! Go! Go!"

One after another they jogged down the ramp, leapt onto the cave's dusty stone floor, and fanned out. I unclipped my own particle rifle from the floor and fell in behind Javelin, Thomason, Canada, and Kohrana.

We were in the cave no more than a few seconds when the echo of particle fire sounded ahead, from where the entrance funneled down into a narrow gallery. I darted to a wall, hunkered down, and read the screens in my HUV. "Hurley? Report?"

"Snipers. Hit-and-run. Think we wounded one of them, but we got one dead, two wounded ourselves."

"Get them up here." I looked to Kohrana. "Medevac."

He nodded and made the call while I studied a 3-D map of the entrance. As expected, those Alliance snipers were jamming my HUV and effectively concealing themselves from detection. The fact they had detected us meant that they had either made visual contact, or someone had given them our encryption codes so they could detect our communications or tac signals. Whatever the case, we had lost the element of surprise, and they might even be tracking us.

"Medevac's en route, but are you sure you don't want to leave them?" asked Kohrana. "Let the magic caves do their work?"

I matched his cynical grin with one of my own. "No."

"Got another question. If the caves heal people, then every time we shoot the enemy, he lies down and gets healed. Then he's ready for more. So we can't kill him."

"And maybe he can't kill us."

"This is nuts."

I chuckled under my breath. "Now you're making sense."

"What if we dismember them? You think the caves can put bodies back together?"

"Forget that. Let's establish where we are: they're expecting us and regrouping, trying to reinforce their positions, which is why we're going in now, full force."

"You're insane. We'll draw too much fire."

"Hey, man. When they're shooting at you, they're telling you where they are."

"Screw that. We have to—"

"First, Second, Third Squads?" I called, getting quickly to my feet. "Hard and fast. Flush them out. Let's go!" I took off toward the gallery, leaving a stunned Kohrana in my wake.

"You can't do this," he cried.

"I know," I called back. "I'm insane. Follow me!" Though I never glanced back, I suspected the color had faded from his cheeks.

4 › I raced by one of the markers left several decades prior by a speleological team. The little hemisphere had been flashing all that time, marking the path. The tunnel grew more narrow, a lot more damp, then, as I remembered, it sloped down in a thirty-five-degree grade, with the ceiling just a meter above my head. More gunfire punctuated the whistling wind and quickened my pace.

"Captain?" gasped Kohrana, trying to keep up with me. "You're taking us right into those snipers!"

"Like you said, they'll all just get shot and healed. Either way, we got no time for cat and mouse. There's an Alliance fleet in orbit. We have to flush out these Marines and get the hell out of here." There was another thing I wanted to do, but he didn't need to know about that.

"If the Alliance is going to win back this moon, then who cares if we do this?" asked Thomason, who had obviously been monitoring my command channel. "We've already lost."

"We don't know what's going to happen up there, so we do our jobs. And we do them quickly. Canada, you copy?"

"Yes, sir! Just hitting the Great Hall now. Jesus, this place is big. Lots of stalagmites for them to set up sniper nests."

"Move in, three by three. Close proximity. Tight to

the wall. Listen to Hurley. He knows what he's doing. And set your particle range for two meters, nearly point-blank. You're going to have ricocheting like you wouldn't believe if you open up."

"Copy that, sir. Seen some already. Moving out."

"Javelin? You with me?" I called, waited, was about to call again when:

"I'm here, Captain. There's another tunnel about ten meters ahead, right near the entrance to the hall. Heads off to the right. Can't bring it up on the map, but I want to take Second Squad in there."

"Do it."

"Sir, are you sure, sir?"

"What do you mean, Lieutenant?"

"I mean, sir, this is my idea. You're going along?"

I regret what I said next. It was unprofessional, but it just came out. "Javelin, *do not* fuck with me. Get in there and kill anything that moves. Copy?"

"Uh, copy, sir."

Kohrana cleared the skin near his face to reveal his frown. "You okay?"

"Yeah, I'm okay. You people piss me off, you know that? Just hold your position."

And the fool in me took over once more. I brought my rifle to bear, scaled the wall, then, hanging inverted from the ceiling but feeling not a single graviton's pull, I bolted off for the Great Hall, negotiating around stalactites, which, from my point of view, rose from the floor.

I sprinted into the vast chamber of the Great Hall, glanced down at First Squad as they spread out, dashing from stalagmite to stalagmite, working themselves deeper into the gloomy orifice.

Then, gunfire erupted from at least a dozen points ahead. My tactical computer immediately traced the beads and singled out fourteen Western Alliance Marines who had taken up positions at the far end of the hall.

Three of Hurley's people took left flank, and another three took right. Good plan. They'd drive those snipers away from the main exit and toward a far corner. I opted to take out the four Marines in the middle, and I'd do that quietly, before they knew what had hit them.

The first Marine who had been firing then ducking back behind a narrow stalagmite glanced up at the rush of wind behind him. Exploiting the bond to penetrate his combat skin, I drove the butt of my rifle into his face as I dropped on him. We collapsed and still disoriented but gripping his weapon, he rolled away.

But I had already abandoned my weapon and had the blade of my Ka-Bar sticking from the bottom of my fist. He got a nanosecond look at me before I punched the blade into his heart, withdrew it, and, panting, snatched up my gun and dodged to a glossy stalagmite a few meters to my right.

Listening only to the sound of my breathing and trying to ignore the voice in my head that whispered, "Murderer . . . murderer . . ." I reached the stalagmite, paused, then spotted movement just ahead, near the next pillar of stone.

"Sir! We're taking heavy fire in here," cried Javelin over the channel. "Request permission to A-3 them, copy?"

"Negative." Javelin wanted to use acipalm-three grenades, which would spread their incendiary black goo all over the cave after exploding, killing the Marines in there by working at the subatomic level to rob the gluons from their bodies. Problem was, that same theft would also destroy a portion of the cave. Our orders dictated that we preserve as much of the rock formations and alien ruins as possible.

"Sir, I've already lost three people!" Javelin argued.

"Then fall back!"

Silence. Then, finally, "Aye-aye, sir! Wait a minute . . ."

"What is it, Javelin?"

"Sir? They've ceased fire. *They're* falling back."

"Pursue!"

"Aye-aye, sir!"

I took off running for that next pillar, got there, found nothing. "Canada?"

"Copy, sir. Got seven Marine casualties so far. Rest here are falling back."

"Very well. Let's go get them."

The next tunnel, a ragged triangle just two meters wide near the base and about three meters high, led to an abandoned Racinian hangar, a vast, empty chamber with stone walls blending seamlessly into polished metal. I met up with Kohrana near the tunnel's entrance, and he hesitated before going inside.

"Something you want to say, Captain?" I asked.

His eyes grew narrower, more menacing. "No." He hustled by and jogged off into the gloom.

We crossed the hangar without incident, reached the conduit of stone on the other side, then ducked down and shifted at double time inside. All three of our squads lay ahead, and reports from Javelin, Canada, and Thomason came in, along with further

observations from the squad sergeants. After about
ten minutes of hunchbacked travel, we reached a familiar cavity about five hundred meters across and
ringed by a natural catwalk. The moment I caught
sight of the place, I remembered the woman we had
chased there, back when I had been a cadet:

*Her eyes widened, the irises a weird, deep shade of red,
her head haloed by that mop of coarse white hair. She shifted
her gaze a little, inspected us, then spoke in a rapid fire that
we could barely follow. "Toroidal Curvature of the contain-
ment field allows the formation of the mediators and the es-
tablishment of a stable family of Primal Space Time Matter
particles. The main TAWT drive computers, networked in a
Quantum Communication Array allow the so-called
faster-than-light computations to be made, which in turn
collapse the wave function of any and all present conditions. As the ship's computer observes the conditions, it in
effect can answer questions before they are posed."*

Jarrett frowned at me.

"Why is she reciting a page from colonial history?"
asked Dina.

"And why is she wearing our utilities?" Clarion added.
"Unless—"

"You're not them?" the woman cried, then grabbed Jarrett's wrist with a bony hand. "You haven't come to take me
back?"

Jarrett tugged himself free. "Take you back where?"

"Better yet, who're you talking about?" I asked.

"Twenty-two-sixty-six. Mining of bauxite begins on
fifth planet in Ross Two-forty-eight solar system," the
woman replied, her ruby eyes going vacant. "Inte-Micro
Corporation CEO Tamer Yatanaya names planet Allah-
Trope and declares it retreat for Muslims persecuted by

Eastern Alliance powers. Allah-Trope becomes first off-world colony with predominately one religion. By year's end, floating research operations are dropped onto planet Epsilon Eri Three—a world entirely covered by warm oceans whose salt content is only slightly higher than Terra's. Thousands of new microorganisms discovered. Aquacultural experiments yield new food sources for a human population that now numbers twenty billion, with six billion living in Sol system colonies and nearly five billion in extrasolar settlements."

"What's the matter with you?" Jarrett asked.

"I . . . it won't . . . I can't . . ."

"Are you a cadet?" Clarion demanded.

Dina crouched down and took the woman's hand in her own. "Are you a third year? A fourth year?"

The woman's eyes glossed with tears, and as she tried to answer, Jarrett checked her pockets for anything that might reveal her identity.

Now, as I stood on the catwalk, it was clear to me that that old lady was my destiny—unless I handed myself over to Breckinridge and allowed her and the Wardens to recondition me.

"What is that down there?" asked Kohrana, staring into the vast pit before us. "I'm scanning it, and I get nothing."

With my tactical computer feeding me infrared images in my HUV, I studied the curving metallic surface, which, the first time I had seen it, reminded me of a missile's nose cone. "I don't know."

"Want to send a rappelling team in there?"

I studied the pit, and in my mind's eye I saw that old woman leap into it. I repressed a shudder. "No. We keep moving."

We forged on for another fifty or so minutes, through more modest-sized tunnels connected by more caverns of flow- and dripstone. Kohrana took lead, sweeping his rifle across the path and hugging the shadows near the wall. Feeling yet another rush of déjà vu, I tried to forget about my first journey into the caves and just listened to the skipchatter on the squad channels:

"J.T. switch to tac five, copy?"

"Going to five."

"Anything on thermal, Canada?"

"We're cold so far, copy?"

"Copy. Lowe and Rammel, you're getting too loose. Tighten those lines."

"Aye-aye, sir."

A rock dropped just behind me. Nothing large, just a stone the size of a baseball. I whirled and studied the cavern, with its dozens of dark hiding places reaching beyond my night-vision's scope. Nothing. I probed once more, looked back, saw Kohrana now some ten meters ahead and shifting left, toward a large seam in the rock wall leading to the next tunnel. I threw a final look back at the cavern, glanced up to the stalactites, which seemed to close in on me for a moment.

And that's when a cold, wet hand penetrated my skin and wrapped around my mouth, even as an arm slipped around my chest. I was dragged back, toward the cavern wall. With both hands locked on my attacker's wrist, I struggled to pry free. I could feel the bond, but I still couldn't budge the hand. That could only mean my assailant was conditioned.

"Shhh. It's me."

Suddenly, the hand slipped away, and I found myself standing in a tunnel just a meter wide. I spun, saw who had grabbed me, and the words just slipped out: "What the fuck?"

Rooslin Halitov stood there, his utilities ruffled and dripping wet, as though he'd been swimming in them. He cocked a brow and nodded. "Yeah, that's just what I said when they contacted me: 'what the fuck,' only it wasn't a question, just an okay. Now give me your wrist."

Still stunned, I raised my hand without question. He waved a small pen over my new tac, one issued to me just before we had dropped onto Exeter. The status lights faded, as did my skin. I noticed that his tac had also been deactivated, which was a violation of standing orders and punishable by imprisonment. We were out of contact with the Corps, and it would be very difficult to trace us. "What a minute—"

"C'mon. They're waiting."

"Who?"

"Who do you think? Come on."

"Activate my tac. Right now."

"Are you kidding?"

"I got a whole platoon here."

He smirked. "This place is crawling with Marines. They'll be busy. Trust me. And I'm sure that asshole Kohrana won't miss you. They'll report you MIA, just like me."

"What's going on?"

A round of particle fire ricocheted just outside the tunnel, followed by the low rumble of falling rock.

Halitov widened his gaze on the tunnel entrance. "No time for a heads up. Just follow me. You'll be glad you did." He started off, hunkering down as the ceiling closed in.

I didn't move. "So you're AWOL—is that what you're telling me?"

"Yup. And now so are you."

"What the hell are you doing here?"

He stopped, turned back. "Geez, I thought you'd be glad to see me. No, 'Rooslin, you're alive!' or 'Rooslin, you don't how much I've missed you. You're like a brother to me.' Shit."

"Will you tell me what's going on?"

Another round boomed outside.

"Goddamn it, Scott, come on! I found Paul. Actually, he found me, but who cares. Come on!"

And that set my boots in motion. "You found him? What about Dina?"

"You want to know about her? Then move your ass!"

Both of us tapped into the bond and maneuvered swiftly through the narrow tunnel, reached an oval-shaped cavern dimly lit by Halitov's light stick. He directed me toward a pool of calm water, about twenty meters across.

"Is she alive?"

"Just get in the water."

I grabbed his damp collar. "Fuck, man, you tell me right now. Is she alive?"

"Let him explain it to you."

"Who? Paul?"

"Just get in the water."

"Why all the secrecy?"

"Just get in the water!"

I splashed in and swore. "Jesus, it's ice!"

"You want a hot tub? Go to Club Io. Now listen to me. Swim straight out to the middle, then dive. Go down a couple meters. Feel your way to another tunnel. Go in. It turns right, then comes back up. You'll need the bond, or you won't make it."

After taking several deep breaths and reassuring myself that the bond was, in fact, tingling within me, I dived and followed his instructions, shivering as much from the cold water as from the thought that Dina might still be alive. The tunnel grew so narrow that I barely fit through, began to feel claustrophobic, panicked, kicked even harder, pushed myself up even faster, then, nearly out of breath, bleeding every ounce from my muscles but unable to will myself to the destination because I didn't know where we were going, my head cleared the surface. I took in a huge breath, blinked hard, saw lights flashing near me, heard voices, felt hands reach under my arms and begin dragging me toward the shore.

There, I looked up at the person who had set me down, but a light stick blinded me. I shielded my eyes from the glare.

"Sorry," came a familiar voice.

The light stick came down, revealing Lieutenant Paul Beauregard, son of Colonel J.D. Beauregard of the Colonial Wardens, once boyfriend of Dina and colleague of mine at the academy. He leaned over me, his now-bearded face tight with concern. Other than that beard and his long, ragged hair, he looked no worse for wear. Surprisingly, he had not aged like Rooslin and I had, with no crow's-feet near his eyes or gray at his temples.

"Paul," I said, still out of breath. "You made it."

His tone grew solemn. "I guess you could say that." He hunkered down, proffered his hand. "Come on. We'll get you dried off."

Behind him stood six or seven other guardsmen, their utilities ripped and dust-covered, with two sporting black bandanas. One, a pale redheaded guy who glanced suspiciously at me, turned away, splashed into the water, and helped Halitov to the shore.

"Who are they?" I asked Paul.

"We've set up a little camp. I'll tell you everything when we get there."

"And Dina?"

"Come on."

With a deep sigh over the continued secrecy, I took his hand, and he helped me up. Shivering and seeing my breath, I welcomed the blanket someone threw over me. We started along the shore, heading toward the entrance of a deep tunnel about a dozen meters ahead.

Rooslin jogged up next to me, clutching his own blanket and trembling. "He made it. You fuckin' believe that? He hijacks our ride, slips in past their defenses, and gets all the way here. That's courage, man. I knew we should've went with him. I knew it." I just shook my head as he added, "And have you seen his face? No accelerated aging. Nothing. Must be these caves."

"We'll see."

Paul led us through the tunnel, which forked into three more tunnels. We took the center shaft and walked for another ten minutes until Paul shouted, "Caveman!"

A voice came from the distance. "Caveman, acknowledged. All clear."

I realized he had just checked in with one of his perimeter guards so that we could pass. Very efficient. We moved under that guard, a dirty-faced guy no more than twenty who lay across an outcropping of stone some five meters above. As we turned a corner, sunlight poured into a wide chamber ahead, and the promise of warmth drove me past everyone else and alongside Paul.

"We found this place a few weeks ago. Moved our camp here," he explained, as we reached a gallery whose curving walls raced up perhaps one hundred meters to a natural skylight at least fifty meters in diameter. We were ants rummaging about the bottom of some enormous, dried-up well with a massive fissure wandering through its center. "Watch your step," he said, as we walked parallel to the fissure. "We've thrown rocks down there. They just drop away. No bottom. Or so it seems."

He led me across the chamber to their camp, a rather standard-looking military bivouac. Sleeping gear lay strewn about, along with several cargo containers bearing Western Alliance insignia. Several battery-powered portable heaters stood nearby, their tubes extending a full meter and glowing brilliantly.

I took a seat on the floor next to one of those heaters. "I was going to ask how you've been managing down here," I said, still examining the camp as he found a duffel, removed several towels, and tossed them to me. "Looks like you've been doing a little hit, grab, and run."

He crossed to one of the containers, removed a loaf

of real bread, tore it in half, and handed me a piece. "They keep sending Marines in here. We take out as many as we can, then we take their supplies. It's not genius work. Just survival." He handed the rest of the loaf to Halitov, who sat near me, took a barbaric bite, then stole one of my towels.

Paul's crew gathered around us, though I suspected he had left the sentries in place. Those with us didn't seem too pleased by my visit. One of them, the redhead who had pulled Halitov from the water, actually glowered at me.

Noticing this, Paul said, "Scott, this is Tommy McFarland. He and most of the others here were second years when the academy got attacked. They didn't get out like we did. They've been hiding here ever since, living off what they could steal and waiting for the counterattack."

I nodded to McFarland, whose glower did not soften, then I turned to Paul. "I do something to piss him off?"

"We know what you're going to do," said McFarland. "And we ain't going to let you do it. Without Paul, most of would be dead. We owe him our lives."

"What're you talking about?"

"I went AWOL," said Paul. "Of course, now we're all hoping to get out of here, but they know that when we do, you're going to turn me in. I'll be court-martialed, imprisoned, maybe even brainwiped. I don't think my father can help."

"Maybe he can."

He shrugged. "Point is, I know you, Scott. Always the code. You'll do the right thing. Turn me in."

"Excuse me, but last time I looked, there were Marines everywhere," began Halitov, still chomping on his bread. "We're debating what's going to happen after we escape. Let's worry about getting out of here first."

"Why don't we start from the beginning," I said, eyeing Halitov. "What happened to you?"

"Not his fault," Paul said. "We scored some short-range communications and monitored your drop here. When I found out you and Halitov were actually leading a company, I thought either the universe or Ms. Brooks was responsible, probably the latter. So I contacted Halitov, let him know where we were, told him I could deactivate his tac. We set up a meeting."

"Why didn't you contact me?" I asked. "I would've come."

"Like I said, Scott, I know you. I asked you to go AWOL when I wanted to take Dina here. You wouldn't come. I seem to remember your knife at my throat. So why would I expect you to go AWOL now? If anything, I figured you'd tell your CO that I was here in the caves so you could get permission to come and arrest me." Paul turned a mild grin on Halitov. "But he wanted to come the first time."

Thankfully, Halitov just nodded and didn't try talking with a huge chunk of bread in his mouth.

"So you thought he'd help you escape, only you didn't expect me to lead a special op in here," I concluded.

"That would be Ms. Brooks trying to help again. And you're right. I didn't expect you here, in the caves."

"So if I'm a threat to you, which explains all the looks your people are giving me"—I glanced to Mc-Farland—"then why'd you bring me here?"

Halitov backhanded bread crumbs from his lips, then wriggled his brows at me. "That's where I come in. I told him I wouldn't help unless it was you and I, together. I remember what you told Breckinridge. Figured I owed you."

"Thanks," I said with mock enthusiasm. "We can break the code together, become just like Breckinridge. Lie, cheat, steal, screw over our families . . ."

"Shut up with the fucking code," Halitov snapped. "There's so much dissension now, maybe there ain't no code anymore."

I grew deadly serious: "There is."

Halitov threw up his hands. "I don't get you. Why's the code so important?"

"It just is."

"No, that's not good enough. I've listened to that for too long. And don't give me that shit about being loyal." He marched up close and leaned into my face. "Well?"

I spun away. "My mother left when I was three. Know why? 'Cause of this." I whirled back and pointed to the birthmark on my cheek. "She couldn't hack a commitment to a kid like me. When the going got tough, she bailed. And you know, every time someone asks me why I'm so loyal to the code, I think about her, about what she did, and I know now I'll never turn my back on my family—and that family is the Corps."

"Look, we don't have time for this," interjected Paul, then he raised an index finger at me. "Your platoon is pushing back the Marines. We've been getting pretty good at tracking them, predicting their movements, but now they're on the run, and it's not safe anymore. We have to move out within the hour. What I'll need from you is a tawt-capable transport, preferably something small, like an ATC."

I couldn't stifle my chuckle. "You're crazy if you think I can get you one. And you're even more crazy if you think I'm going to let you leave without telling me what happened to Dina."

He nodded. "It's easier if I show you."

5   As Paul, his crew, Halitov, and I were about to depart the camp to see what had happened to Dina, Paul handed me a bandana. "Blindfold. Put it on."

"Why?" I asked.

"You trust me, I show you. You don't, you get nothing."

"I don't understand."

"I don't care."

I looked to Halitov, who had already donned his own blindfold. "Scott, just put the damned thing on, will you?"

I hardened my gaze on Paul. "Too many secrets."

"And too little time."

Swearing under my breath, I tied the bandana around my eyes. Paul checked to make sure the fabric fit snugly around my eyes, then he grabbed my wrist and we began a trek that lasted nearly an hour, with me stumbling all the way.

I thought it painful how in all that darkness I found it hard to summon up a clear picture of Dina's face. I wondered if that inability said something about my feelings for her. Did my heart ache from love, or guilt? I wasn't sure.

"Okay," said Paul. "Take off your blindfold. Let your eyes adjust."

I complied, and brownish gray walls undulated

around me until I realized that I was inside a tall, cylin-
drical chamber whose ceiling tapered up into a cone.
The walls were not brown or gray or made of stone but
comprised of some burnished alloy. I chanced another
glance to that ceiling, saw just how vast the place was,
and with a tingling sense of familiarity that finally
warmed into full-on recognition, I realized where we
were. "The pit with the catwalk around it and the big
missilelike structure down below. We're inside that
missile, aren't we?" I asked Paul.

"That's right. But it's no missile. And you'll never
find your way back in here without me." He tipped his
head to the opposite end of the cylinder, where, from
behind a long bank of electronic equipment with oc-
tagonal displays, I caught sight of Dina. And gasped.

"Oh my God," was all Halitov could say.

"What is this?" I asked, barely able to look at her.

She hung above us, a frail, unconscious, naked
woman attached to a gelatinous disk by thousands of
hair-thin gossamers that reminded me of the tiny
tubes inside the conditioning machines. If she was
alive, there was no clear indication. She looked like an
anorexic puppet crucified against a throbbing, pul-
sating drape of green and orange and black. Remarkably, the slash across her throat was fully healed, with
no evidence of a scar. I suspected that the stab wound
to her back was also gone, along with any signs of her
decompression.

"Is she alive?" I asked.

"Barely," Paul replied, his eyes glassing up as he
stared at her. "For the past few days her pulse has
been growing weaker."

"But her wounds are gone," I said, gazing upon the

miracle as though it were a dream. "How did you know to get her here, to this place? What is it? A Racinian hospital or something?"

"I didn't bring her here. When I landed outside, Marines were right on my tail. I took a couple of rounds, got Dina near the catwalk. And that's the last thing I remember. I must've passed out. I woke up in here. My wounds were healed, and I found Dina up there."

"Someone must've helped you," I said.

"I don't know, but Dina's been here ever since." He spun to the bank of electronics. "I think there's a problem with this equipment. Until you guys arrived Alliance scientists over at the conditioning facility were trying to get the place back on-line. I think their experiments affected this place. I've tried gaining access, but even knowing the language doesn't help. Could be codes or DNA or something." He closed his eyes, rubbed the bridge of his nose. "We've turned these caves upside down looking for an answer. I still think maybe it's not the caves that have healing properties—it's this equipment. Maybe this whole place is emitting a fluctuation in the space-time continuum that allows it to reorganize the particles of your body to heal you."

"Look at us, Paul," I said. "Me and Halitov. We're getting old."

"I didn't want to say anything."

"You went through the same conditioning. You should be aging like us. You're not."

"Which supports my theory. But maybe the effect is only temporary. Maybe if I leave, the rapid aging will begin."

I gave a long, weary sigh. "Burning twice as bright . . . it's no fun at all."

"How long you think she's going to be up there?" asked Halitov.

Paul frowned. "Who knows. I thought about cutting her down, but I'm afraid that might kill her. These machines, they brought her back to life. But now . . . it's like she's dying on me all over again." With that, he slammed a fist on one of the alien panels. "Fuck!"

My gaze swept the room. "There has to be something we can do."

He stared gravely at me.

"I say we leave her up there," said Halitov. "Maybe her pulse is getting weaker 'cause it's supposed to. Maybe that's how the machine works. Just leave her up there until the machine releases her."

"Or till someone comes and takes her down," I said.

"Who?" asked Halitov. "One of the Racinians? Some old alien who's the guardian of this facility?"

"Maybe."

He made a silly face. "Fuckin' fantasyland you're living in. Probably some Racinian drone or something scooped them up, brought them here, hooked Dina up to the machine. Now a drone I can believe. We've already found evidence of drones in their ruins. At least all that history they dumped in my brain says so. Best thing is to leave her. See what happens."

"You mean we wait here in the caves?" I asked. "For how long?"

"As long as it takes," answered Paul, shifting to get in my face. "But not we. Me. You'll lead my people out, but I'm not leaving her."

A cadet named Hollis, a hard-faced woman with dark hair pulled back in a ponytail, came forward. "Sir, with all due respect, sir. I speak for the others when I say that if you stay, we stay. Sir."

As much as I disagreed with Paul's decision to go AWOL to try to save Dina's life, I admired his loyalty to her and the loyalty he inspired in his crew. You could see it burning in Hollis's eyes. She would give her life for Paul in a heartbeat, and that was just the kind of fierce dedication I needed from my own people.

Paul's tone grew sympathetic as he gripped Hollis's shoulder. "When we get back to camp, you're all getting out with these guys."

"No, sir."

"C'mon. All you ever talk about is getting out of here. What about that slice of New York pizza you said you were going to buy? What about your parents? You don't think they're waiting for you? You don't think the brass'll issue you a leave so you can see them? Your entire life has been put on hold. You've been living in a cave, for God's sake."

"But sir—"

"No. I won't have it. I owe you a ticket out. And you're getting one. End of discussion."

Paul's little speech doused the fire in Hollis's eyes. She swung away, dejected. "Yes, sir."

I cleared my throat. "Of course, I can't allow you to stay," I told Paul.

"Of course."

"So where does that leave us?"

He cocked a brow. "At war, I'd say."

I closed my eyes, stiffened. "Paul, I have to do my job."

"Your job," he began darkly, then shouted, "Look at her! Open your eyes and look at her! People are what's important—not duty, not honor, not the Corps. My father was wrong. Everything they told us at the academy is wrong. It's all bullshit. In the end, we're all we got."

After glancing painfully at Dina, I narrowed my gaze on him. "What if she doesn't love you?"

"You asked me that once before. And my answer's still the same: I know she doesn't love me. But I don't care."

"You're a fool," said Halitov.

Nearly in unison, Paul and I told him, "Shut up!"

"I was going to say you both are fools," Halitov said. "Scott, if Paul wants to stay, let him stay. We take the rest out. We don't have to lie. We just don't volunteer the fact that we ran into him. That's all."

"And that's all I'm asking," said Paul.

"See?" said Halitov. "One big happy family again."

I glanced at Halitov, then at Paul, wondering whether I should keep the secret because I understood how Paul felt about Dina, understood it as intimately as anyone could.

Then, fortunately, I realized I didn't need to make that decision. "Paul, if I leave you here with her, I'm signing your death tag. There's an Alliance fleet up there. Chances are high they're going to drop a major ground force here and take back this moon. That happens, the only way you'll get off this rock is as a POW. And since you're conditioned, I'm betting they'll brainwipe you and put you back out there, fighting for the wrong side. We have to get out. Now."

"I'll take my chances. But you're right. You do need to leave. Blindfolds on. Let's go."

"Fuck the blindfold," said Halitov. "If you can't trust us now . . ."

"I got very little to bargain with," he said. "The way in here stays with me."

I looked at Paul, saw that for the time being there would be no more arguing with him. I figured that once we returned to camp, I'd try one last time to convince him. If he did not comply, then I knew, God, I knew, what I had to do.

I didn't plan on passing out, just five minutes into our trek back. A wave of dizziness hit, a tingling rose through my spine, and I swore as I surrendered to the inevitable.

"Holy shit. Scott, wake up."

There are many faces I can appreciate after a stretch of unconsciousness—but Rooslin Halitov's isn't one of them. He gaped at me, all big jowls and pointy jaw.

"I'm awake," I said. "What's going on? We blacked out, didn't we?" My gaze focused, and I got a better look at him. "Holy shit is right."

Halitov appeared as fresh and young as the first day I had met him at the academy. No gray. No wrinkles.

"Fuckin' fountain of youth, man," he cried.

"No," said Paul, now hovering over us. "If I'm right, that machine is just correcting a problem. Like you said, when you leave, the aging might return."

"Then it's just a damned tease," Halitov said, bolting to his feet. "Damn! But then again, maybe it isn't!"

I glanced up, saw the stars peeking through a twilit sky, and got my bearings. We were back in Paul's camp. "What time is it?"

"About twenty-one hundred local," said Halitov.

"Twenty-one hundred? Damn, we have to get out of here." I sat up, touched my eyes, which didn't feel very different, the skin near them perhaps a bit smoother.

"Want to look?" asked Paul, tossing me a standard-issue pocket mirror. Sure enough, my own gray and wrinkles were gone. I even felt more agile. "You got thirty more seconds to admire yourself," he continued. "Then I'm reactivating your tacs, and you're taking my people out."

"Okay."

He did a double take. "Okay?"

"Yeah. I'm going to leave you here. With her."

"You're bluffing."

"I'm not." I rose, faced him squarely. "You know, Jarrett used to talk a lot like you. He never believed in any of the things I believe in. He never wanted to be a soldier. But you . . . you've always struck me as hard-core."

"Yeah, when your father's commanding the Colonial Wardens, everybody thinks you're going to follow in Dad's footsteps. I've always hated not having a choice."

"Guess I'd feel the same."

Perhaps my lingering bitterness over my brother's death—or supposed death—made me strike back at the Corps by doing something I swore I'd never do: let Paul stay. Or maybe I just felt sorry for him, for a life dictated by his father's choices, not his own. To this day, I'm still uncertain what really made me change my mind, but the act would later have an interesting and unexpected effect on Paul.

"All right, people," Paul called in a familiar command tone. "Take them up through tunnel eight."

McFarland and two others nodded, as Paul waved his little magic wand over my tac, reactivating it. He did likewise to Halitov. I immediately skinned up and called upon my tactical computer to show me the whereabouts of my platoon.

The image of two ATCs already airborne robbed my breath. The entire platoon had already evacuated the caves. "Kohrana, copy?"

"Is that you, St. Andrew?"

"Affirmative."

"Thought we lost you, just like your XO."

"Negative. Tac malfunction. And I've located my XO and about a dozen cadets who've been hiding here since the first attack."

"Get up to the main entrance. We're coming back for you."

"Negative. What's the status on that Alliance fleet?"

"Troop carriers en route. They'll make moonfall in approximately twenty-one minutes."

I ordered my computer to pull up a satellite image of those carriers. My God, there must have been a thousand of them, each jetting a full platoon toward the academy grounds.

"Just get back," I told Kohrana. "I know another way out of here. And do me a favor: relay my status to Disque. Ask him to hold back one ATC for us. Have it wait out in the canyon below Whore Face."

"Aye-aye. And hey, St. Andrew. You're an asshole . . . but good luck."

"Yeah," I said with a snort. "Thanks."

I de-skinned, glanced around at Paul's ragtag

team. "There's a tunnel that'll take us all the way back to the academy, out near Whore Face."

"They know it," said Paul. "But from here it'll take at least an hour to get there. I'll contact the pilot for you, tell him to hang low until you're almost there."

"Thanks." I regarded the group. "All right. Let's gear up and go." Abruptly realizing that I might never see the colonel's son again, I offered my hand. "Come with us."

He took the hand, shook firmly. "If she does wake up, I don't want her in there alone. I have enough supplies to last a couple more months. They won't find me in there."

"I hope you're right." I turned, accepted a particle rifle from McFarland, then started off.

"Scott?" Paul called after me. I glanced back. "If you ever run into my father, don't tell him what happened here. Don't tell him anything."

I nodded and almost wished I had shared with him how the Wardens wanted to recruit me as part of their plan to push the new colonial government in the right direction. But telling him that his father was organizing a "mild" coup would only deepen his disillusionment.

We moved as quickly and stealthily as we could, though Halitov and I could have accessed the bond and traversed the passageways in seconds instead of minutes. McFarland assumed command of the cadets, and while he wasn't thrilled about still answering to me, he behaved professionally and even thanked me for allowing Paul to remain behind. Five minutes into our trek, we reached an intersection, where a much wider tunnel cut at a forty-five-degree angle across our path, and smack in the middle of it lay a hole with a diameter of about two meters, with an identical one bored into the ceiling. "What do we got?" I asked McFarland, as we paused and hunkered down near the wall.

"The machines below us emit some kind of a pulse wave, which comes up through here. I wouldn't get too close to that hole. There . . . there's one now."

The ground rumbled for a moment before a shimmering blue-green orb shot up from the floor and passed through the hole in the ceiling. Two seconds later, another one came. Two more seconds, and the third rocketed skyward. They kept coming at two-second intervals.

"I've seen this before," I said, remembering the night Dina and I had jogged out to the canyon. We had been getting ready to leave when she had spotted the light show in the distance. Now I stood directly over the source.

"We've thrown rocks at them," said McFarland. "And they get vaporized."

"You got point," I told him. "Let's move."

He rose and dashed off, with Halitov just behind him. I waved on the others, then pulled up the rear. I neared the pit and paused as the orbs shot past me. A strange compulsion to touch one drew me toward the hole, my arm extended, fingers twitching as they neared the eerily beautiful light. Just a few inches away. One inch. A hairsbreadth.

Suddenly, the quantum bond surged within me. At the beginning of the universe, all matter was one. All time was one. Time and space have expanded, but at that moment I found myself watching nebulae coalesce into stars and black holes grow bright as they returned to their original states. Billions of galaxies gathered toward a central region as I surveyed it all from a spectacular vantage point. McFarland, I realized, had been wrong about the rocks. They were not vaporized but transported to another space, another time.

Over the years I've shared the experience with close friends, but I'm often told that it was either my imagination or, perhaps, an image put in my head by the machines. In any event, the vision seemed to confirm what we suspect about the origin of the universe and how the mnemosyne allow us to tap into that most basic, most powerful of forces. I've come to theorize that the emissions are not created by the machine but represent a natural seam in the fabric of the space-time continuum. The ancient Racinians located this seam running through Exeter and opted to build their conditioning facility and machines close to it, perhaps in an attempt to harness its power.

And what power I sensed, though the entire experience lasted no more than a few seconds. Multiple rounds of particle fire jarred me away from the orbs and toward the tunnel ahead, where Paul's people were shouting.

More gleaming rounds split the air just a quarter meter left of my head as I reached the rearmost cadet, a scrawny woman whose name I had already forgotten. She had skinned up but had kept the shield near her face clear. She looked scared. "McFarland says we got two snipers up ahead."

"And I say we got no time for this." I found the

bond, skinned up, and bolted past the line of cadets, running directly into the snipers' fire.

Either McFarland or Halitov called me, I wasn't sure. My name echoed through the tunnel as the snipers' beads narrowed and struck my abdomen for all of two seconds before I willed them away, bending them back toward their sources.

I saw the first sniper to my left. He had scaled a stalagmite and had roped himself tightly to it, up near the tunnel's roof. His own stream of fire burrowed into his combat skin, weakened it, broke through, then tore apart his chest—before he knew what had happened. I didn't spot the second sniper until I heard the death groan, off to the right. I jogged a few meters farther, saw him scrunched into a shallow depression in the cave wall, near the floor.

Rooslin came running over, raised his brow at the dead Marine. "I still have trouble doing that. One of these days you're going to teach me."

I sighed and scanned our course. "All clear. Move out."

Once again, I pulled up the rear, and occasionally I'd look up to see my brother leading the way, with Dina and Clarion just behind him. I'd shiver off the déjà vu and the memories and warily keep moving.

No light poured into the tunnel to indicate we neared its end, but we had been traveling for nearly an hour. McFarland called for a halt. I double-timed up the line and joined him and Halitov as we dropped to our bellies and crawled outside, onto the bluff opposite Whore Face. We shifted past the wide lip of rock that concealed the tunnel entrance from the riverbed below. I skinned up and zoomed in on the canyon floor below Whore Face, not far from the spot where Cavalier had died.

"C'mon, Disque, you old prick. Don't let me down," I muttered as I panned the area, searching for the quad-winged silhouette of an ATC.

And wouldn't you know, an ATC came roaring over old Whore Face, turned on its starboard wings, and descended smartly toward the canyon floor.

"Paul must've gotten through to the pilot," said Halitov.

I scrolled through a communications data bar and locked onto the pilot's frequency. "ATC Delta Five-Six, copy?"

"Copy, Captain. Ready to load and dust off in one mike, copy?"

"Copy. We'll be there."

"Better move, Captain. We got troop carriers dropping all over the place."

"I hear that. Stand by."

Two things happened at once. Actually, three things, though the latter was less alarming.

Even as the ATC's skids touched ground, an artillery nest on our side of the riverbed opened up on the ship, launching heavy particle rounds that struck and began weakening the vessel's combat skin.

Behind us, back in the tunnel, that familiar and dreaded sound of rifle fire returned, along with a scream: "I'm hit! Oh my God! I'm hit! I'm hit!" Paul's people began pouring out of the tunnel, with a few trailing behind, shifting backward and firing wildly into the darkness.

I traded a look with Halitov, realizing with a start that he was returning to his aged self right before my eyes. I opened my mouth, about to mention it as I sprang to my feet and brought my rifle to bear.

An explosion below stole my attention.

The ATC had been trying to climb away from the mortar fire when its shield had finally succumbed. Our ride out burst into dozens of fire-licked fragments that lit up the canyon wall as they plummeted toward the riverbed.

I whirled away from the destruction, even as an Alliance Marine darted from the tunnel, took a half dozen rounds from Paul's people, then fell—but not before spraying the area with a wild bead. I craned my head, even as McFarland, who was just skinning up, took a round just above his Adam's apple. Direct spine shot. No chance of resuscitation.

"There's a whole squad in there," cried the scrawny woman I had been following. "Here they come!"

"Fuck. What do we now?" Halitov asked darkly.

I gave him a funny look. Wasn't it obvious? "Run!"

6 ❯ I waved on Paul's group, ordering them to take the rocky path down toward the riverbed, where our ATC lay burning and strewn across the dust. Halitov took point, which he wasn't thrilled about, but he and I were the only conditioned officers, and I planned on stalling those Marines still inside the tunnel.

We had already lost McFarland and two other cadets, but the rest made it out and charged in behind Halitov. As the scrawny woman passed me, she asked, "What do we do now, sir, with no ride home?"

"Not your problem. You worry about dropping more Marines and clearing our path."

"Aye-aye, sir!"

For a nanosecond, I wished her problems were mine. I was the one who had to find us another ride, and as my gaze lifted skyward, all I saw were the running lights of Western Alliance crab carriers and smaller troop carriers descending like multicolored meteors in slow motion. Antiaircraft guns operated by tactical computers, their human operators already aboard escape shuttles, sent streaming globules of white-hot fire toward those colorful lights.

Crouching tightly against the lip of rock, I braced myself, planning on using the bond and the quitunutul arts to launch myself at the first Marine to exit. With the *gozt* I'd take him out, even as I aimed my rifle at the next soldier. The maneuver and its result shone so vividly in my mind's eye that when I caught my first glimpse of the Marine, his combat skin fluctuating from black to a dusty brown, I gave little thought to the fact that my conditioning might fail me. I saw what I needed to do. Waited. Spotted him.

I sprang from the rock, launched myself into the air, and felt nothing but a meager rebound from the bluff. I rose a couple of meters and would have made a respectable *gozt* into the Marine's chest, had he not easily dodged my advance and opened fire.

Two more Marines joined the first, adding twin thunderclaps of fire that riddled my combat skin with rounds and set alarms flashing in my HUV. The tactical computer reported evenly, "Skin at forty percent and falling. Estimated penetration in nine seconds. Eight, seven, six—"

I tried rolling out of their beads.

"Five, four, three—"

Tried to reach the path, where the nearest boulder shaped like a blunt arrowhead stood, offering good cover.

"Two, one—"

My last word was nothing profound, just a simple recognition of the inevitable: "Shit."

A slight sting rushed through my shoulder as I came out of the roll, bumped my head on the boulder, then saw the three Marines drop, all shot in the back by someone inside the tunnel. A skinned figure charged out, his shield glistening a moment before trickling away.

Even as I stared at my rescuer, data bars flashed, reporting that my shoulder wound was only superficial and being attended to by the suit.

"You all right?" Paul asked, lowering his rifle, his cheeks red and tear-stained. He grabbed my wrist, yanked me to my feet.

"You coming with us?"

"Yeah. It was like she knew," he gasped.

"What're you talking about? Who knew?"

"Dina."

"What happened?"

"She's gone, Scott. I went back to check on her, and I thought I heard her in my mind. She told me it was all right. She told me to go. Then the machine just . . . stopped. I checked her pulse. She's gone." He choked up once more. "I guess even the Racinians can't raise the dead."

I nodded. "I'm sorry, Paul."

He wiped off a tear. "I tried to get her down from the machine. I couldn't detach those tubes, those things. We'll come back for her body. I swear. Let's get the hell out of here."

We hightailed it down the path, exploiting the boulders for cover and catching up with the rest of the group within a few minutes. Halitov and the others were as surprised as I was by Paul's appearance. Whispering, I told Halitov of Dina's death, and he nodded and went to Paul.

"I'm sorry," Halitov told the colonel's son.

"Let's get to that talus and scree near the base. It'll make good cover," Paul said quickly, burying his pain in the business of escape. He craned his head toward me. "If that's okay with you?"

Had he uttered his last sentence with sarcasm, I would've returned the same, but he had said that in earnest, remembering that I was senior officer. "You're used to being in charge. Don't let me stop you—and you're still in command of these people. Just answer to me."

"Thanks."

Down below, hidden behind cracked shoulders of stone that had dropped off the hillside, we stared gravely at the dying embers of our ATC.

"Situation assessment," said Halitov, glancing around for effect. "Multiple enemy carriers dropping hundreds of troops. Friendlies have already evacked. No chance of another ATC getting through their defenses and said troops dispersing to terminate remaining enemy personnel—meaning us. Short version: we're fucked."

"That's correct, Mr. Halitov," said Paul in a tone so formal that it reminded me of our academy days. "And they're hitting the jackpot, taking three conditioned officers into custody."

"That can't happen," I said.

Paul nodded. "We'll kill ourselves first."

"Fuck that," cried Halitov. "You want to join your girlfriend, go ahead. We're not following."

"Hey, *Captain*," I said, reminding the whiner of his rank. "Have you looked in the mirror? You're dying anyway."

"And not alone. But I'll take whatever time I got left. I want to get back. Get a couple of hookers and go on a two-week R&R. I want to die while getting laid. And I want Breckinridge to watch, so she can see what she could've had."

"Wait a minute," I said. "Maybe we have an ace in the hole—if she's still talking to me." I ordered my tac to show me classified comm channels and found the one Kristi Breckinridge had used to contact me. Time for a long-distance call with the minutes billable to the Seventeen System Guard Corps.

The link established, despite the enemy's jamming the standard battle frequencies, and the time delay was reduced significantly by new communications technology inspired by the Racinians and having something to do with rerouting the signal through a space-time fluctuation field. At that moment, I could have cared less about the physics.

"St. Andrew. It's about time," she said, her voice cracking ever so slightly. "I've been monitoring your progress."

"Our ATC got tommyed."

"I know."

"Can we bum a ride?"

"That's pretty glib for a man who's surrounded by over ten thousand enemy troops."

"Forget the details. Concentrate on this: I found Halitov. And Paul. They're both safe and with me."

"What about Dina Forrest?"

"She's dead."

"All right, then. The rest of the fleet's getting ready to tawt out, but one of our endo/exo skimmers has just tawted in to cover the retreat. I'll contact the colonel and have that ship punch a hole in the Alliance's artillery and send down a dropshuttle for you."

"Were it that easy. ETA?"

"Give me about twenty minutes."

"Uploading coordinates now."

"Receiving. Just stay alive."

"Oh, we will. Just don't leave us here. Understand?" I broke the link before she could reply and shared the news with Halitov and Paul.

"Now we're really in bed with her," said Halitov.

"What are you bitching about?" I asked. "Isn't that what you want?"

He rolled his eyes, checked the charge on his rifle.

"Those skimmers are pretty awesome," said Paul. "Lightest, fastest ships in the fleet. Our taxi blew up, so they're sending down a limo. Not bad. That Breckinridge sounds like a player."

"Yeah, she's a player, all right. And she works for your father."

Paul sobered and shifted off, spying the riverbed.

"Well, all we have to do is wait," said Halitov. "And not get—"

Particle fire boomed over his words and sheared off gaping pieces of rock. We ducked behind a long slab of stone, about bench height, and I crawled toward its edge, even as the incoming continued. Peering around the edge, I zoomed in on our attackers: a squadron of Marines lying on their bellies and strung out along the top of Whore Face.

Fire punched gaping holes in the ground just a meter from my boots, and our cover began crumbling before our eyes. I crawled back to Halitov and Paul and reported the squadron.

"They know if they keep firing, we won't stay here," Paul said.

"I'm surprised they haven't used any A-three," said Halitov.

Paul and I put our index fingers to our lips. The big

guy was going to jinx us. Too late. We heard the in-coming round's whistle, saw the characteristic flash of the acipalm-three explosion—

Then ran like there was no tomorrow because in 3.98 seconds there wouldn't be.

The scrawny woman and another cadet, Adams, a tall guy with a thick neck, caught the tail end of the round. The acipalm worked quickly on their skins, and as they fell, writhing, screaming, knowing they were going to die, I kept running parallel to the slope, dashing from boulder to boulder, kicking over cairns placed years prior by academy cadets marking the trail. The screaming stopped, and, finally, I paused to catch my breath near a split boulder with a top that hung over like an awning. Halitov was there, panting. "Where's Paul?" he asked.

I craned my head, shot a glance back to the path I had just beat, saw Paul about fifteen meters back, kneeling over the scrawny woman. I called out to him.

He got to his feet, and, remaining hunched over, darted warily toward us.

And that's when another acipalm-three grenade whistled in and struck, no more than ten meters be-hind him. Even at night you could see the shattered rock and dust and black goo heave up, block the stars for a terrifying heartbeat, then fall in an inescapable and deadly rain.

"Paul!" I cried again. "Run! Run!"

He didn't need me to tell him. I assumed he tried to find the bond, but his conditioning had failed, be-cause he sprinted toward us at a normal pace until a scintillating piece of acipalm struck his left arm and began bubbling and chewing into his skin.

Even as he reached us, he wailed, trying to brush off the burning goo, but his hand came up fiery as the skin over it began to succumb.

I grabbed his wrist, then grabbed Halitov's, ordering our tacs to transfer as much energy as possible to Paul's combat skin. As our fields grew dimmer, Paul's brightened and began to throb over his arm and hand. His eyes rolled back in his head, and he collapsed.

Halitov yanked his hand free. "Don't ever do that again," he shouted. "You know how I am about sharing this skin. No one comes in here with me."

At the moment, the last thing I needed was him reminding me of his boyhood trauma and the fact that he had refused to transfer his own energy to Dina when she had been stabbed the first time and had been dying.

The rest of the cadets gathered around me as I crouched down near Paul, and for a few seconds, the world went dreamlike, my senses overloaded by the battlefield. Another round of acipalm-three fell wide, melting into the mountainside. Particle fire sewed ribbons a couple meters below us, the rhythm reminding me of a weird dance song Dina was fond of. More artillery boomed in the distance, accompanied by the multiple pitches of turbines from over a dozen classes of assault craft flying overhead. And lying before me was my friend, with nearly fifty percent of his arm burned down to the bone and only the thumb remaining on his right hand. I'll never forget that stench. I kept telling myself it could've been worse had we not helped him, but the sight of his burned hand and arm was just horrible. Just horrible.

"Lieutenant," screamed Hollis. "Lieutenant, come on, sir." She looked at me. "If we get him back to the cave—"

"Yeah, I know. But our ride will be here soon."

"And if it isn't?" asked Halitov, crouching down beside me.

I waved off his question, focused my attention on Hollis. "You people got packs. What do you got in them? Any medical supplies?"

"I've got some cling and four-by-fours," said Hollis.

"Then while we're waiting, you dress those wounds. Best thing for burns is cold water. Get one of your canteens."

She glared at me, then turned for her pack.

I dropped to my hands and knees, crawled toward the edge of the rock behind us, and surveyed the canyon. The Marines atop Whore Face had moved out, heading east, toward the winding, cliff-side trail that would take them down, across the riverbed, and toward us.

"Why couldn't they just stay up there?" groaned Halitov, hovering at my shoulder.

I glanced dubiously at him. "You thought this was going to be easy?"

"Guess I'm always asking for too much. Shit."

I ducked behind the rock. "All right, here's what I'm thinking. That skimmer'll get through. No doubt about that. But the dropshuttle they're going to send won't last five minutes against that artillery fire."

"Yeah, it's going to blow up, just like our ATC," he reported matter-of-factly. "Your point is?"

"That we're going to be thieves in the night. I count

two bunkers. We'll take them out quietly. And if we spot any SAM sites, we're taking them out, too. Remember when Pope used to say no superhero bullshit? Well, if he were sizing up this grid, he'd tell us it's time to use superhero bullshit. You with me?"

"I guess so."

"Hell, it's not like your life depends on it."

"Like you said, we're all dying."

"What's the matter now?"

He closed his eyes. "I've been thinking a lot about my sister. She could be up there, aboard one of those ships, fighting for the alliances."

"Rooslin, man, we have a job to do. I'm going over there to tell them our plan and have them sit tight with Paul."

"Yeah, whatever."

If Halitov had any team spirit and will to survive, he had left them back inside the caves. I needed him one hundred percent. I was lucky to get fifty. But when push came to shove, he would come through. In fact, he wouldn't be my problem, Hollis would. When I returned to the cadets, she and Paul were gone.

A second year named Bell, with bright green eyes and an impressive goatee, huddled behind the scree and turned glassy eyes on me. "Sir, Hollis said she was taking him back to the caves. I'm sorry, sir."

I nearly lost my breath. "Did you try to stop her?

"Not physically, sir, but—"

"Shut up." Using infrared I scanned the slope behind us and picked up Hollis dragging Paul along the path. I patched into Halitov's comm. "Rooslin, you're going to take out those bunkers by yourself." I told him about Hollis, then, "Can you do it?"

"I guess so."

"No, you tell me you can do it."

Dead air.

"Rooslin!"

"All right! On my way."

After glancing once more to Hollis and Paul, I took a chance, reached into the bond, and willed myself to their location. A wave of dizziness passed through me as I realized I was standing just ahead of them, with Hollis's back to me as she dragged Paul. "Hold it right there."

She jerked her head, shocked by my presence. "Where did you . . ."

"Never mind. What're you doing?"

"The caves can make him whole again; otherwise, if the nanotech doesn't take, he'll be stuck with prosthetics."

"That's not your decision to make."

She set Paul down and faced me. "He would want this."

"We're taking him back. Right now."

"Sir, please—"

"Our ride's going to be here. And we're all going to get on it, including him. Those are the facts. Let's go."

"Sir, I love him, sir."

"We all love him. Move out!"

"No, sir. I *love* him. And what he did for Dina is what I want to do for him."

Only a few times in my life have I seen an expression as determined as hers was. And that expression gave me pause—a pause that saved our lives.

A shell exploded over the remaining cadets, and with a start I recognized the sound. Smart schrap. *Oh,*

God. With dread I craned my head toward them. Computer-controlled fragments needled into their combat skins. I had all of three seconds to watch Bell and the others die before particle fire pinged and ricocheted all around us. The Marines from atop Whore Face had reached the slope.

Hollis and I grabbed Paul and carried him toward the nearest boulder. We set him down, then crouched low, the dusty stone at our shoulders. "Thanks," I told Hollis.

"Sir?"

I wanted to answer, "For listening to your heart," but all I said was, "Forget it." I felt like a shuttle passenger who had missed his flight, only to discover the shuttle had crashed.

"We can't stay here," she said, her eyes shifting as she read the information pouring in on her HUV.

"Rooslin?"

"Little . . . busy . . . right . . . now." I heard a scream, thought I heard a bone or a head or something crush. Particle fire thundered.

"Captain St. Andrew?" came a voice over my channel. "This is CW Pilot Kenner, copy?"

"Copy you, Lieutenant."

"We've just left the skimmer. Punching the hole now. ETA to your location: two minutes, copy?"

"Copy. We're taking out some bunkers down here, but we still got a ground force. Got them on your scope?"

"Got 'em. We'll lay down some suppressing fire."

"Copy. Flare's up now."

"See you on the ground. Kenner out."

I reached into a small pocket built into my boot,

withdrew the microflare, thumbed a switch, tossed the flare straight up. It took off like a rocket, leaving a brilliant green streak that Alliance Marines could not erase.

Of course, that streak gave up our location to those Marines, and they opened up with everything they had. I wanted very badly to charge them, turn all of their beads back toward themselves, but the bond felt weak. I agonized over taking the chance, then just remained with Hollis, huddled behind the rock, as rounds chiseled away at our cover.

Paul's eyes flickered open, and he raised his head, took one look at his bandaged arm, and shuddered violently. "Fuck it, Scott. Leave me here. Dina's gone. There's nothing now, man. Nothing. It was all for nothing."

"No, it wasn't. You have to come back with me now. You have to tell your old man the truth."

"Yeah, and stand court-martial."

"Don't worry about that now."

He was about to say something, but the approaching whine of our dropshuttle overpowered even the incoming. I caught a glimpse of the silver ship, its boxy nose and heavy landing gear making it look more dog- than birdlike as it zeroed in on the Marines opposite us. A salvo of acipalm-three bombs dropped from its belly, struck the ground, and heaved all hell in a rumbling wave. You could hear the Marines screaming, smell the flesh melting as the dropshuttle's exhaust turned the dropzone into a sandstorm.

"Rooslin?"

"Yeah, I see our ride," he said. "Don't leave without me."

The dropshuttle had not taken any artillery fire, so I had to assume he had neutralized the bunkers. Even as the ship landed and its bay door cycled open, Halitov appeared through the whipping dust. He limped forward a few steps, stumbled, fell onto his stomach.

"Go!" I ordered Hollis, as two Colonial Wardens dressed in navy blue utilities jumped out and jogged toward us.

She looked at Paul, saw that the Wardens would carry him, then ran toward the ship.

I sprinted back for Halitov, reached him, then rolled him over. Shit. Round in the leg. Round in the shoulder. Gaping cut across the forehead. With help from only my surging adrenaline, I dug hands under his arms and dragged him back toward the ship. I didn't realize that I was being fired upon by two Marines who had escaped the acipalm-three strike. Later on, the pilots would tell me that those rounds had chewed into my back, weakened my skin, and torn through my shoulders. All I knew was that by the time I got on board, I couldn't understand why I felt so weak. I remember thinking, *Good-bye, Dina*, as the ship blasted away.

The ride back was equally dramatic, though I couldn't describe it with much detail since I passed out even before we broke atmosphere. I heard that we had taken several direct hits, that our landing gear and guidance systems had been destroyed, and that were it not for the expert piloting of the skimmer's captain, who managed to scoop us out of orbit with the ferocity of a mother bird saving her young, we'd all be dead. She was the first person I thanked with a bottle of expensive bourbon. Kenner, the dropshuttle's pilot, preferred Tau Ceti vodka. Hollis, the only cadet to escape Exeter, had trouble meeting my gaze when we were wheeled into the *Auspex*'s sickbay. I thought of reassuring her that I wouldn't report her insubordination, but I didn't get the chance. She was examined, extensively debriefed, then shipped out, all while I spent the next forty-eight hours recuperating. She didn't even come to say good-bye. I thought for certain she'd at least bid farewell to Paul.

At my request, they put my gurney next to Halitov's, and beside him lay Paul, whose temples were going gray.

"Three stooges, huh?" I said.

"Who?" asked Halitov.

"Stooge. What does that mean?" added Paul. "Is it like a musketeer?"

"Just forget it." My father was a film buff who really enjoyed the old comedies; I shouldn't have expected them to understand the reference.

Kristi Breckinridge entered the bay, lips glossed and hair freshly gelled. I didn't feel much for beauty marred by cunning. However, Halitov examined her every curve as she nodded to us, then approached Paul's bed. She knew we would listen in, but she didn't seem to care.

"I've sent word to your father," she told him.

He threw his good arm over his eyes. "So?"

"So he'll be thrilled that you're alive."

"Now he can watch his son get thrown in jail for going AWOL."

"Well, if it's any consolation, you've got three things on your side: a good lawyer, a famous father, and a war in which every conditioned officer is needed. If you do any time, it'll be short. And your father will do everything he can to get you reassigned to the Wardens."

"Just what I've always wanted," he said grimly.

She pursed her lips. "You've been through a lot. The doctors say you're responding well to the nanotech repairs. That's good. And you'll come around. Get some rest." She was about to leave, then stopped. "Oh, one more thing. I'm sorry about Dina."

"Get the fuck out of here!" he suddenly screamed, then rolled over and buried his head in his pillow.

She shook her head and started out. As she passed my bed, I gestured her over. "Don't we have anything to discuss?"

"Like what?"

I scrunched up my eyes, turning my gaze into an old man's. "Call me insane, but I don't think any of us wants to be flapping our gums and using a cane before we're twenty-five."

"I told you that the aging's not that predictable and that the meeting's being rescheduled."

"When and where?"

"I don't know yet. We've had some problems."

"Like what?"

"Like in a few minutes, Disque is going to come in here and relieve you of command of Zodiac Company."

I sat up, winced as the synthskin over the wounds on my back pulled a little. "Say again?"

"You've lost Zodiac."

"Why?"

"Apparently somebody high up, maybe your friend Ms. Brooks, wants you and Halitov running Special Ops. They say you work better with small teams."

"So I'm getting transferred to the Wardens," I concluded.

She shook her head. "The Seventeen's putting together a new special forces group, codename Rebel ten-seven. We think it's in reaction to the rumors that we're tying to manipulate the government."

"So our new government doesn't trust its own special forces and decides to create another unit . . . to do what? Combat the first one?"

"Maybe."

"Jesus . . . divided we fall."

"Yeah, well, you and Halitov are being groomed to become key players in this new Rebel ten-seven, but we'll keep doing everything we can to get you transferred to us."

"I thought that wouldn't be a problem."

"So did we. But like I said, somebody upstairs is really pulling some strings. The colonel's pushing hard but getting nowhere. We'll need you to put in your own transfer request."

"Let's have that meeting first."

She nodded. "I'll get back with you as soon as I have something. And by the way, your AAT will start up tomorrow."

"Combat training? I'm not even healed yet."

"You will be. And I hope you'll be ready for me. While you were down on Exeter, I came up with a new move I want to show you."

"Can you show it to me, too?" asked Halitov, his salacious tone making me grimace.

"With pleasure. Of course, it could make you sterile."

He frowned.

"Kidding," she finally said, then turned to me, her lip quivering. "Say hi to your mother for me." She hurried toward the door.

"Captain?"

She froze, didn't look back. "What is it?"

"Maybe one day you can tell me about your brother . . ."

She faced me, shook her head, then left.

"What a nice ass," said Halitov. "What a very nice ass."

"Yeah, on a woman we can't trust," I reminded him.

"What do we got to lose?" he asked.

I glanced past him to Paul. "Hey, Paul. You all right?"

He rolled back over but kept his arm over his eyes. "Oh, yeah, I'm fucking great. How're you?"

"Stupid question. Sorry. Dina was a hero. You know that, right? You know that."

"Yeah, well now she's a corpse."

Halitov looked at me, shrugged. "You had to ask, huh?"

I thought a moment, decided it best to change the subject. "Paul, what do you think about Breckinridge? About the Wardens?"

"I don't fucking care about any of that," he said. "I need to get back to Exeter. Dina deserves a proper burial. I should've tried harder to get her off that machine. I should've carried her out of there."

"There wasn't time," I told him. "You did the right thing."

"No, I didn't."

"How're you going to get to Exeter now?" asked Halitov. "Go AWOL again? To do what? Bury her?"

"If I have to."

"Paul, we'll work it out. I'll send word to Ms. Brooks. She'll come up with a plan to get Dina. If you can't get there, I will. You'll just need to tell me how to get inside that machine. We'll bring her back and bury her properly."

He tightened his lips, then shifted over, his back to us.

"Far as I'm concerned, I never want to see that rock ever again," said Halitov. "Never again."

"Yeah, but you never get what you want," I reminded him.

He looked at Paul, then at me. "Neither do you."

I lay back on my bed, closed my eyes, thought of Dina hanging on the wall. Although I had said the words—Dina is dead—the reality of her loss finally took hold. Back at the academy, she had been my counselor, my savior, my strength. Though she had rejected me at first, she had spoken so gently and honestly that she had made me love her even more. I'm not sure how or why, but she understood me when no one else could. "There's something about you," she had said. "I don't know what it is. I just get the feeling that I was meant to know you. And that mark on your face? I think it's a blessing. You just don't recognize it." I'll never forget those words. And knowing her was the greatest blessing of all.

Good-bye, Dina.

My thoughts shifted to Paul, to the guilt I felt for having fallen in love with his girlfriend, and I knew then what our relationship would be. No matter how jovial we appeared on the outside, we would always feel the burn of jealousy and mistrust. Still, I felt like I owed him something, an apology at least. Then again, I wasn't sorry for what I had done. I had always thought of him as the privileged one, the guy who had no trouble with women. He would find another love. I was a gennyboy. Who would understand me the way Dina had?

"Captain? I got some bad news for you and good news for me."

Slowly, I opened my eyes and glanced at Disque's ugly face. "Want to trade?" I asked.

He smiled darkly. "All right, son. Listen up . . ."

A few years ago, I ran into Disque at a veterans' benefit. They wheeled what was left of him into the hall. The son of a bitch didn't even remember me.

PART 2

⊘ ⊙

Treading Water

10 **Just two weeks** after our narrow escape from Exeter, Halitov and I found ourselves running like hell across the deck of the *Eri Flower*, a floating research vessel nearly two kilometers long and sailing at four knots through the great Northern Vosaic Ocean of Epsilon Eri III. We weren't running for our health; then again, maybe we were. Our cover had been blown, and four Alliance Marines skinned up and were charging after us. Particle fire punched through a pair of life tubes just ahead on our right and purple coolant spilled through the Swiss cheese of their bright blue hulls.

"They're going to run our tac codes through their system," cried Halitov, sprinting a few steps ahead of me. He hit the coolant, fell on his ass. Swore.

I helped him up. "We're done here."

"But how do we call for extraction? They'll be jamming our comm now."

"We're not calling."

"The hell you talking about?"

"This is a recon mission," I reminded him breathlessly. "We already got off the signal. The brass have everything they need about the Alliance's occupation here."

"So we're expendable."

"Says so on our résumés."

"Not on mine."

III

We kept running, dodging the fire and squinting against the planet's bright, K2 orange star. I had no plan, and I suspected Halitov knew I had no plan. We had been told that if we were discovered, we should use any and all means necessary to escape. And if we were captured, a single coded message to our tac's computer would put us in cardiac arrest with no chance for resuscitation. As we continued toward the ship's bow, I thought it might very well come to that.

Four scientists in lab coats stood near the railing ahead, measuring something with small instruments. The *Eri Flower* was an aquacultural researcher's paradise, and over fifty thousand brains from nearly all seventeen systems lived aboard her to study new ways to improve cultivating marine or freshwater food fish or shellfish. Those brains were instrumental in improving food supplies in over half the colonies, and consequently, the side who controlled the ship gained a valuable proving ground for both the academic and business communities. We had lost the *Flower* during the first month of the war. Only now was the new colonial government interested in recapturing the ship. It seemed obvious to me that without a strong food supply, you couldn't fight a war. I would've defended the food and other supplies first, but that idea was naive and made too much sense. I've learned without surprise that government officials are sometimes bribed by representatives from conglomerates like Exxo-Tally and Inte-Micro. In fact, scuttlebutt had it that we had lost the *Eri Flower* because most of the troops assigned to defend her had been moved to Drummer Fire, a terrestrial planet well-known for producing an expensive lubricant called Crude 57A. We saved the production plants on Drummer Fire. The crude continued to flow. Colonial profits continued to be made. And the *Eri Flower* fell into the hands of the alliances.

But now, Halitov and I were part of an intelligence-gathering mission to win her back. We had tawted in posing via expensive DNA forgeries as Western Alliance security officers attached to a government research team from Luna. We had reveled in the idea of running an op on Epsilon Eri III, a world whose continents were entirely covered by seas and whose breathable atmosphere was purportedly the result of Racinian terraforming efforts. Neither of us had ever seen a real ocean, and we had both been disappointed when we learned that we wouldn't get a chance to see AQ-Tower, a modest-sized province whose largest buildings rose up through shallow waters. AQ was still held by colonial forces, as was Jones Rigi-Plat, an experiment in creating a kind of massive raft of biologics on which a city of two hundred thousand had been constructed, a city whose limits constantly grew. Both were impressive sights to see, but we weren't on vacation.

And the rounds buzzing near my ears continually reminded me of that.

The scientists craned their heads as we thundered by them, and I figured our gray security uniforms said we were responding to a call and not the reason for one. I caught up to Halitov, and as we sprinted on, I couldn't help but notice the calm, endless sea ahead of us, the water supposedly the same color as Earth's

Pacific Ocean near the California coastline. A great wedge of sunlight lay across the waves and narrowed toward the horizon. The open space, very uncharacteristic of the mines where I grew up, had made me feel warm and at peace from the moment I stepped aboard the ship. Now it reminded me of how cut off we really were.

"Aw, shit," moaned Halitov as four Marines rounded a corner ten meters up the deck and leveled their rifles at us. We could've run perpendicular to the rail, if we hadn't reached Research Platform Skid #17, a launching ramp for jumpsubs and other small water craft. I looked at the placard identifying the area as such. Escape Plan B, though pathetic, took hold. Maybe all that water held the answer.

"Let's go," I told him, throwing one leg over the rail.

"We're jumping overboard?" he asked.

"Abandon ship."

"Let's steal a jumpsub."

"No time."

The fact that the *Eri Flower*'s deck stood nearly four hundred meters above the ocean's surface probably had something to do with his reluctance, as did the *hirosasqui*, who ruled the planet's seas. Indigenous fish often compared to Earth's great white sharks, the *hirosasqui* are three times as large as the great whites and have seven dorsal fins. Halitov and I had been aboard the *Eri Flower* for about a week, and nearly every day one or both of us had spotted one of the beasts hunting smaller bait fish near the ship's hull. Combat suit or no, entering those alien waters would test our bravery and sanity.

But it was either that or take on all the Marines, pray the bond wouldn't fail us, kill them, and reveal that we weren't just spies but conditioned officers. Maybe we could hit the water instead, swim under the ship to an access point before they were able to launch a jumpsub. We'd find a dive hatch, get back on board, and evade those Marines long enough to find another way to signal for extraction. Pretty naive thinking, now that I consider it.

I didn't give Halitov a chance to argue further. I jumped, and even as I fell, I yelled, "Come on!"

He released a long cry, and I knew he had gone over the side. My security uniform flapped violently against the wind, and I had trouble forcing my head down to look at the ocean rushing up at me. I skinned up, and the tactical computer issued a mindless proximity alert that had me telling it to shut up. I wondered what it would feel like to hit the water at such a high velocity while skinned. They had not subjected us to anything like that at the academy. My curiosity wouldn't last long.

Reflexively, I held my breath, though my skin would recycle my air supply and keep me comfortably warm and dry. I hit the waves, and the water enveloped me with a dull force as I immediately weakened the skin to decrease the rebound. Surrounded by curtains of bubbles illumined by the phosphorescent green emitted by my skin, I sank three, four, maybe five meters, then the inertia wore off and the bubbles cleared. I whirled to get my bearings. There was the ship, off to my left, its dark gray hull curving down into the water so far that it blended seamlessly with the darkness. Out of the corner of my eye, I spotted Halitov, swimming toward me like a shimmering jellyfish. I opened a channel. "Stay close to the hull."

"I don't like it here," he said. "It feels kinda closed in, you know?"

"What're you talking about?" I argued, trying to shift his thoughts away from his phobia. "This ocean covers the entire planet."

We kicked hard, heading back to the ship, when a gauntlet of particle fire triggered from above streaked into the water. Glowing rounds chased away from me and dematerialized into the depths. I sighed with relief as I found the bond and torpedoed forward, feeling at least two rounds strike and rebound off my combat skin before I reached the algae-slick hull and began floating up. I increased the strength of my skin at my shoulders, and the force kept me submerged.

I shared the finding with Halitov, who swam up next to me and did likewise. "Nice trick," he said. "But floating down here begs the question, what now?"

"Working on it." My HUV shimmered to life, and I called up the *Eri Flower*'s schematics, zeroed in on our location, and scanned for dive hatches.

I didn't hear them at first, just felt the dull impact of the water they displaced as it reached me. Then I looked away from my HUV and saw the bubbles. Four Marines were in the water, their skins brightening as they drew closer.

"Fuckin' pool party," said Halitov, swimming past me toward our pursuers, who opened fire with QQ81 aquatic rifles that I had never seen in use. The weapons' highly accelerated rounds traveled through the water as though no drag were being placed upon them. The laws of physics were not being violated; those rounds were just god awfully powerful and fast. Halitov swam right into them.

"Uh, Rooslin?"

"I'm tired of running."

"But you're not running, you're . . ." I didn't finish. Nothing I could say would stop him.

After a huge breath, I stiffened and reached for the bond, diving beneath one of the Marines until I turned and shot straight up from below. He got off a round that struck the skin over my left eye and made me flinch a second before I wrenched the gun from his hand and found his tac. Off came the tac. And his hand. His drowned cry amid a swirl of rising bubbles faded as he floated toward the surface, blood jetting from his stump.

Two meters directly below us, Halitov wrested away another Marine's rifle, then did as I had taught him: he tore the tac from the Marine's wrist. She, like her comrade, screamed and trailed blood as she fought her way to the surface. The other two Marines were already retreating as I headed back toward the hull, with Halitov just behind me.

"We should've killed them," he said.

I reached the hull, pivoted to look up at the Marines heading toward the surface. A great, oval-shaped shadow glided near them. "We did kill them. You, me, and the *hirosasqui* that's up there now."

"Oh my God," he said, craning his head back.

With mind-boggling speed, the massive fish circled once, twice, then broke from the spin and launched it-self toward the Marines. The water displaced by the *hirosasqui's* powerful tail blew us back, into the hull. We couldn't see its face or its teeth, just all those dorsal fins cutting through the water like old-fashioned saw blades, sharp and relentless. The fish rose faster and faster. And though we couldn't hear them, you just knew those Marines were shrieking, watching this incredible maw some five or six meters in diameter rush up at them. I couldn't take my eyes off the scene as the carnivore made one quick lash of its tail and lunged at two of the Marines, swallowing them whole before it darted off and vanished.

Halitov and I floated there, breathing, not saying anything, until the *hirosasqui* pushed through the shadows and showed itself once more. For a terrifying moment, it took interest in us, barreled forward, came within a dozen meters, its cold, gray eyes the size of my fists narrowing on us. Then its head twitched, and it steered left, speeding toward the remaining Marines.

In the blink of an eye, the whip of a tail, those Marines were gone. Only this time, one of them hung limply in the animal's jaw, his head and arms flapping violently as the fish arrowed down, into the gloom.

Halitov's voice came thin and shivery. "What are we doing here, man?"

A chill wove up my own spine as I pulled up the schematic once again, this time ordering the computer to scan for entrances. A dive hatch about twenty meters away and located about ten meters below the ship's waterline appeared in a databar. "Found a way inside. Follow me."

Haunted by what we had just seen, we found the bond and broke all swimming records getting to that hatch. Once there, I punched in the code, one of nearly twelve thousand sets of numbers I had cerebroed prior to coming on board. We had also downloaded the ship's schematics, but we had later learned that the prints were outdated and that many of the ship's features had been upgraded after the alliances had taken control. Only data collected by our tactical computers would be useful, and that certainly proved correct as the doors parted, letting ocean water flood inside the lock. I waved Halitov in first.

As he pulled himself inside, something slammed into me. My head jerked. My back felt as though it had snapped. The force of rushing water pinned me to a smooth, rubbery surface. It was, arguably, one of the strangest sensations I have ever felt, and when I realized what had happened, none of it seemed real. A second *hirosasqui*, this one slightly smaller than the first, had caught me in the corner of its massive jaw.

"Scott? Jesus, Scott? Are you there?" Halitov screamed.

I forced my head down, saw that my combat skin held off the fish's razor-sharp teeth, though they hung just a few centimeters above my uniform. I drove my hands down, pressed palms onto its lips, and tried prying myself free against the awesome strength of its jaw.

"Scott? Where are you?"

"Rooslin, man. This thing's got me."

He didn't reply, but I could hear him hyperventilating.

The *hirosasqui* slowed almost to a stop, then shook

its head violently like a dog playing with an old sock. Though my skin blunted some of the force, the pauses and jerks sent the world spinning.

"Scott, use your skin, man. Full power. Full power!"

With palms still placed squarely on the fish's lips, I counted three, two, one, and did as Halitov had instructed. The repulsor field that rippled through my combat skin blasted open the fish's mouth and sent me tumbling away from it.

Panicking, I swam upright, whirled, searching for the *hirosasqui*.

And there it was, about twenty meters out and shooting straight toward me, mouth open, triple rows of beryl-like teeth clearly visible against the blackness of its gullet. I reached into my boot, withdrew one of my Ka-Bars, and even as I came up with it, the fish was on me.

"Scott, are you there?"

I slammed a fist into the thing's stout nose, then punched my knife home beside one of three nostril-like orifices. I dragged the blade a little, but the fish's skin was so thick that I hardly caused much damage. Surprisingly, though, the pain I inflicted was enough. The fish whipped its head around and retreated, my Ka-Bar sticking from it like an antenna.

"Scott? Are you there?"

I looked around. Nothing but ocean. The ship's hull was gone. I tried pulling up my location on my HUV, but all GPS signals were being jammed. "Hey, Rooslin. I'm okay, but, uh . . . I'm lost."

"Yeah. And it looks like the pool party's still not over . . ."

My gaze lifted to a whirring sound from above: a two-man jumpsub was plunging toward me, its yellow, bullet-shaped nose painted with a blue 6.

"Hold your position," came an unfamiliar voice over our private channel. "Or we will fire upon you."

I thought of the tac code that would end my life as I watched the jumpsub slow a little. Something flashed off to the right. The jumpsub exploded in a bubbling cloud of debris and dark liquids.

I paddled around, toward a different whirring, much lower in pitch, coming from behind me. Three skinned-up people riding a fast-moving skiff glided forward. I couldn't tell from their nondescript dry suits if they were military personnel, civilians, or even what side they were on, though the bubbles still pouring from one of their cannons indicated they had just taken out the jumpsub. One of them, the pilot, waved me on.

"Scott? There's a skiff here. They want me to get on board."

"Got one here, too. I think they took out that jumpsub. Let's take a chance."

"Aw, shit. All right."

The skiff, a long, sledlike vehicle with a clear, curving water shield that wrapped over us, seated up to six, and its cockpit and compartment remained open to the sea. The one I strapped myself into had seen better days and made me suspect that maybe, just maybe, these people were locals with no love for the alliances. I noted that much of their equipment was fishing-related, with several types of harpoons and spear-type weapons, along with the more contemporary particle and skin-powered devices.

As we started off, I looked at the woman seated next to me, her face barely visible through her skin. I tapped my ear, gesturing that I wanted her to open a channel and talk to me. She shook her head and grabbed an old-fashioned water board with pencil from a pocket behind the forward seat. CLOSE ALL CHANNELS, she wrote. NO SIGNALS.

WHO ARE YOU? I wrote.

She cocked a brow at me, wrote: CLASSIFIED.

ARE WE POWS NOW?

NO.

WHO ARE YOU?

She ignored the question and shoved the board and pencil back into their pocket.

I rolled my eyes, then leaned back and took in the view as we descended toward an amazing trench several kilometers deep and at least a half kilometer wide. The skiff's pilot switched on the headlights, and off to the left, another pair of lights clicked on and drew near. That'd be Rooslin's ride. I wasn't sure how deep we were descending, but one of my databars noted the increased water pressure on my skin. Soon, the water grew even darker, near black, and, finally, there were only the twin beams of light, twinkling with billions of tiny particles. We whirred on for at least another thirty minutes, and I began to drift off. After all, we'd had a busy day . . .

A nudge to the shoulder woke me, and my gaze focussed ahead on an exceedingly impressive sight that answered at least one of my questions. I recognized the ship immediately from my cerebroed data, the CWVN *Charles Michael*, a Valiant-class submarine equipped with the latest in Racinian-influenced technology, including a tawt drive capable of allowing the ship to jump even while submerged. As we drew closer, I gasped at her two colossal cylinders joined at their bows and sterns by wedge-shaped cross members that gave her the appearance of a submerged catamaran, sans the sail. If one of her cylinders was damaged, the other could detach and operate independently, making her in effect two submarines. Dim lights from hundreds of portholes shone like glowing rivets across her dark green hull.

As we maneuvered into our final approach, it dawned on me that once the brass had received our intelligence transmission, they might have decided to move the *Charles Michael* into the area as part of an extraction plan. When we didn't call, they had ordered the ship's captain to send out a recon team. But that seemed too easy, and the timing of our rescue was just too damned coincidental. Someone knew we had jumped ship. Someone knew we were in the water and needed extraction. I hoped my questions would be answered once we were on board.

We traveled up, into a docking pool located near the stern of the ship's port cylinder. We rose vertically, broke water, and glided toward a dock. I de-skinned and caught a whiff of seawater and a burning smell from the skiff's turbine. We bumped against the dock, and two crewmen began mooring the skiff while a third helped us out. I crossed to a rail and turned back to marvel at the huge docking station, with its sweeping overhead and half dozen pools where more skiffs, all of them as old as ours and betraying no evidence that they were being piloted by military personnel, were either arriving or prepping to head out. Above the pools, a command box jutted from the bulkhead, its wide windows revealing dozens of officers orchestrating and monitoring the activity via holos and conventional displays.

Halitov's skiff arrived, and I offered a hand, helping him onto the dock. He de-skinned, had a look around, regarded me with a crooked grin. "And I thought our luck sucked. Here we are. Rescued. How 'bout that?"

A tall, bearded man in his forties and wearing a dark blue command uniform came down a catwalk and toward us. A slightly shorter man, a lieutenant in his late twenties, trailed him. "Captain St. Andrew? Captain Halitov?" called the bearded officer. "I'm Commander Eric Main, ship's XO."

Halitov and I snapped to and saluted. "Sir," I acknowledged, wondering if I should follow with: "What the hell's going on, sir?"

The XO returned the salute. "As you were. I'm sure you have a lot of questions. I can take you up to C&C, but first, if you're hungry or you want to rest, I'll have Lieutenant Feers show you to our guest quarters."

"Sir, I'm hungry, sir," said Halitov.

"You can take us up, sir," I corrected.

Halitov shot me a dirty look. "I guess you can, sir."

A smile nicked the corners of the XO's mouth. "Very well then." He withdrew a pen scanner from his breast pocket. "Gentlemen, your tacs please."

"Sir, you're deactivating?" I asked.

"A security precaution. I insist."

Halitov stuck out his wrist, and the lights faded on his tac. Resignedly, I raised my arm, watched my tac wink out.

The XO pocketed the scanner and tipped his head. "Follow me."

Neither Halitov nor I had ever been aboard a submarine. I noted that corridors seemed a little more narrow, the hatches much more reinforced than those aboard your average interstellar craft. Other than those differences, the two were remarkably similar, and by the time we reached Command and Control, I had already forgotten we were deep within a submerged trench.

I felt a little awkward as the officers seated at their stations turned their heads to regard us. But the awkwardness quickly turned to sheer awe as I took in the view through an enormous, wall-to-overhead window that curved lazily around the forward half of the bridge. Beyond us lay the rocky walls of the trench, lit up here and there by dozens of skiffs coming and going. A pair of *hirosasqui* strayed near one of the skiffs. The pilot discharged a reddish brown ball that sent the carnivores veering after it. Still more sea life, colorful fish and a few aquatic creatures I'd never seen before, occasionally wriggled by the window. I could have remained there for an hour, just watching.

The XO led us down a short staircase to the captain's station, a long, U-shaped bank of displays behind which stood the woman herself.

"Skipper," began the XO. "This is Captain St. Andrew and Captain Halitov. Gentlemen, this is Captain Ves Angelino, Colonial Wardens."

We stood rigid and offered our salutes. She answered with a perfunctory salute of her own, then told us to stand easy as she blew an errant wisp of short brown hair from her eyes. It was hard to tell how old she was, maybe thirty, maybe even forty. Her gaze seemed wise and practiced, but her skin looked smooth and cast a faint glow. At least her deportment was easy to pin down and seemed friendly enough. "Gentlemen, I understand you've been running an intel op aboard the *Eri Flower*."

"Ma'am," I began tentatively. "I'm supposed to say that information is classified."

"Supposed to say," she echoed. "Very good, Captain. You've just covered your ass, but I'll save you the trouble of having to do that again. Let's get right to it. We've been running our own operation for several months now. We already have four people aboard the *Flower*. One of them was keeping tabs on you."

Halitov closed his eyes, and his shoulders slumped. "Begging your pardon, ma'am, but are you telling us that the Wardens are already gathering intel here and that our mission was redundant?"

"I'm afraid so, Captain. It's a classic case of one hand not knowing what the other is doing—and that's because the new colonial government doesn't trust us anymore."

"Then you knew we were being sent on this op," I said. "You knew all along."

"Of course we did, Scott." That reply came from behind us, the voice painfully familiar.

I glared back at Captain Kristi Breckinridge, who came down the stairs and raised her brows at me.

"We even have an operative working within Rebel ten-seven. We know exactly what the Seventeen is trying to do, which is all the more reason why you need to be with us. They send you down here on a wing and a prayer and with no backup plan for extraction. You should thank God we've been monitoring your progress."

My next came through clenched teeth. "Because we're valuable commodities, right?"

"You need us as much as we need you."

Angelino shifted between me and Breckinridge. "I suggest you continue this conversation in the wardroom."

"Yes, ma'am," Breckinridge replied.

Angelino hoisted her brows at me and Halitov. "If there's anything you gentlemen need, don't hesitate to ask."

We nodded, saluted, got out of there.

After a long and silent walk to the aforementioned room, Halitov and I entered. Breckinridge sealed the hatch behind us. I collapsed into a chair. "If you knew, why didn't you tell us? Why did you let us spend a week aboard that ship, risking our lives and wasting our time?"

"It's not that easy, Scott. I could've tipped you off, then I'd be tipping off the Seventeen as well."

"Hey, we would've kept your secret," said Halitov. "Remember, you've still got something we want."

"Yes, but we needed you to go through the motions and send that intel back to the Seventeen. We don't want them to know we've been in contact with you or that we have a presence here. The situation has grown even more tenuous, I'm afraid."

"How can the Seventeen not know you have a presence here? I'm thinking it's a little difficult to hide a ship this size."

"We're cloaked, and this may come as a surprise, but the *Charles Michael* was destroyed on Sirius BI while trying to defend one of the oil rigs there—at least that's what the Seventeen believes."

"How many other ships were reported destroyed and are now being used by the Wardens?"

"I'm not a liberty to say."

I folded my arms over my chest. "Do you people realize what you're doing? You're weakening the Seventeen. You're going to make us lose the war."

"That'll only happen if we don't act. We're the only hope."

"Don't hand me that melodramatic crap. You're getting ready to mount a coup. And I don't want any part of it."

She came behind me, stuck her head over my shoulder. "You don't know what you want anymore. If I were you, the first thing I'd want is to be reconditioned, to find out what really happened to my brother, and then, if I had to say thank you by doing everything I could to become a member of the Wardens, that's just what I'd do. What's so terrible about that?" She shifted around the table to face me. "Your friend Paul Beauregard has already been transferred. He's en route to Aire-Wu right now to be reconditioned."

"That's a lie. He would've had to stand for a general court-martial, and there's no way they could've convened one this soon."

She shrugged. "Believe what you want."

I shot to my feet. "If you don't mind, we need our tacs reactivated and a ride out to Nau Dane." That planet was a tenth of a light-year away from Epsilon Eri III, and Rebel 10-7's new command ship, the SSGC *Greenville* was, I had to assume, still in orbit there and waiting to hear from us.

"Right now, you're MIA. And we'd like you to maintain that status."

I snorted. "Translation: we're POWs."

"No. I just need you to come with me to AQ-Tower."

"Why?"

She started for the hatch. "Because your life depends on it." With that, she left.

"I'd like to do her," said Halitov.

I just looked at him.

"Hey, don't you think about it?"

"Excuse me if right now I'm little preoccupied by the fact that we're being held against our will."

He recoiled. "We're not being held. She probably set up that meeting. We even get to see AQ-Tower. This is what we want."

"I'm not so sure anymore."

"Take a look in the mirror, then tell me you're not sure."

I tapped a fist on my forehead, wishing I could drum out all the doubts, all the fears. Breckinridge wanted me to do the same thing to the Seventeen that she had done to her brother, the same thing my own mother had done to me: forget loyalty, turn your back, grasp the opportunity . . .

"So, are we going to stay here? Or get something to eat?"

"Rooslin, let me ask you something. How can you be so nonchalant?"

He ignored my question and opened the hatch. "C'mon. Maybe they got spaghetti and meatballs . . ."

I forced myself out of the chair with a groan. "Yeah, right. Anything but seafood."

8 ⊘

After we ate, or, more precisely, after I watched Halitov stuff down two chicken sandwiches (they didn't have spaghetti and meatballs), Breckinridge met up with us, gave us civilian tunics and pants that were in vogue at AQ-Tower, then escorted us to the captain's gig, a sleek, black jumpsub that seated up to ten and would get us to AQ-Tower in about four hours.

The three of us climbed aboard, and Breckinridge took the controls. Halitov made sure to sit next to her, while me and my depression sat in the back. I stared through the canopy, watched the water rush by, and listened to him ask Breckinridge about her first boyfriend and her opinions about monogamous versus open relationships. She giggled as he turned up the smooth talk, and the two of them made me more ill.

"You've been quiet for a long time, Scott," asked the devil herself.

"Just thinking."

"His greatest downfall," added Halitov.

I almost smiled. "How much longer?"

"ETA's about twenty minutes," answered Breckinridge. "Now, Scott, when we get there, my contact will get us through customs without the usual DNA scan."

"You've got it all worked out . . ."

Halitov looked back at me. "Why are you being such a prophet of doom? Hey, man. I want to solve this aging problem and get on with my life, you know?"

"Yeah, I know," I answered, though I doubted he understood what I really meant. I knew exactly how self-centered he was being. To hell with the Seventeen. To hell with all the other conditioned soldiers who were aging like us.

Deep down I was jealous that I could never allow myself to be like him, even though part of me kept wanting to. He gave in to it, and in doing so, carried very little guilt. I was the martyr. Perhaps the fool. But in the end, my reservations about the Wardens were not unwarranted.

The water near AQ-Tower's northeast docking port was so murky that we could barely glimpse the main tunnel as we neared it. Breckinridge relied upon her instruments and explained that a recent construction accident had released ten million tons of raw sewage into the ocean. The damage to the surrounding reef and sea life was so extensive that the *Eri Flower* herself was being called in. Her scientists and crew would assist with the cleanup.

"The ship'll be here in two days," said Breckinridge. "And that's our ticking clock. We need to be out of here before she arrives."

"What do you mean?" asked Halitov.

"They've been calling this place a province since the beginning, but over a million people live here now, under the protection of the Seventeen. Magnesium and bromine exports are up. The place is turning a nice profit, and that money needs go to back into the hands of the alliances."

"They're going to invade?" I asked.

"Had you spent more time aboard the *Flower*, you would've learned all about it. There's an invasion force waiting belowdecks, and they're going to go in under the guise of the cleanup operation. That construction accident was no accident."

"Then we need to warn the Seventeen," I said, grabbing the back of Breckinridge's seat.

"No, Scott, we don't. All they would do is divert forces from Nau Dane and leave the colos there vulnerable to attack. That's just what the alliances expect the Seventeen to do."

"So we just sit back and let them take this place? I don't believe this. Do you know how many guardsmen and civvies are going to die?"

"The alliances already have control of the *Eri Flower*. We've analyzed the situation and concluded that the ship is a loss. When she arrives here, the *Charles Michael* is going to take her out."

"Are you serious?" asked Halitov.

I began to lose my breath. "We have researchers there who are POWs. You saying they're expendable? And all of the research that ship provides is expendable?"

"There's no other way."

We reached the end of the docking tunnel, rose toward the pool, and glided up to break water.

"This can't be happening," I muttered as I glimpsed the flashing lights and neon signs of Rifka, one of AQ's busiest commercial ports.

Breckinridge steered us to a low-lying pier, where her contact, a man wearing a brown-and-gray customs uniform, stood and lifted his chin at us.

We docked, got out, and Breckinridge exchanged a few rushed words with the man before she waved us over. "We're all set. Let's go."

After double-timing it through a crowded terminal with guardsmen posted at every corner, we reached one of many long lines of people waiting to pass through customs. The guardsman nearest us looked strangely familiar, and when he noticed me noticing him, his gaze suddenly brightened. "Lieutenant? Is that you?"

Halitov, Breckinridge, and her contact all froze as the guardsman—whom I now recognized as Jama Chopra—came toward me, looking a little worse and somewhat wiser for wear. Chopra and I had served together on Gatewood-Callista, where he had been a squad sergeant under my command. He obviously didn't know I had been promoted to captain.

I glanced at Breckinridge, who warned me with her gaze, then I faced Chopra. "No, sorry. Think you got me mixed up with somebody else."

"No way, sir," Chopra said, then grabbed my hand and shook it heartily. "Man, I can't believe it. Where's your uniform? What're you doing here? You on leave?"

I scowled at Breckinridge, threw an arm over Chopra's shoulder, then led him back toward his post. "Sergeant, you didn't see me, okay?"

"Sir?"

"You didn't see me. And Sergeant, the *Eri Flower*'s coming here."

"Yeah, everybody knows. The whole place is on alert. I'm working back-to-back shifts."

"They're not just coming to help with the cleanup. They're bringing an invasion force. Do whatever you can to get out."

"Sir, with all due respect, don't joke like that."

"I'm serious. It's an invasion. And it's coming. Save yourself, buddy." I squeezed his shoulder, then shifted off to catch up with the others, who were moving between lines. I chanced a last look at Chopra, whose eyes had grown wide and glassy as he stared off, into nowhere.

"What did you say to him?" Breckinridge asked, as I reached her.

"Just told him I was on leave."

"I hope so," she said menacingly.

Her contact showed several identicards to another customs officer near a side gate. That second officer waved us past the DNA scanners. Breckinridge said good-bye to her contact, then said we needed to catch a taxi and that our meeting was fifteen minutes away, in a little community known as Sobrook's Dome.

We were in such a rush that I barely took in the place, which, after we left the terminal, reminded me of the mining towns on Gatewood-Callista, though on my world you'd be hard-pressed to find a natural skylight that let in real sunshine. One such bubble, located nearly a hundred meters above us between two towering skyscrapers, glowed a powdery blue, and all that light pushed back some of the well-worn street's darker corners.

The taxi, a small ground vehicle painted yellow in the age-old tradition, carried us on a freeway built within a transparent conduit that, according to the driver, had once provided spectacular views. The sewage now formed a milky brown cloud obscuring everything. We sped toward a small group of people, tourists probably, who were standing atop a foot-bridge over the freeway and pointing up at all the pollution. The driver said the accident had really been bad for business. It was about to become bad for existence.

We exited the freeway, navigated through the traffic of several narrow, garbage-lined streets, then rolled up to the curb outside a dilapidated old office building located within one of the smaller domes encircling the main tower. While Halitov and I had both longed to see the tower and its environs, we both now wore the same long expression. Sobrook's Dome was old, dirty, and economically depressed. I guess it was off the beaten path enough for Breckinridge, who paid the driver, then told us to follow her inside.

"Look at this place," said Halitov, kicking a dirty water container out of his way. "I thought you said profits were up here."

Breckinridge glanced back at him. "Where do you think those profits have been going? Back into social programs to revitalize these cities? I think not. They're helping to pay for the war."

We followed her inside, into a gloomy complex that more closely resembled a warehouse, with broad, open spaces and piles of abandoned office furniture lining the walls. Meager light from the alley outside sifted in through a long row of windows on the far wall. To the right of those windows lay the entrance to a corridor toward which Breckinridge steered us.

"They're really rolling out the red carpet," Halitov quipped.

As Breckinridge muttered something in reply, my gaze alighted on a tiny flash of reflected light coming from the opposite corner. I looked again.

Four pale white spheres about two meters in diameter hovered at eye level and rotated once before they buzzed toward us. Small, whiskerlike sensors sticking out from their poles twitched with lives of their own, and at least a dozen particle points scattered over their hulls flared open to reveal short muzzles. My cerebroed data told me they were Alliance Anti-Personnel Drones, most frequently used for riot control and sentry duty on some of the lesser-populated colos. What they lacked in appearance they made up for in the weapons department.

"Shit!" Halitov cried. "APDs!"

As the drones issued a thundering report of automatic weapons fire, we charged toward the corridor, the wall behind us exploding in showers of shattered wood and metal.

"Are they the welcoming committee or what?" screamed Halitov.

As we reached the corridor, Breckinridge stopped short and turned back. "Look!"

A lithe young woman of Asian descent, with black hair braided into a ponytail that reached her waist, plunged down through a ceiling panel and landed just behind the drones. She wore nondescript black utilities and brandished a QQ60 particle pistol. As she rebounded from the floor, she leveled her weapon on the far left drone and fired. The machine took the hit, then wheeled back to charge her, as the other three arced high over her head. One drone remained at her twelve o'clock, while the other two found positions about three meters away from her, at her flanks.

The drone she had struck continued forward. She pumped one, two, three rounds into the thing, but it kept coming.

I reached out, into the bond, figuring I'd move in to assist, but she had found the bond herself and, with the world shifting slowly around us, she leapt up, dropkicked that relentless drone out of the way, even as she reached up and latched on to the whiskers of the drone above her head. Swinging it like a balloon on a string, she batted the other two drones away, then kept spinning like a top, spinning faster and faster, turning herself into a bizarre propeller that whirred across the room and smashed apart the three drones, along with the one in her hand. She broke out of the spin, then tumbled forward, launching into a series of one-handed cartwheels that abruptly ended just a meter from my face. I jolted, took a step back.

She stood there, panting, her brows raised, the teardrop-shaped birthmark on her lower left cheek glistening with sweat. She gave me the once-over, her gaze hanging a second on my own birthmark before she looked to Breckinridge. "Good enough?" she asked sarcastically.

"That was . . . weird," answered Breckinridge. "But yeah, good enough."

"So this is him," the Asian woman said, cocking a thumb at me. She eyed Halitov. "Then who's he?"

"I'm Captain Rooslin Halitov," he said, matching her sarcastic tone. "Who are you?"

"Gentlemen, this is First Lieutenant Katya Jing, Colonial Wardens."

"Guess you owe us a salute," Halitov told the lieutenant.

"Yeah, right," she said, not bothering to lift her hand. "I only salute Wardens."

Halitov and I traded a look, then I twisted my lip and faced Jing. "So this is her," I said, tossing a quick glance back to Breckinridge. "I'm unimpressed."

"You are?" Jing asked.

"You got more attitude than skill."

A grin flickered across her lips. "I'll show you what I have." With that, she grabbed my shoulders and hurled me into the air.

I couldn't believe the force she had mustered, and I found myself halfway across the room before I tapped into the bond, regained control of my body, and back-flipped onto my feet—

Only to find her standing right in front of me, smiling a second before she broke into a move I had never seen before. She lifted her elbows to her ears, then abruptly somersaulted to bring those elbows down onto my shoulders. I crumpled to my knees as stinging pain shot through my neck and chest.

Then she just booted me in the forehead, knocking me onto my back. She pinned my arms to the floor with her knees, and bond or no, I could not pull myself free.

Breckinridge called out from the corridor: "Like I said, Scott. Her conditioning is flawless, and her assimilation is complete."

"If you don't mind, I'd like to have a little talk with him," said Jing, bolting to her feet.

"Then meet us upstairs," Breckinridge answered. She and Halitov headed into the corridor.

I sat up, rubbing my arms and shoulders, sensing the throbbing pain in my head.

"Do I still have more attitude than skill?" she asked, striking an exaggerated yet sexy pose, with hands on her hips, medium-sized breasts thrust out.

"You're mostly attitude. But you just happened to have enough skill to kick my ass."

"I'll take that as a compliment."

"It's not." I stood, groaned off the pain.

"Getting too old for this shit?" she asked, then reached up to stroke my graying temple.

I grabbed her wrist. "How many other freaks like us do they have working for them?"

"Just us."

"Just you."

"Look, I know how you feel. Of course they want to use us. You don't have to like it. I don't. But they fixed my conditioning. And some of the things I'm able to do now . . ." With that, she vanished, appeared behind my shoulder, whispered in my ear. "Did you miss me?"

"Is this what they're paying you to say?"

She pulled away, crossed in front of me. "The only thing they wanted from me is that demonstration with the drones. I'm talking to you right now because we're the same, gennyboy, gennygirl, picked on all our lives because of these fucking birthmarks. And now we get the last laugh."

"Is that all this is to you? Revenge?"

"Oh, come down from your moral high ground. My sister died because of who I am. You know what this is to me? My way of saying thank you and letting her know that she died for something. I'm wanted now. I'm respected. I'll make a difference."

"My brother died for nothing," I retorted.

"That's not what I heard."

"Oh, yeah?"

Her gaze swept the room. "We're being monitored. I can't say anything."

"They're just using my brother as bait. And I can't tell you how much I resent it. He's dead."

She shook her head, ever so slightly.

I went to her, grabbed her shoulders. "Tell me!"

She ripped out of my grip. "C'mon. They're waiting for us upstairs."

"Just like the rest of them, huh? Know what? I've already heard enough. And I'm amazed that you condone this."

She frowned. "You're amazed? You don't even know me."

"I know you swore an oath to the Seventeen, and now you and the rest of them are just opportunists, turning your back on the Corps and breaking the code."

Her laughter caught me off guard. "The code? This is war. You want to play by the rules?"

"What's the alternative? Chaos? Anarchy?"

"How 'bout victory?"

"You ever think that what's going on between the Wardens and the Seventeen is a ploy by the alliances? The age-old strategy of divide and conquer?"

"Or maybe there isn't a coup. Maybe the whole thing's been set up by the Guard Corps to test our loyalties."

"That's ridiculous."

"More ridiculous than what you're saying?"

"In two days the *Charles Michael* is going to arrive here and take out the *Eri Flower*. Stand there and tell me that that action has been approved by the colonial government."

"Scott, I don't care what you do, but one thing's for sure: if you don't join us, you're going to die way too soon. And for someone who's just like me, that'd be a real shame. I'm going upstairs. You can come, hear them out. Or you can try running. They'll just send me after you."

I might very well have tried to run, but I thought of Halitov and, resignedly, followed Jing upstairs, where Breckinridge and two gray-haired men in civilian clothes sat in a small, dingy room. Halitov lounged across from them, leaning back, hands behind his head, looking a hell of a lot more relaxed than I felt. I gave him a quick glance of reproach before I found a dusty old chair and slid it beside his.

"Scott, this is Lieutenant Colonel James Abronoff and Major Tom Smiteson," said Breckinridge.

I was about to snap to and salute, then I remembered Jing's comment about only saluting Wardens and thought I'd return the favor. I gave each man a passing nod, then leaned forward. "Gentlemen, ex-plain to me why you don't consider yourselves trai-tors."

Abronoff, the older of the two officers, drew his head back, eyes bulging. "Explain to me, son, just who the fuck you think you are?"

"Easy, Colonel," said Major Smiteson. "She said he'd be difficult."

I glowered at them. "Gentlemen, I *start* at difficult."

"Are you threatening us, son?" boomed Abronoff.

"No, *Dad.* Just relaying the facts." I'll admit that my behavior was far from professional and quite unchar-acteristic of me, but my patience had worn thin. I couldn't bear to listen to any more lies.

"Scott, shut up, man," said Halitov. "Just hear them out. Let them show you the holos. You're not going to believe what's going on. We haven't been following the news."

"So what're you going to do? Go AWOL to join them?" I asked.

"Show him," Halitov told the officers. "Just show him."

Smiteson retrieved a small holo projector from be-hind his chair and activated the device. For about fif-teen minutes I sat there watching a montage of news footage shot at over a dozen colonies on half as many worlds. All of it was the same: Alliance Marines dropped in crab carriers, stormed the cities, mur-dered civilians, and seized territory. I watched moth-ers carry dead children in their arms and fathers struggle in hand-to-hand combat with Marines. I watched families get torn apart. The images brimmed with pathos, the horror pushed to its limit. When the projector finally winked out, I nodded at them. "Nice movie. Who made it for you?"

"What you just saw is legitimate, verifiable by twenty-one sources," said Smiteson. "We anticipated your response. If you'd like, I can take you through the verification process right now."

"Scott, they're not lying about this. *Eight*, count them, *eight* of the Seventeen systems have already fallen to the alliances."

"What about—"

"Gatewood-Callista?" Halitov finished. "They've taken it back."

"But rest assured, Captain, that a contingent of Wardens ran a rescue Op before that invasion. Colonel Beauregard himself saw to it that your father was among those rescued."

"So now you have my father," I said, gasping with incredulity. "What're you going to do? Kill him if I don't join you?" I shot to my feet, hands balling into fists, my heart drumming, my mind's eye flashing with an image of me murdering Jing, the two officers, and Breckinridge. I shuddered.

"Your father, along with the rest of the refugees, was taken to Kennedy-Centauri," explained Abronoff, now on his feet to meet my gaze. "We saved his life. And we're not using him to bargain with you. We're trying to make you understand that working with us is the right thing to do."

"Captain, the remaining colonies can't support the Seventeen's war effort for much longer. If they're going to remain operational, they'll need to begin a raiding campaign more extensive than they could possibly handle."

"You're talking about hijacking transports and robbing alliance-held colonies . . ."

"Exactly—just to get the needed supplies. But we've already cut deals with over a dozen minicorps sympathetic to the colos. They'll smuggle out the materials we need. We can maintain the war effort without having to risk Guard Corps lives. It's a better plan than anything the new colonial government has put together."

"Why not just go to the new government and tell them the plan? Why does everything have to be so clandestine?"

"There are too many egos involved, and way too much partisanship. Anyway, it's already too late for diplomacy." Abronoff returned to his seat.

The man was probably right. And maybe they had saved my father. Maybe they would recondition me. I suddenly felt cold and weak, and for a second, I thought I'd surrender to them. Then I remembered my father's expression every time someone would mention my mother.

"I won't break the code," I said, eyeing all of them. "I made a commitment to the new colonial government, and I won't betray it."

"We're not betraying anybody," snapped Halitov. "The Seventeen can't do the job anymore. So we help the team that can. Forget all that crap about your mother and the code being so important. One hand washes—"

"No."

Halitov swore under his breath. "Are you nuts?" He faced the group. "I'm sorry. My friend is temporarily insane. Give me a minute while I beat some fucking sense into him." He rose, grabbed me suddenly by the throat, and forced me toward the back of the room. "What're you doing, man?"

I wrenched his hand away. "We have to choose sides. Again. I swore that if I joined the Seventeen, I'd remain loyal till the end. I'm not a quitter."

"Hey, asshole. The end's going to come sooner than you think. We join them, get reconditioned—"

"Get caught by the Seventeen and either brainwiped or executed," I added.

He lowered his voice. "We're too valuable. That won't happen."

"You don't know that. And okay, their offer's tempting, but we don't really know how much of it is true. The answer is no. And we're leaving. Right now."

He stared gravely. "I want to stay."

"No, you don't. Not really. You're just thinking about all the promises they've made and the fact that you want to screw Breckinridge. You're not thinking about the consequences. We're soldiers. We dig in. We don't run away."

He shut his eyes, rubbed them vigorously. "I swear to God, when the time comes, I'm going to tell you so, and you're going to say I was right, we should've stayed. But then it'll be too late. And we'll be fucked."

I pushed past him, regarded Abronoff and Smiteson. "I'm sorry, gentlemen, but we're commissioned officers in the Seventeen System Guard Corps assigned to Special Forces Unit Rebel ten-seven, and we were just leaving . . ."

"If you leave now, Scott, you'll never find out what's happened to your brother," said Breckinridge, her voice full of false sympathy.

"My brother is dead." I gestured to Halitov, and we started out.

"Captain St. Andrew," called Abronoff. "I'm sorry we couldn't reach an agreement."

As I reached for the door, I muttered to Halitov, "Get ready. They won't let us go."

9 ❯ To my surprise, Halitov and I were able to slip into the hall without being stopped.

"See, you were wrong about them," he said, as we hustled toward the stairwell. "They were being honest. And they're letting us walk right out of here . . ."

Had we been back in the room, we would've heard Abronoff order Jing to stop us. The order made perfect sense. They couldn't allow what we knew to fall into the Seventeen's hands. Before the meeting, I had been unsure how forthcoming they would be, and I didn't want to believe they would hold us against our will. As we hit the stairs, I wondered if my mistake would cost us our memories at the least, our lives at the most.

I reached for my tac, wanting to skin up. A chill struck me as I remembered the tac had been deactivated.

"This can be simple or difficult," Jing hollered from the top of the stairwell.

"I take it back," Halitov shouted to me. "You were right about them. Shit. You were right."

"Wish I were wrong."

We reached the ground floor, burst through the rickety old door, and raced through the corridor, venturing into that warehouselike room.

Jing was waiting for us at the front door, arms outstretched, hands clutching her pistol. "Geez, how'd she do that?"

Halitov attempted to skin up, grimaced at his deactivated tac, then slowly raised his hands.

"We just want to help," said Jing, sounding remarkably earnest. "Don't do this. Don't let them brainwipe you."

Tingling with the bond, I willed myself behind Jing, and even as the wave of dizziness washed over me, I grabbed the muzzle of her pistol and forced her hands up as a round exploded from the weapon. "Go!" I ordered Halitov.

He charged past us as Jing leaned forward, then yanked me into the air, over her back. In doing so, she lost her grip on the pistol, and I tumbled to the floor with the weapon in my hand. I rolled, faced her, aimed the pistol with a shaky hand.

She shrugged.

I looked at the pistol, saw the flashing red light that indicated the weapon was set to user-specific mode. But even if I could have fired, she would have skinned up. I was about to throw away the gun, then realized she could still use it, and tucked it into my boot.

In that instant, Halitov, who should have been running his ass off in escape, launched into a *dirc*, the somersault and kick, from behind Jing. His boots caught her squarely in the back of her head, and down she went as the rest of him collided with her back. He had executed the move rather sloppily, but the distraction bought me time enough to launch forward, sliding in the *shoru* until, with one leg bent back, I came down and thrust out my boot, slamming Jing's head back into the floor.

Halitov clambered away from her, and we both got to our feet and dashed for the door. I repressed the urge to look back, but I imagined her recovering and sprinting after us.

Once on the street, we darted to the next intersection, turned right, and passed a row of machine shops with their garage doors open. We ducked inside one, drawing the confused stare of an old man in a soiled work uniform. "You," I called, shifting behind a workbench cluttered with the parts of some big machine, perhaps a jumpsub's engine. "Do you know where the Seventeen's garrison HQ is?"

He just looked at us.

"Do you understand?" demanded Halitov.

Whether the guy did or not, we didn't have time to wait. We crossed through the shop, found a rear exit, and rushed into a back alley where a small group of young people, early teens from the looks of them, were lying with long tubes attached to their arms. Drug users, no doubt. Even as we left them, I heard that rear door slam open, chanced a look back, and saw Jing. Our gazes locked for a second, then I joined Halitov in a mad rush up the alley.

Two blocks later, with Jing narrowing her gap, we reached a thoroughfare with ground traffic backed up in both directions. A few taxi drivers had already exited their vehicles and sat on their hoods, shouting obscenities. Halitov and I ran straight up the middle of the street, weaving between the transports and leaping over doors twice as they swung open.

We neared the next intersection and saw what was holding up traffic. About two hundred or so antiwar protesters had filed into the middle of the street. Some sat cross-legged and weren't going to move, while others carried makeshift signs, a few of which read

STOP THE BLOODSHED! WE BELONG TO THE ALLIANCES! and SEND THE GUARD CORPS HOME!

We couldn't help but slow as we neared the crowd, and to our right, a wall of guardsmen dressed in orange riot gear and gripping opaque shields advanced toward the protesters. I shot a look behind us, saw Jing weaving forward, and when I turned back, a young woman with blue hair and yellow eyes was shoving signs into our hands. "Come on," she told us. "Show them we mean business!"

I thought I was dreaming, thought that perhaps I had been transported back in time to the war protests on Earth during the 1960s or the Martian revolt during the 2270s. Halitov and I were thrust into the crowd, our elbows forced up so we could wave signs demeaning the very force we served.

Jing reached the edge of the crowd and stopped, saw the wall of guardsmen, saw the hundreds of witnesses all around us, and I assumed they were why she did not pursue us. But before she turned and left, she met my gaze and . . . winked.

I returned a confused look as she jogged off.

"She's leaving?" asked Halitov, lifting his voice over the shouting protesters.

Maybe her wink meant nothing. Or maybe the Wardens had staged the whole thing and had deliberately fed us information they knew we would take back to the Corps. I would get a headache trying to consider all of the possibilities.

"Let's talk to one of those corporals," I told Halitov, pointing to a pair of soldiers on the other side of the intersection.

He nodded, and we elbowed our way through the

picketers, not realizing that the situation had already turned violent. Just ahead of us, the shouts had become screams as a chaotic thumping followed by multiple whistling sounds drove our gazes skyward.

"Fuck, Losha Gas," yelled Halitov, as we watched the pellets explode into crimson chemical clouds that would render us unconscious within sixty seconds. People ran in all directions, and Halitov and I got swept toward the corner, where we fell over two women screaming and crawling to get away.

I got my first whiff of the gas and retched over its sulfurlike odor. Halitov's face swelled like a balloon. The streetlights exploded with color. The street turned into an oily black river, and I had forgotten how to swim.

A voice sounded from the darkness, an unfamiliar voice, deep and presumably male, with a strange accent I had never heard before: "It's the water, the water, the water, you think it's not the water, but it's the water, the water, the water, because it's wet, you know, too wet to comprehend."

I opened my eyes. Leaning over me was a young woman, maybe nineteen, her head shaven, a fine layer of what might have been salt covering her entire face like a weird mask. She widened her eyes. "It's the water, right? The water."

"What the hell are you talking about?"

That voice I recognized as Halitov's. I sat up, and there he was, standing near a force fence that encompassed a huge, vacant lot between a string of office complexes. The curving ceiling indicated we were still somewhere in Sobrook's Dome, I didn't know where. We were two among the hundreds milling about or coming to behind the fence.

"Welcome to paradise," said Halitov. "I tried talking to one of those grunts over there. He won't listen."

"Did you show them your tac?"

He brightened over the idea. "No, I didn't. That's why I got you to do the thinking." He helped me to my feet.

The bald, salt-covered woman rushed to me, put her hands on my shoulders. "It's the water. You can tread it. But don't drink it."

Halitov pulled me away from her. "Fucking place has gone crazy."

I looked back at her as Halitov shoved me forward. She made a drinking gesture with her hand, then waved her index finger in warning.

The grunt posted at our corner of the fence wouldn't give us the time day, even after we showed him our tacs. He dismissed us and the devices with a word: "Forgeries."

"Who's your CO, private?" I demanded.

He ignored me.

"Private, if you don't answer me, I'm going to jump over this fence and choke you to within a second of your life."

"Good luck," he said. "That's a three-meter force fence with a nine-point-seven-five rating."

His mouth fell open when I bent my knees, found the bond, and leapt over the fence, hitting the ground before him. "Now I could choke you, but I just want to talk to your CO."

He staggered back, lifting his rifle. "Don't move." His skin rippled to life, and he immediately called for his sergeant as Halitov took his own flying leap over the fence, making a more graceful landing than I had.

The sergeant, an overworked NCO with bloodshot eyes, asked for our ID numbers and operating codes, which she said would still need to be verified via DNA scan since our tacs were deactivated, but she was willing to take us to her command post around the corner.

There, we met with two second lieutenants, one of whom checked us out with his portable scanner, then abruptly snapped to and saluted us. I told him we'd need immediate transportation to the garrison's HQ, where we could speak directly with Lieutenant Colonel Pauson Drage, operational commander. Five minutes later, an airjeep arrived and whisked us off.

The HQ was located on the north side of Pier 81A, where ground and marine traffic was restricted to military vehicles. As we got closer to the complex, I stopped repeatedly looking over my shoulder, feeling a bit more at ease. We made a vertical descent outside the single-story building's main entrance, thanked the corporal for his smooth piloting, then hurried inside the office, where administrators monitored activity on literally hundreds of displays. A second lieutenant led us into Drage's office, where we took seats and waited for the man's return.

"How much are we going to tell this guy?" Halitov asked.

"I'm not sure."

"We'd better get our story straight before he gets here."

"Let me do the talking."

"Gentlemen," said Drage, parading quickly into

the room. Dark-skinned, with cool, blue eyes and an old-fashioned crew cut that squared off his head, the lieutenant colonel dropped quickly into his chair and leaned forward. "You guys are part of some new special forces group, aren't you?"

I glanced to Halitov. Drage knew more than I had thought. "Uh, that's classified, sir."

"Not at my clearance it isn't."

"Sorry, sir. Yes, we're part of a special forces group."

"So you were working undercover as war protesters . . ."

"Not exactly, sir. That was . . . an accident."

"Really?"

I could tell he wanted to pursue that subject, but I didn't want to waste time. "Sir, we need to record a message and tawt it out to Rexi-Calhoon. It's urgent, sir."

"We can arrange that, but I have to tell you that since the war broke out, we're running only two comm shuttles per local week. You just missed the last one. The next one won't be here for about seventy-six hours."

"What about commercial exporters? Can we run a chip out on one of them?"

"You could probably get a skipper to do that for you, but those people don't work cheap when they know you're desperate." His frown deepened. "What's going on?"

"Sir, you understand that our mission here is classified."

He smiled darkly. "Captain, I really don't have time for this. I have the *Eri Flower* en route, a major sewage spill, and a security problem to handle. If all you want is help sending off a chip, I'm sorry, but you're on your own." He stood, getting ready to dismiss us.

Halitov gave me a pleading look, and I realized that even if Drage didn't believe me, I couldn't leave his office without warning him. I needed to do that, not for him or for me, but for the thousands of civilians who might die. "Sir, intel provided to us by the Colonial Wardens indicates the *Eri Flower* is carrying an invasion force."

"Nonsense. Our intel indicates she's carrying a Marine detachment of about eight thousand troops, which is just enough to secure her. I'll trust my own recon officers before I trust anything gathered by the Wardens—if you know what I'm saying."

"I understand, sir, but I wanted to let you know that once the ship arrives, the *Charles Michael* is supposed to take her out before those invasion troops can launch."

Drage reached for a tablet on his desk, called up information on the *Charles Michael*, then scanned the page. "She's listed as destroyed."

"I know, sir. She's being operated independently by the Wardens."

"And how did you come by this information?"

"Sir, we were aboard the *Charles Michael*. She's out there in the Vzyk Trench, cloaked and waiting to strike."

"I'll need a cerebral scan to verify this."

I knew he would say that. And I knew that if we submitted, he would learn more about Rebel 10-7 and about the Colonial Wardens than he needed to. "Sir, please. Just trust me on this."

He thought a moment. "If what you're saying is true, then all I need to do is sit back and watch the fireworks."

"Yes, sir. But there's always a chance the *Charles Michael* won't take out the *Flower*, and if those Marines arrive, your garrison will be massacred. You can't get reinforcements here in time. I respectfully suggest that you begin evacuating as many civilians as you can. Get them out on every ship you have."

"Do you know what you're asking? Do you know the kind of panic an evacuation like that would cause?"

"Sir, how many civilians will die if those Marines invade? I also suggest that in preparation, you shut down this HQ, shut down all your command posts, and purge all data."

He looked to Halitov. "You haven't said a word, Captain. You concur with everything your partner is saying?"

Halitov's gaze turned steely. "Yes, sir. I do."

"Well, then. You've given me a lot to consider." He was hardly convinced.

I rose. "Sir, I'll submit to a cerebral scan right now."

"Are you sure, Captain?"

"Yes, sir. But I have to warn you. What you're going to learn could put your life in danger."

"That's a guardsman's job, isn't it?" he asked. "If you'd like, your partner can record that message while I'm scanning you."

"Thank you, sir."

I told Halitov to address the chip to our friend, Colonial Security Chief Mary Brooks, who would share the information we had gathered with her council of senators, though I wondered if our intel would simply be too little, too late.

Drage took me over to the HQ's single interrogation room, handed me the C-shaped cerebro, and promised he would focus the scan on military-related activities and do his best to ignore personal memories. He spent about ten minutes watching the monitor. I didn't feel a thing, though I still worried about him respecting my privacy.

When it was over, the grave look on his face and his distant gaze made me nervous. "Sir, are you all right?"

"Yeah, I just, uh, I didn't realize that eight of the seventeen worlds have already fallen. The reports we've been getting have obviously been censored."

"Sir, will you begin an evacuation?"

"Yes, I will. We'll concoct some story. An airborne virus, maybe. Something related to the sewage spill."

"You've got less than two days."

"In two days we'll be lucky to evacuate ten percent of the population."

"I know, sir. You should probably concentrate on getting the children out first."

He nodded, slapped palms on his hips, then stood. "Well, then, I'll have your tacs reactivated. If you want to ship out on a military ride, you'll have to wait for that comm shuttle; otherwise, you'll have to try cutting your own deal with a barge or freighter pilot."

"If you'd like, sir, we'll wait for the shuttle. In the meantime, I don't think our CO would mind if we helped you out." Even as the offer came out of my mouth, I remembered that Jing could still be waiting to capture me and Halitov. Still, I needed to think like a soldier. I had sworn to protect the colonists here and in the sixteen other systems. We would follow the code. We would help Drage.

"Two conditioned officers from a special forces group volunteering to help? Only a fool would turn down that offer," he said with a wan grin. "I'll put you in touch with the skipper of a mineral barge who owes me a favor. I'll have him get your chip to Rexi-Calhoon."

I stood. "Thank you, sir."

"Also, I'll call over to the supply desk, get you fitted with some new utilities and gons."

"I appreciate that, sir." I saluted and went for the door.

"Captain?"

"Yes, sir?"

He hesitated, then slowly reached for his cheek. "I have a cousin who has epi. I wish he could meet you."

I nodded awkwardly, then left to find Halitov waiting for me outside the room. I summarized my conversation with Drage as we headed down a hallway toward the supply officer's desk. When I finished, he stopped dead, looked at me. "You volunteered us? You idiot."

"We can't just leave."

"The hell we can't." He held up the tiny comm chip, no larger than the size of an old penny. "I say we tawt out with this, go to Rexi-Calhoon ourselves, and personally deliver it to Ms. Brooks. And while we're there, we tell her about this second conditioning facility on Aire-Wu, and we tell her we want to be brought there and reconditioned. Maybe you don't have a problem with our grandpa syndrome, but I do. I really do. And so will the Seventeen. They need us. They'll find a way to get us there."

I started forward again, and he double-timed after me. "Rooslin, I want to be reconditioned, too, but not by becoming a traitor. Look, we give Drage a couple of days. Then we leave. And by the way, getting to Aire-Wu is one thing. Finding the conditioning facility and gaining access to it is another."

"Two days, huh? Shit. That's two days too many. And I'm sure the Wardens still want to get their hands on us."

"All of them except Breckinridge, right?"

He made a lopsided grin as we reached the supply desk, where the sergeant, a rawboned nineteen-year-old with fuzz on his chin, looked as tired as every other soldier we had seen. He saluted, cleared his throat. "Captains St. Andrew and Halitov?"

"That's right," I answered. "We were recently mistaken for war protesters. I'm wondering if you have any clothes that might help . . ."

He ran his gaze over our civilian outfits and snorted. "Yes, sir."

We received the fresh utilities, along with new boots, boxers, and socks, then used Drage's private billet to change. I looked in the mirror, reached for my breast, and leveled the gold octagon pin with the diamond in its center, the "captain's gon." I never thought slipping into military-issue clothing could feel so good. And wouldn't you know, I didn't look much older. Still a touch of gray, yes, but our accelerated decrepitude had slowed, at least for the time being.

*   *   *

About thirty minutes later, Drage called and told us where to meet his friend. In the company of a trio of heavily armed guardsmen, we airjeeped down to Pier 56F, where we delivered the chip. The skipper told us that he and Drage went way back, that they had even gone to high school together. That made me feel slightly more at ease. Still, we were turning over highly classified information to a stranger. Sure the message was encrypted, but any rogue decrypter worth his salt could break into it. We had to trust Drage and his friend.

After that, the lieutenant colonel put me in charge of a company stationed within the main tower. Halitov remained, of course, my XO, and we immediately realized that our unit was spearheading the entire province's defenses. Drage, it seemed, had a lot of faith in us.

From the main observation post located on the tower's roof, we squinted against the wind and looked out at domes peaking up here and there, at the tops of pyramid-shaped structures, and at the circular, flat-topped roofs of still more buildings half-submerged in the brownish gray amoebae that encompassed the province and gave off an unholy smell. Our skins filtered away the stench once we had found the proper purification setting. We spent the better part of the afternoon checking in with the company, running drills, and familiarizing ourselves with the junior officers. During all of that, my mind worked overtime on something Breckinridge had told us, something that I had initially accepted without a second thought but now didn't make much sense.

By the time night fell, the fixed geometry that had once cut across the wavelets had reduced itself to the twinkling of thousands of randomly positioned lights. The sea had grown eerily calm, the light of twin crescent moons casting a faint sheen across its surface. I stared through a pair of binocs, believing I could pick out the distant lights from the approaching *Eri Flower*. A hazy smudge of black obscured the horizon.

"Well, we wanted to see the tower," Halitov said, his skin shifting from phosphorescent green to transparent over his face. "Can't see it any better than this."

"What do you think is going to happen?"

"Who knows . . ."

"Breckinridge said that when the *Eri Flower* arrives, the *Charles Michael* is going to take her out. I've been wondering all day about the logic of that. Why are they waiting until the ship arrives? Why not just blow it up out there?"

"I don't know. If they destroy her while she's docked, they're bound to cause major damage to the port and the nearest domes."

"Exactly. Why would they let the *Flower* get so close?"

"Maybe they want some people to get off first. Their operatives, maybe?"

"No, they could jump ship the way we did. Or take a jumpsub or something."

"They said they've already written off the *Flower* as a loss."

"And maybe they've written off AQ as well," I said.

"Could be. Maybe they're going to kill two birds

with one stone. I mean, it's not like most of the citizens want us here."

"Yeah. And hey, that holo we saw a little while ago, remember? What was that poll?"

Halitov squinted hard in thought. "I think they said eighty-one percent of the people want us to leave. These people never wanted to secede from the alliances. This place reminds me of Mars."

"Maybe the Wardens consider AQ and the *Flower* as a double threat."

Halitov's expression soured. "Two birds, one stone. Or in this case, tactical nukes."

I took a long breath. "If this place is a target, then we're standing right in the bull's-eye."

He grinned crookedly at me. "And you volunteered us for this shit."

"We have to find Breckinridge," I said.

"What?"

"Come on. We'll see if Drage can loan us a jumpsub." I started toward the hatch behind us.

10 ❯ **Lieutenant Colonel Drage's** evacuation was in full swing and playing out on big-screen news monitors hanging above most of the major piers. Nearly every watercraft available was departing for Jones Rigi-Plat, even though the floating colony lay over two weeks away via the fastest jump-sub. Some civilians in smaller or older ships would run out of food, fuel, and oxygen long before they reached safety. Thousands of those ships would float aimlessly on the waves like old lifeboats carrying the survivors of some horrendous sea disaster. I couldn't help but imagine that scene as the high-speed lift carried Halitov and me down to the main floor.

"What're we going to do?" he asked. "Surrender to the Wardens?"

"If we have to."

"Good."

"What?"

"If we're right, they're the only people who are going to survive this thing."

"This 'thing' has to be stopped."

"And you think we can go there and talk them out of it? This goes way up, way beyond them. We have to leave—preferably before this place blows."

The lift doors opened, and we jogged across a circular terminal, where one of our privates waited with an airjeep. He flew us over to Drage's HQ, and we found the man in his office, frantically packing his belongings into several rucksacks. "What're you two doing here?"

"We could be wrong," I began slowly, "but we think the *Charles Michael* is going to take out a lot more than just the *Eri Flower*."

"Figured it out, huh?" he asked grimly.

I exchanged a puzzled look with Halitov. "Sir?"

"The sub's skipper contacted me about an hour ago. The moment the *Flower* is moored, everything you see here will be gone. They're going to use low-level nukes with limited fallout, but they'll do the job, all right."

"We can't let this happen."

"Too late. Angelino has her orders, and Drummer Fire Command won't divert any capital ships here. They already got their hands full."

"Sir, wait a minute. I don't understand. Why did Angelino contact you?"

"She's sending over nearly every jumpsub she has to help evacuate my garrison. She has no intention of killing any member of the Guard Corps."

"Just innocent civilians—including children," I amended.

"St. Andrew, love it or hate . . . it is what it is. And we can't change it. Yeah, we swore an oath to protect these people, but these people are already dead. Our job now is to save ourselves so we can go on fighting the good fight." He didn't sound very convincing and probably didn't believe the words himself.

I was about to exploit that doubt when Halitov butted in. "Sir, with all the activity that's going on around here, won't the intel people on the *Flower* realize something's wrong?"

"They must assume we know they're carrying an

invasion force, thus we're evacuating the city. We have to assume they don't know about the *Charles Michael* because they haven't altered course."

I shook my head. "But, sir, if they observe we're evacuating as well, and they track those jumpsubs back to the *Charles Michael* . . ."

"We'll be evacking as quietly as possible. And we'll be rendezvousing with the *Michael* at a point deep in the trench, just after she retreats from her attack."

"If we leave the city completely undefended, they're going to know we have an ace in the hole," Halitov pointed out.

"Which is why I haven't bothered to tell you about any of this," Drage said with a nod, then turned a hard gaze on me. "I'm leaving your company and one other behind to man the tower and all perimeter bunkers."

"Sir?" Halitov asked, utterly dumfounded. "You're ordering us to die?" He looked at me. "Fuckin' volunteer mission, huh?"

"When the *Flower*'s a couple kilometers out, the Marines will launch their hovercraft. When they do, that's your cue to withdraw. Jumpsubs will be waiting for you at the main pier below. You'll have thirty minutes to get to the trench. Coordinates will be uploaded into the subs."

"Sir, why do I get the feeling you're making this up as you go?" asked Halitov. "You're telling us anything you can to get us out of your face. Maybe there won't be any jumpsubs waiting for us, huh? Just another day where you send good people to their deaths . . ."

Drage finished filling one rucksack, hoisted it over his shoulder. "I guess you'll have to trust me, won't you, Captain? Now take your insubordinate attitude back to your station before I have you locked up."

"Sir, we'll do what you want, sir," I said quickly. "Just make sure those subs are waiting for us." I could not have looked more serious.

His gaze didn't flinch. "They'll be there."

He rushed out of the office, and Halitov and I remained a moment, letting it all course through and contaminate us like the radiation soon to come.

"Well, at least we know the Wardens have a conscience," said Halitov. "Sure, they'll kill civvies, but they won't kill guardsmen. Can't say I have any major problems with their priorities . . ."

"You know what I really want right now?" I asked. "Just a straight fight. Tell me I have to secure a location. Show me where the enemy is, let me coordinate my people so we can get the job done."

"Yeah, don't lie to us about who the good guys and the bad guys are. Don't lie about the location. Don't lie to us about the mission," he added.

"Can I tell you something? This whole Op has been so drawn-out and depressing, it's making me question whether anyone believes in the code anymore."

He raised his brows. "I know one idiot who does."

"Yeah," I said, grinning faintly.

"So, can we even believe this guy now? Are we really going to sit up there until the very last second? Tell you what? I like your original plan a lot better. Let's go throw ourselves on the Wardens' mercy."

"What about those people still up there? Two full companies of guardsmen. We just abandon them?"

"Uh, let me think about that. Yeah. And do you see any guilt on this face? No."

"I think we should tell our people what's going to happen," I said.

"Okay, you do that while I find us a jumpsub."

"You know it seems like a long time ago, that night at the academy, when we were leaving Pope's office, just after I was going to dust out? You asked me to teach you how to put others before yourself. I guess we never got to that lesson."

"Look at my face. I'm telling you, there is no guilt."

I stared at him, stared a moment more, widened my eyes.

"Oh, fuck you, man," he said, looking as guilt-stricken as ever. "I can't believe I'm going along with this."

I smiled inwardly and followed him out.

Once we were back up top, I got on the companywide frequency and addressed my people. "Ladies and gentlemen, scuttlebutt aside, I'd like to confirm a few things for you and clarify our mission here."

Halitov lifted his chin, and I switched to our private channel. "Careful, Scott. You tell 'em too much, and some of them might desert."

"I'm aware of that," I said, then returned to the company channel. "All right. The *Eri Flower* is en route to us. She'll arrive sometime tomorrow. She's carrying an invasion force. Our job is to remain at our posts until her hovercraft launch, at which time we'll withdraw down to the main pier and board jumpsubs. Nav systems will have your coordinates. Understand this: we're not running from the enemy. We are, as always, part of a much larger plan." I hesitated, then: "The truth is, we want them to believe that the entire garrison is still here. We'll be jamming their scans, so they'll have to rely on visual contact. We're the bait, and we can fool them. Now then, direct all questions to your squad corporals and hang tight. I'll deliver the evac order myself. That is all." I went to the railing ahead, looked off, past the city's lights, to that impenetrably dark horizon.

"Well, no deserters so far," said Halitov, his gaze distant as he read his HUV's screens. "Everyone's still in position. Three hundred and twenty lives putting on a show. Chezower says she's had no problems with her company."

"Good. Third watch begins. Why don't you get some sleep? I'll take next watch."

"Okay. And Scott? If anything bad happens? You'll take care of it, right? I don't want to be disturbed."

I smiled tightly. "Right."

He went below, where in the corner of a small C&C room we had set up our bunks.

During the night, I scanned the horizon at least a dozen times while listening in to the company's skipchatter. Then, just as the sky began to wash into a deep, early-morning blue, one of my platoon commanders abruptly reported in: "Sir, I think we've spotted her, sir."

I bolted to the rail, jammed my binocs to my eyes, and saw the faint outline of a massive, pointed bow. Then I skinned up and ordered the tactical computer to show me a digitized image of the approaching ship within a 3-D grid that pinpointed her position and marked her ETA. She had increased speed and would arrive by midday. For the hell of it, I tried a low-emission scan of her hull to see if I could detect any chemical residue from weapons within, but, as expected, my scans were jammed. For all of three seconds, I entertained the idea of willing myself into her hold to learn the truth, but I feared the drain on me would be too much, and if the bond failed me there, I might be trapped aboard a ship about to be destroyed. I thought of Jing, of how she so effortlessly shifted her body across the bond. If I envied one thing about her, that was it.

"Hey, Scott," Halitov called on our channel. He was still down in our C&C room, but he sounded fully awake. "You have to see this report I just recorded. Transferring to your tac."

A data box opened in my HUV, and within it sat a handsome, young news reporter seated behind his desk, delivering a special report in exaggerated tones. ". . . and while we still haven't received official confirmation from the military or pier command, witnesses do report sighting the *Eri Flower* in the southeast. She's best viewed from anywhere within the main tower. And as most of us have heard, the *Flower*'s arrival represents a long-awaited rescue from the sewage spill that has plagued our community and recently resulted in a massive evacuation because of the spread of contaminates into the main water lines. Those of us still here can breathe a little easier. Help *is* on the way."

I switched off the data box, wincing over the irony, then I opened the command frequency. "All right, Poseidon Company, let's start the show. Activate the holos and make yourselves as visible as possible."

I've waited for a lot of things in my life, but waiting

for that ship to arrive ranks right up there with some of the most difficult. Her bow grew out of a morning fog hugging the water's surface. And as the sun began to burn off that fog, more of her incredible girth lumbered into view. A half dozen tugs launched to meet and guide her toward the docking platform about a quarter kilometer out.

To play it safe Halitov and I charged a pair of second lieutenants with procuring some backup transportation, in case Drage had been lying to us. Unfortunately, they had come up with a single, small ferry that could only carry about fifty people and whose engine wailed as much as it smoked. So we gave up on that idea and placed the two lieutenants on a recon at the main pier. When the *Flower* was just an hour out and about to launch hovercraft, one of those lieutenants frantically reported in. "Sir, jump-subs arriving, sir!"

"Copy," I said, gasping with relief, my gaze still fixed through my binocs. "Tell 'em to stand by."

"Jesus, I'm shaking," said Halitov, clutching the rail to my right.

"I don't see any hovercraft," I reported.

"Here's one for you: maybe there is no invasion force. Maybe that's just an excuse the Wardens are using. Maybe they don't want the alliances to control this city and that ship. Period. Maybe the *Flower* really has come on a humanitarian mission, and we're here, drawing her in, helping the Wardens to blow her up."

"I'd say you might be right, but I'm looking at hovercraft launching right now!"

He raised his own binocs, took a look. "Son of a bitch."

While those low-tech hovercraft were not the most swift or efficient troop carriers for launching an invasion, they were the most portable. A steady stream of them poured from the *Flower*'s port and starboard launching platforms. The three lead craft skipped across the water, jetted past the tugs, and swiveled their main guns into firing position.

"Company! Light up those autoseekers and fall back! Fall back!" There was the order I had been waiting all morning to give. And mere seconds after I gave it, the sky between the tower and ship lit up in a gleaming storm of crossfire. Our autoseeker guns would automatically track and fire upon the incoming ships, but they would only ward them off until the enemy's own tactical computers got a positive lock and destroyed them. The guns would, however, buy us the time we needed to—as the brass might put it—"commence in an orderly withdrawal."

What I didn't count on was the mob of civilians held behind force shield barricades just outside the main pier. They saw the jumpsubs. They saw members of my company climbing into those subs. They saw that they were being abandoned, and all Halitov and I could do was run across the pier, trying to ignore their screaming. I noticed a young woman standing at the barricade, crying, a small boy and a small girl clutching her hips. I started toward them, visualizing myself leaping over the fence and leaping back, carrying all three in my arms toward a sub.

"Scott?" Halitov called. "Come on!"

He grabbed my shoulder, pulled me back. I

whirled to face him but found Katya Jing staring back at me. And over her shoulder stood Kristi Breckinridge. The two of them had just stepped out of a jumpsub.

"See? Everything works out in the end," Jing said brightly, then her expression darkened. "Now let's go."

"Not before you see what you're doing here. Take a long, hard look."

"I'm just a soldier," she said. "Just like you."

"You seeing this?" I asked Breckinridge, shouting over the crowd. "You seeing this?"

Breckinridge marched up to me. "Get in the fucking sub. Now!"

I glanced at the woman, the children.

"I'm not kidding, Scott."

I turned back to them, saw Halitov gesturing emphatically with his hands, and mouthing the words, "Come on!"

Even as I chanced another look back to the force fence, the ceiling above it exploded and collapsed on the screaming crowd, crushing them where they stood as a dense cloud of debris rose and blanketed the sudden horror.

Jing grabbed my wrist and, exploiting the bond, dragged me back to the jumpsub and threw me into a seat beside Halitov. She and Breckinridge sat up front, and as a second artillery shell blew through the northwest wall, sinking two jumpsubs with it, Breckinridge slammed down the canopy and submerged.

I threw my head back on the seat and thought of that woman, those kids, and muttered epithets, muttered that I'd had enough, that I couldn't take any of it

anymore, that duty, honor, and courage had nothing
to do with this. The war was the real pollutant . . .

When the water finally grew clear, Halitov called
my attention to the right, where dozens of torpedoes
armed with low-level nukes came within a hundred
meters of us and arrowed by, leaving dense trails of
bubbles in their wakes. Ten or so other jumpsubs kept
tight to our heels, and Breckinridge repeatedly ordered their skippers to tighten up the patterns, lest
they accidentally travel into a torpedo's path.

"Impact in five, four, three, two, one," Jing said
calmly as she watched a monitor.

Nothing for a moment. Just the whir of our engine.
Then a dull thud seemed to reverberate over the hull,
followed by another, more powerful one, then another that actually kicked the sub forward, and Breckinridge fought with the control stick. "Damn it," she
gasped.

"The tower's coming down," said Jing, pulling up
a satellite image.

I leaned forward and watched on the small monitor as the very tower atop which Halitov and I had
stood leaned precariously to the north, then splashed
violently into the murk.

"And there goes the *Flower*," added Jing, switching
to another image of the great research ship. Flames
pouring from jagged holes near the *Flower*'s waterline
licked at her port side. She listed hard to that side,
where scores of life tubes dropped into the water near
the docking platform, itself exploding under the on-
slaught of torpedoes.

"Sink, you bastard," said Breckinridge. "Sink."

"You have no idea what's going on here, do you?" I asked her.

"Oh, I know exactly what's going on. We're scoring a major victory for the colonies."

I fell back into my seat. "If you say so."

"Scott, you don't know the details. Let's just say that this needed to be done. There was no other way, believe me. And with the *Flower* and AQ destroyed, the alliances' research and development teams have been set back six months, maybe even a year. They planned on seizing AQ and using it as a proving ground for new aquatic weaponry and biologics. We couldn't let that happen."

"Tell that to survivors of all those families you killed. Tell that to all those people floating out there, trying to get to Jones-Rigi. Thousands more are going to die."

"You know I don't usually jump up and preach it with him," said Halitov. "But this time, I have to. AQ Tower was a free colony at the time you destroyed it. History repeats itself. They burned the village in order to save it."

"We burned the village to save the Colonial Alliance. Slight difference, don't you think?"

Halitov threw up his hands. "I don't know."

"What about those refugees?" I asked.

"Hey, Scott, you're not the only one who knows how to cut deals with mineral barge skippers," Breckinridge said. "We have twenty or thirty of them standing by to rescue those people. Yeah, a lot of civvies died, but we saved as many as we could."

"Does that really make you feel better?" I asked.

"As a matter of fact it does. And as a matter of fact, I've grown pretty fucking tired of defending our actions to you and listening to your personal attacks." She glared back at me. "Just shut up. And enjoy the ride."

"Enjoy the ride?"

"Scott," Halitov warned.

I balled my hands into fists and stiffened. Halitov gave me that "just relax" look.

With a snort, I shifted away from him, staring fiercely through the canopy at the icy depths.

▐▐ ❯ **We rendezvoused with** the *Charles Michael* at the designated location, nearly a half kilometer below the ocean's surface and walled in by the trench. Assuming that word of the destruction would quickly reach the alliances, the docking procedures were rushed to get everyone on board so the ship could tawt out.

"What now?" I asked Breckinridge as I stepped onto the pier. "You have us escorted to the brig?"

"If that's necessary. If you choose to remain civil about all this, you'll stay in officers' quarters until we tawt out. After that, the *Charles Michael* will get her new orders, and we'll take an ATC to meet up with *Vanguard One*."

"Colonel Beauregard's ship?" I asked.

"The colonel's disappointed in your reaction to our offer, and he wants to talk to you himself. I have a feeling that if you're more open to the idea of joining the Wardens, he'll take you to Aire-Wu. It's up to you."

Halitov came up behind me, put his hand over my mouth. "It's a deal. We're in. And we won't give you any more trouble."

"God, I hope so," she said with a sigh. "I've been getting some of the worst migraines I've had in years."

I pulled away Halitov's hand. "Maybe it's not us. Maybe it's the guilt."

"Just go. Find an ensign with a tablet. One of them will take you to your quarters."

"Thank you, ma'am," Halitov said, a little too politely.

"Oh, and Rooslin, if you'd like to join me for a drink in a few hours . . ."

"Yeah," he replied, looking thrilled until I dampened his enthusiasm with my stare. "A drink to fallen comrades," he added softly.

She nodded. "I'll call."

We found an ensign who led us to our quarters, where we spent a moment buckling into jumpseats that folded down out of the bulkhead. Angelino's voice echoed through the shipwide comm as she announced the oncoming tawt. The Trans Accelerated Wave Theory drive went to work, twisting our stomachs into knots as it booted us a tenth of a light-year away, to the terrestrial planet Nau Dane, a solitary world orbiting a red, M5 star. The planet's rolling uplands were strangely devoid of impact craters, despite its thin, hydrogen-argon atmosphere. We had no idea why we were going there, but once we settled into a polar orbit, Halitov unbuckled and headed into the shower. I fell back onto a gelrack and closed my eyes.

Sometime later, the hatchcomm beeped. "Rooslin?"

He didn't answer.

I rose. "Who is it?"

"It's me. Dina."

Stunned, I opened the hatch, and there she was, dressed in dark blue utilities, looking a little pale but very much alive. "Oh my God."

"Can I come in?"

"Uh, yeah." I shifted aside, let her pass, shut the hatch, and just stood there, gawking at her.

"I guess I owe you an apology," she said, beaming.

"For what?"

"For dying, of course." She came over to me, stroked my cheek. "I'm sorry, Scott. I'm so sorry."

"You're not here. I'm just dreaming. You're still back on Exeter."

"Am I?"

"You have to be."

"Then how'd I get here?"

I half shrugged. "You tell me."

"Maybe Paul lied to you. Maybe I'm not dead. Maybe they sent a commando unit back in to get me. Maybe the machine finished healing me, and they arrived just in time. And maybe that's why I'm here."

"No, I think you're here because I need you to be here. I guess . . . I don't know what I'm doing anymore. I don't know who's right and who's wrong. And all I really want to do is just follow the code, be a good soldier—and not abandon the people and the cause. But no one else seems to care about the code or about anything else—except winning the war."

"Isn't that why we're here?"

"I don't know. There's just so much bullshit out there. You kind of lose hope in the human race, you know? I keep thinking that if I perform my duty to the best of my ability, if I remain loyal to the Corps and to myself, then I won't just know what honor means, I'll be living it."

"Scott, that sounds . . . a little corny."

"Yeah, you're right. Maybe no one can live that perfectly. Makes me think there's something out there better than the human race, and it's just waiting for us to find it."

"The Racinians?"

"Maybe. Maybe we can learn something from them. And I'm not talking about technology. I'm talking about living without killing each other."

"Is this what you really want to talk about? Or do you want me to tell you it's okay."

"What do you mean?"

"It's okay to get on with your life. Just remember me. Can you do that?"

The hatchcomm beeped. I shuddered awake. Another beep. "Who is it?"

"It's Lieutenant Jing. Can I come in?"

"Rooslin?" I called. Silence. He had probably gone off for that drink and who knows what with Breckinridge. I pulled myself out of the rack and dragged my feet to the hatch, opened it. "What?"

"You look terrible," she said, inviting herself inside.

"What do you want?"

She turned back, wriggled her brows, and I finally noticed the alcohol on her breath. "I was just wondering if you . . . if you wanted to work off some of that anxiety."

"You're drunk."

"I had two drinks. It's not like we haven't had a hard day. Work hard, play hard, right?"

"So you thought you'd come in here and ask if I want to have sex? Huh? Just like that?"

"Sex? With you?"

"Yeah, with me. What? I'm not good enough for you?"

She chuckled under her breath. "I was going to invite you down to the low-G sphere to work on some of the arts. Work out that anxiety. Sex wasn't part of the invitation."

I averted my gaze, feeling like an idiot. "Sorry."

"I guess we could have sex, if you really want to . . ."

Gritting my teeth, I reached for the door. "Let's go see if I can kick your ass."

She smiled. "Kristi told me you were a dreamer."

"Yeah," I said, opening the hatch. "I definitely am."

Twenty minutes later, Jing flew through the air, spinning in a well-executed *chak* that she turned into a floating kick, counterkick, the *ai*. I dropped and rolled under her, stood, whirled, then launched myself headfirst toward her in the *biza* as she turned back.

We had set the sphere to one-quarter G, and within the broad chamber with padded floor, we had already pounded the hell out of each other. Every time I struck a solid blow that I assumed would finish her, she'd suggest another attack.

So I spun out of the *biza*, driving both boots toward her face, but she caught and spun them as though she were turning a wheel, rolling me away, off to the side. I collided with a breath-robbing thud against the wall. As I gasped for breath, she materialized right in front of me. "Maybe we should've had sex . . ." She dragged me to my feet.

"Let's take a break," I said, grunting as I turned my head, working out the kinks in my neck. My right shoulder throbbed, and even in the one-quarter G, my body felt heavy, bloated.

"Feeling any better?" she asked.

The irony of her timing left me grinning.

"Well, that's good. Exercise always improves my mood. And I have to say I've been feeling pretty sorry for myself lately." She went to a wall panel, increased the G setting, then sat, pulling her knees into her chest.

"What's there to feel sorry about? Your conditioning's not making you grow old . . . seems like the Wardens are taking good care of you . . ."

"It's my parents."

"You miss them?"

"They were killed on Tau Ceti Eleven. They worked in the agridomes. My father was an arborist. I don't even know what happened to their bodies."

"I'm sorry."

"Thanks."

"When I was at the academy, they showed us a holo of that attack. I'd never seen so many crab carriers."

Her gaze drifted to the floor. "My father was always such a pacifist. He wanted to hide from everything. Pretend the war was never going to happen."

"My father's like that, too."

"My mother . . . she knew. She was always so strong. She's the one who pushed me to go to South Point. I graduated the semester before you arrived."

"You got out as a second lieutenant. Not too many promotions since then, huh? Why are they holding you back?"

"When you say 'they' do you mean the Seventeen or the Wardens?"

"Both, I guess."

"As far as the Seventeen is concerned, I'm MIA. The tac I'm wearing has been reprogrammed. I can only be traced by the Wardens. I run special ops for them, and they pay me really well. I'm saving the money, so when I get out, I won't have to work. Rank doesn't mean anything to me, so long as they keep the payments coming."

"Well, at least you're honest. You're a mercenary."

"That's right. And I don't feel guilty. They owe it to me, and it's about time someone in my family rose above the middle class. My grandparents worked in those domes until they were hunched over. My parents would've done the same. And even though they took a lot of pride in their work, I watched it suck the life out of them. Maybe the attack helped end their pain."

"You know, I used to think my life back on Gatewood-Callista was pretty bad. I figured the only future I had was working in the mines until the numox poisoning finally got me. But when I think about it now, it wouldn't have been so bad. Just a simple life. Honest. No secrets. You'd get up in the morning and you'd know what to expect. Maybe that's boring, but boring sounds pretty good now. I'm tired of playing these games."

"Yeah, I guess we're a couple of statistics. You know, disillusioned soldiers beaten down by the system."

"And I keep thinking there's a way to rise above this shit. Maybe I'm kidding myself. And that scares the hell out of me."

She stood and put a hand on my shoulder. "Scott, no matter what happens, no matter what you choose to do, I think we should . . ."

"What?"

Pulling away, she turned back to the wall. "Forget it."

"You think we should be friends?"

"Yes, I do."

"Misery loves company?"

She faced me, her eyes welling up. "No, because you know what it's like to be me. You *know*."

I thought about my life, about the epi we had both endured. "I'll be your friend. Just don't lie to me."

"Okay."

Perhaps I was undermining the moment, but I saw an opportunity, and I took it. "Tell me the truth about my brother."

She sighed deeply. "I'll tell you what I've heard. But I can't tell you if it's the truth."

"Just tell me."

"They're probably monitoring us, and I'm going to get in trouble for this, but you know what? Fuck it. Here it is: even before the war the Wardens knew the Guard Corps wouldn't be able to stand up to the alliances, especially under a new government's direction. So they began increasing their numbers quietly, through diversions, sabotage, whatever they could come up with. The conditioning accident on Exeter that apparently killed your brother? Well, the Wardens knew the alliances would try to seize control of that place. So they sabotaged it and basically kidnapped as many cadets as they could. There was a massive cover-up. The cadets were listed as KIA, but they were given new identities and recruited into their ranks."

"Were they brainwiped?"

"Most weren't, but I heard some of the extreme cases were."

"How could they be given new identities? DNA forgeries last for like what? Six months? A year at the most?"

"We've addressed that problem, but the details are trivial. The point is, your brother is alive. And he's one of us."

"But you can't prove that."

"I wish I could. He has a new identity now, but I've heard his old name mentioned several times. It's Jarrett, right?"

"That's right. But I still don't understand. You're saying the Wardens staged the accident on Exeter so they could kidnap personnel, among other things."

"Exactly."

"Then why didn't they take me? Doesn't my epi make me more valuable?"

"Yeah, and much more high-profile. They probably kept a tight watch on you. Getting you would have been a lot more difficult, so they probably didn't bother and figured they'd use your brother to get to you later."

The hatch opened, and we both turned as Breckinridge and Halitov stepped inside. "Oh, you're already finished," said Halitov, clearly disappointed.

"We thought we'd come by and watch the show," Breckinridge explained, shutting the hatch and following a perimeter walkway toward us.

"You didn't miss anything. I kicked her ass, and she begged for mercy," I said, deadpan.

"That's right," Jing said. "I didn't know he had it in him."

"Are you serious?" Halitov asked.

"You guys look drunk," I said.

Breckinridge winked. "We'll be shipping out in a couple of hours. Got coordinates in Ross one-fifty-four, where *Vanguard One* will meet us."

"You still won't let us send word to our CO?" I asked.

"What do you want to tell him? Uh, sorry, sir, but we can't report for duty for a while because we're considering an offer from the Wardens. Mind if we take some time off?"

"Our tacs have been reactivated. They can track us now."

"Doesn't matter. They can't spare anyone to come searching for you."

"How are we supposed to explain this when we get back?"

"Get back? Scott, by the time you're finished talking with the colonel, you'll understand that working for us is what you need to do. And if the Seventeen won't transfer you, then you might have to return to MIA status so you can work for us."

"Which'll probably include brainwiping so you can turn me into a good little Warden, huh?"

"Listen to the whiner over here," said Halitov. "We have a chance to help ourselves and help the colonies."

"You've been spending too much time with her," I told him, widening my gaze on Breckinridge.

"At least Rooslin's keeping an open mind," Breckinridge said.

I could remain there, brooding, or get a shower. I moped over to the hatch.

"It's all going to work out, Scott," Halitov called after me. "Stop worrying."

A few hours later, my expression long and my heart turning black, I stepped aboard an ATC with Halitov, Jing, and Breckinridge. The pilots got their clearance, and we rose and glided forward through the bay as the doors ahead rumbled apart. I gripped the safety bars pressing on my shoulders and glanced across the hold at Jing, who took a deep breath and closed her eyes. I did likewise and barely noticed the tawt drive kicking in until a sinking feeling overcame me.

"Tawt complete," reported one of the pilots. "Entering Ross one-fifty-four. Right on the grid. Uh, Captain Breckinridge?"

"What is it?"

"No sign of *Vanguard One*. Picking up another ship tawting into the system. Goddamn it!"

"What?"

"It's the capital cruiser *Rhode Island*. She's launching an attack wing. Activating her beam."

"Get us out of here!" cried Breckinridge.

"Engaging emergency tawt sequence," the pilot said. He barely finished when a thundering blow struck the ATC, slamming all of us into our bars.

"She's got us in her beam," said the pilot.

I leered at Breckinridge, who said, "You were worried about being brainwiped? Now's the time to worry . . ."

"Can't launch a boat?" asked Halitov.

"If this ATC can't pull free from their beam, you think a lifeboat can?" Jing snapped.

"Full power now," hollered the pilot. "Captain? They got us. They got us good. Orders?"

Breckinridge bit her lip, staring hard in thought.

"You're not thinking about suicide, are you?" Halitov asked her.

"We're carrying information that can't fall into their hands," she said.

"Fuck that! Let them take us into their bay. And let's fight them. That's the way to go out," he said.

"They'll have orders to take us alive," she countered.

"I'd like to see them try."

"If this goes bad . . ." She tapped an index finger on her tac, reminding us of the termination code. "So we fight. But we don't let them take us."

Breckinridge looked to Jing, who nodded. Then she looked to me. I added my nod to Jing's.

"All right," she said, throwing up her safety bars. "Let's make life a bitch for the Western Alliance Marine Corps."

PART 3

◀ ▶

Defining the Code

12 ▸ **I kept watch** through a porthole while Halitov set a charge just above the ATC's rear hatch. "Hey, nobody's mentioned this, but, uh, I'm wondering . . . what the hell happened to *Vanguard One?*" he asked.

"Excellent question," said Breckinridge, returning from the cockpit. "Somebody must've tipped off the alliances, and the colonel must've found out about it. Maybe he couldn't warn us in time."

"Or maybe we've been set up," said Jing.

"Wouldn't surprise me," I added.

"Thirty seconds till we clear the bay," said one of the pilots.

"You got all the charges set?" Breckinridge asked.

"Yeah," said Halitov. "And if it's okay with you, I'd like to gear up. I understand those Marines will be carrying rifles. Nasty things. They shoot projectiles that wear down your skin and tend to get you killed."

"Gear up, wiseass. All of you."

I yanked a QQ90 particle rifle from its bulkhead clip, checked the charge, set the ID code, then strapped on a smart schrap grenade belt weighed down by two dozen of the deadly devices.

"We have to get pumped," yelled Halitov, as the ship suddenly listed hard to port, and, through one of the portholes, the void of space panned off into an icy, battled-scarred plain of gray alloy. "We're inside now. And we have to get pumped! We're going to kill 'em all, right? Right? Right?"

Halitov's nerves had reached his voice, and I guess working himself into a war frenzy allowed him to cope. To the rest of us, he was just annoying, and, thankfully, Breckinridge talked him down. I went over to Jing, checked her grenade belt, then double-checked her rifle while she returned the favor.

"Scared?" she asked.

"Back when I was a cadet and we got attacked, the Marines caught me. But I got away. Nowhere to run now, huh?"

She saw right through me. "I'm scared, too."

"We'll work together. We'll have to kill a lot of them. Do you understand?"

She tightened her lips, nodded.

"All right, they're going to release the beam," said one of the pilots.

The ship lurched and hit the landing deck with a solid thud. Then . . . silence.

"Signal coming through now," reported the pilot. "On the comm . . ."

"ATC Four-five-zero-niner, this is Executive Officer Haight Vanderson, Western Alliance Marine Corps. Under war declaration sixteen-B we are hereby authorized to board your vessel, seize it and all property contained therein, and place you and anyone in your charge under arrest, copy?"

"We copy that, sir," said Breckinridge. "And we're prepared to surrender ourselves and this vessel. Opening hatch and sending out our pilots."

The two pilots shifted back into the hold, two

young men staring hard at Breckinridge. One, the blond, muttered to her, "This had better work."

Breckinridge took a deep breath, then beat a fist on the starboard hatch control. The door cycled up and away from the bulkhead.

With their hands raised, both pilots hopped down from the hold and started off. We needed to get them as far away from the ATC as possible, and, since they were not conditioned, they, unfortunately, walked point for our "surrender."

Halitov, who peered out through a nearby port-hole, said, "Looks like three squads. Center and flanks. Count three grenade launchers, but I doubt they'll use them. Okay. They got the pilots. Deactivating tacs and taking them away."

"Distance?" asked Breckinridge.

"About thirty meters now. Entering the lift. Okay. We're clear."

"ATC Four-five-zero-niner, we register four more occupants within your vehicle. Leave your weapons inside and come out with your hands extended above your heads."

"Oh, we're coming out," said Halitov. "Don't worry about that."

"Ready on your triggers?" Breckinridge asked us.

My thumb lay heavily on the detonator's button.

"It's Jing and Scott, then me and you, Halitov," Breckinridge said. "Go!"

Jing and I skinned up and burst through the hold, hit the floor, and in that second, as the Marines real-ized we were heavily armed, we both found the bond and leapt up, toward the ceiling. Even as we flew, they opened fire and Breckinridge and Halitov jumped from the hold and rebounded off the floor, joining us in a race toward the overhead, some thirty meters away.

In a pair of heartbeats, all was chaos, with the Marines firing up at us as we rolled to land boots-first on the ceiling and activated our detonators.

The ATC exploded, sending thousands of sharp-edged fragments in all directions. Debris knocked Marines off their feet, cut one man in half, decapitated two others, and set a third on fire. Since his leg had been cut off, his skin had deactivated. Grunts near the back ran toward the lift doors on either side of the hold, but a fireball swallowed them as Klaxons resounded. More Marines shouted, and automatic fire suppressers triggered in the bulkheads, their nozzles spewing a powdery foam all over the bay. A life-support alarm indicated that oxygen was automatically being jettisoned through the locks, effectively extinguishing all flames.

We had just destroyed our only ride out, which, initially, didn't make much sense. However, we had reached the conclusion that even if we could somehow neutralize the capital ship's beam and affect a launch, her fighters would be on us long before our ATC's computer could calculate an emergency tawt. The ATC's armaments were no match for a squadron of atmoattack jets. So we did something the Marines did not expect, something we still couldn't believe.

As we raced across the overhead, toward a crab carrier we had singled out as our holding ground, the Marines answered our explosion with a surprise of their own. A low-level EMP bomb dropped from a hidden tube in the ceiling and exploded in a white-hot flash, kicking out a pulse wave that disrupted all electronic equipment within two hundred meters, according to a databar in my HUV. Our rifles and smart schrap grenades were useless, though at least our tacs and skins—which relied on our own bodies' energy—still functioned. We never suspected they would utilize an EMP charge within their own ship, since the pulse wave would affect all of their own equipment, including life support. Apparently, they were so eager to get their hands on us that someone, maybe the XO, had decided to take the risk.

Though I expected Halitov to voice his surprise and begin moaning about just how screwed we now were, he kept silent as we dropped from the ceiling, onto the crab carrier's hull. Breckinridge led us toward the cockpit, toward a hatch near two thick antennae. We climbed into the carrier and hopped anxiously from the ladder.

"What the hell am I supposed to do now," Jing asked Breckinridge. "I can't even bring up the computer to ID me because the EMP bomb's knocked out everything."

"Mind if you tell us what's going on?" I demanded.

Breckinridge hesitated. "Oh, fuck it. Jing was going to get us in so we could fly this bird out. This ship could hold off a squadron and a beam long enough to tawt."

"How was she going to get us in? You can't fly this bird without DNA recognition."

Breckinridge glanced to Jing, who just returned a menacing stare. "She can bypass."

"That's impossible."

"I can use the bond to temporarily alter my DNA to mimic whomever I want," Jing said. "The computer will think I'm the pilot."

"You're joking."

"The joke's on all of us—unless we can reach another bay out of the EMP's range. I'll be right back." And with that, she dematerialized, and even though I knew she possessed that power, seeing her do it right before my eyes still left me unnerved.

Breckinridge glanced down at her tac, rubbed her fingers over it.

"I know what you're thinking, and I'm not going to kill myself here," cried Halitov. "No fuckin' way!"

Without so much as a whisper or faint puff of air, Jing appeared, pale and gasping. "I did a quick scan of the other four bays. They've added security around every ship, got the cockpits locked up tight. Scott and I can get inside, and I can probably get a ship on-line and launch, but there's no way we can get back here for you."

"Then we'll have to fight our way down there," said Halitov. "You two go ahead and get the ship ready. We'll meet up with you."

"He makes it sound so easy," said Breckinridge.

"What about the pilots?" I asked. "You told them we had a plan for breaking them out of the interrogation room."

Breckinridge's expression soured. "Yeah, I did."

"You lied?"

"They're not conditioned. Maybe they'll get wiped, but they won't be killed."

"How could you do that to them?"

"It's called making tough decisions. As a captain

and company commander, I assumed you'd know all about that."

"Yeah, I do. And now that we're no longer en route to meet the colonel, I'm assuming command."

She chuckled darkly. "We don't got time for jokes."

A loud beep came from the ship's cockpit, and Jing strode off to check it out.

"What?" called Breckinridge.

"They're as crazy as we are. Ship's autodestruct sequence has been armed."

"Shut it down," Breckinridge cried.

"They've locked me out. I can't."

A voice boomed from outside. "Attention, guardsmen. Step out of the carrier with your hands fully extended above your heads. If you fail to comply in one minute, we've been authorized to jettison and destroy the ship. One minute. Mark."

Halitov moved to a rectangular porthole. "They've cleared the hold. Bay doors opening." His worried gaze met mine. "These assholes are serious." Then he glanced accusingly at Breckinridge. "And I thought you said they'd want to take us alive."

"They're bluffing."

"I don't think so." Halitov pointed up, toward a powerful whine emanating from above. "They've brought in some equipment from another bay . . ."

The carrier suddenly buffeted as the talons of a colossal bay crane clamped onto her sides. With a jolt, the ship began to rise.

I turned to Jing. "It's going to put a big drain on me, but come on."

"Where to?" she asked.

"They're controlling the crane from the flight boss's station. Let's raise a little hell."

She nodded, her eyes went distant, and . . . she was gone. I thought hard, felt the bond, and willed myself out of the carrier, out of the bay, and above to the flight boss's station, with its panoramic windows overlooking the carrier and shattered ATC.

As I got my bearings, I spotted Jing ripping the portly flight boss from his chair. She drove a palm up, into his nose, and kept pushing to kill him. He slumped as two Marines guarding the door came forward, leveling their particle rifles. I ran forward and leapt between them, kicking both rifles from their hands as I came down and grabbed their necks, driving them back, toward the door. One of them shouted something as I fumbled for his wrist, tore off his hand and tac, turned to the other, who frantically dug into a hip holster for his pistol. I seized his wrist—

"Scott!" cried Jing.

I looked up, right into the small, dark eyes of a Marine sergeant hovering over me. He waved a pen scanner over my tac, deactivating it. My skin faded, and a horrible smell made me light-headed. Jing rocketed toward us in the *biza*, but the Marine got his scanner close enough to deactivate her tac. As her skin faded, she dropped, began coughing, rolled over, looked at me, eyes begging for help. "Scott . . ."

The humming of force beams came from somewhere, from the darkness, it seemed. Suddenly aware of my aching body, I opened my eyes and saw dust twinkling in the beams. I sat up. They had carried me to a small cell in the brig, lavishly furnished with a narrow gelrack, small sink, and foul-smelling head. A thick band had been placed on my wrist, just above my tac, and I tried repeatedly to rip it off, but I couldn't find the strength. The band was drugging me, I knew, keeping me weak, too weak to will myself out of the cell. I opened my mouth, and the voice that emerged sounded thin, hoarse, nearly unrecognizable. "Rooslin? Jing? Breckinridge?"

I waited for an answer, listened to the beams' incessant humming. I wanted to call again, but my throat hurt.

A little later, I'm not sure how long, the beams trickled out, and in stepped the ship's XO, a tall man with closely cropped hair and a silver goatee. "Captain, you've been placed under arrest by the Western Alliance Marine Corps. Do you understand me?"

Even just a nod brought on pain. A lot of pain.

"My orders are to disregard the war conventions of 2300 and 2301 pertaining to the seizure and treatment of POWs. I understand that your orders are to obey the Articles of the Code of Conduct, that you will not willingly give information or take part in any actions that might be harmful to the colonies. Am I correct in assuming that?"

"Yes, sir," I whispered.

"Well, unfortunately son, we've already scanned you, the other captains, and your pilots, and you've given us more information than we could have possibly hoped for."

My jaw went slack. "No."

He smiled. "A second conditioning facility on Aire-Wu? Conditioned officers with the ability to manipulate their own DNA? A possible coup being initiated by the Colonial Wardens? Some kind of Racinian medical machines on Exeter? Unbelievable. Truly unbelievable."

My eyes welled up. I had not succumbed to their torture. I had not volunteered the information. I was simply foolish enough to let myself be captured. As I gritted my teeth at the XO, I realized that my greatest failure was in remaining alive.

"You're probably wondering what happens now," said the XO. "And though you might be fighting for the wrong side, I admire a gennyboy like you who's managed to become a captain. So I won't keep you wondering. We're transferring you to another carrier. You'll be taken all the way to Earth. I guess the techies want to get their hands on you and your friends. Yes, they're probably going to brainwipe you, maybe turn you into some kind of secret weapon. Who knows, one day we might even serve together."

A tear slipped from one eye, and I quickly backhanded it away.

"Easy, son. You won't remember any of this bullshit. And I'm willing to bet that for the first time in your life, you'll be happy. Hell, at least you'll be on the winning team, because the information you've given us will allow us to dismantle the Seventeen System Guard Corps by year's end." He waved a hand. "Don't get me wrong. I'm not here to gloat. I just came to say . . . good luck."

I glanced at the floor as he left and remained that way for a long moment before I curled up into a ball. The drugs made me feel so emotional, so vulnerable, that I couldn't help but sob.

* * *

They fed me twice per day, and I was able to measure time by those feedings. After the first week I suspected that my body was developing a resistance to whatever chemicals they were pumping into me. I began to feel stronger and more in control of my emotions.

It's interesting how confinement has a way of putting you back in touch with yourself—whether you like it or not. I began a mental conversation in which I sought forgiveness from my friends, but they continually reminded me of my failure. I turned to thoughts of escape, and I managed to focus on them for a few days, exhausting dozens of ideas until I surrendered back into self-pity.

Then one morning, on the eleventh day of my confinement, alarms wailed, and I couldn't understand why. I had grown so accustomed to the world of my cell that I had forgotten I was on board an Alliance capital cruiser and that anything, anything at all, could happen.

13 ❯ After listening to that racket a moment more, I finally realized that the *Rhode Island*'s captain had sounded the general alarm. His voice came loudly and evenly over the shipwide comm: "Battle stations. Battle stations. All hands . . . this is not a drill. Skins up! Weapons charge now!"

Two Marines jogged by my cell.

"What is it?" I cried.

They ignored me and kept moving.

A muffled explosion came from somewhere above, followed by a rumble that might have begun at the cruiser's stern and moved forward, like a breaker, though as I craned my head this way and that, I couldn't be sure. The rumble came again, much louder, and seemingly from all directions. Then, *boom, boom, boom*! The incoming struck hard, and the situation grew more clear. The *Rhode Island* was taking heavy missile and laser fire, probably from one of the Guard Corps's capital ships, a couple million kilometers away. With our tacs deactivated, there was no way of communicating to the attacking ship that we were on board, and I grinned bitterly over the fact that I had been struggling with the idea of betraying the Guard Corps, a force that might very well, albeit unknowingly, end my life.

The wall of force beams that imprisoned me flickered, then blinked out, along with the ship's standard lighting, which reverted to dim crimson. I was free, but an odd feeling, an intense fear of stepping out of the cell, pressed hard, pressed very, very hard. I kept telling myself, *You idiot, come on, run!* But then I'd look back at the little gelrack and sink, at the walls, even at the head, and all of it, the place where I had spent so many hours, continued to beckon with the promise that if I remained there, I would be safe. *Just stay here. This is your home. If you go out there, they'll shoot you, kill you . . .*

"I hear the bar's got a two-for-one special? Want to go?" came a familiar voice.

I slowly raised my gaze to meet Halitov's. He looked a little leaner, his blond beard graying near the jaw. "I want to stay," I told him.

"Like the accommodations that much, do you?"

I stared vaguely at him.

"Let's go." He grabbed my wrist and hauled me out of there, chills needling up my spine as I realized that for the first time in what felt like years I was . . . I was out.

We met up with Jing and Breckinridge in the next cell block. The guards had been called to the upper levels, presumably to man hardpoints or make preparations for abandoning ship. We huddled inside Jing's cell, all of us still wearing the bands that kept us drugged, though the others appeared to have developed a resistance like me. Jing suggested that she run recon, but Breckinridge was worried that in her state she might not return.

"Let's see," said Jing, then she closed her eyes and dissolved.

We just sat there, no one talking, our gazes riveted to the overhead as we listened to the chaotic booming.

After a minute, Jing reappeared and collapsed into my arms, startling the hell out of me. I cupped the back of her head. "That was . . . that was bad," she said.

"What happened?" I asked.

"I shot up to the bridge for a second. They're taking long-range fire from *Vanguard One* and three other ships. The TAWT drive's been tommyed. They're going to abandon ship. *Vanguard*'s on her way. ETA two minutes."

"Where are we? What system?" Breckinridge asked.

I was about to set Jing down beside me, but she struggled against my grip, apparently quite comfortable being in my arms. "We're still in Ross. The *Rhode Island*'s been waiting for the transfer ship that was supposed to take us to Earth. I'm not sure, but I thought I heard a midshipman say the transfer ship was just taken out by *Vanguard*."

"Okay, our buddies up on the bridge probably called for help," said Halitov. "They're getting into life tubes and hoping that their rescue gets here before *Vanguard*."

"I doubt that'll happen," said Breckinridge. "And if I know the colonel, he won't waste any more time with this ship. He'll assume she's going to blow."

"So where's this leave us?" asked Halitov. "Screwed as ever or what?"

Breckinridge narrowed her gaze. "According to an obscure schematic of this ship that I almost wish wasn't in my head, there's a life tube station at the end of this block."

Even as we rose, four Marines burst into our cell,

lifting their rifles. The lead soldier, a corporal, nervously said, "We're going to the life tubes. Now!"

I traded a weak grin with Breckinridge. Halitov chuckled under his breath. Jing, who had just gotten to her feet, fought for balance, then finally smiled herself.

"What's so funny?" demanded the corporal.

"Nothing," I said. "Nothing at all."

He huffed, waved his rifle. "This way!"

The life tubes aboard the *Rhode Island* could carry up to twenty soldiers each, but only the four of us and the four Marines lay strapped in the jumpseats as the corporal gave a verbal launch order to the tube's computer. With a jolt that stole my breath, we ripped away from the *Rhode Island* and joined hundreds of other projectiles speeding from the dying hulk. The ship's long, boxy fuselage spewed all manner of liquids and shed tattered pieces of her hull and innards, which tumbled and flashed against the distant red sun. Even as the strangely beautiful scene collapsed upon a plate of brilliant stars, our evacuation abruptly ceased. A beam from *Vanguard One* or one of the other ships locked on to our tube.

"They've got us," cried one of the Marines. "Aw, man. I didn't want to get brainwiped. Oh, man . . ."

I leaned over and looked at the soldier, just eighteen, maybe nineteen, with real fear in his eyes. I suspected that Beauregard would, in fact, wipe the Marine, turn him into a Warden, and put him back in the field, fighting against the alliances he had sworn an oath to defend. People, it seemed, were now just machines whose honor, duty, and loyalty were not forged over time but programmed. And maybe that was the better way to go. It seemed damned near impossible to adhere to the code when you were tugged at by what-ifs and maybes and lies.

"Hey, Scott? What's the first thing you're going to do when we get back?" asked Halitov, as we glided toward *Vanguard One*, her starboard docking port wide-open and already admitting dozen of tubes.

"I don't know," I said. "Sleep, I guess."

"Okay, Halitov, what is it you're going to do," said Jing. "I know you're dying to tell us."

Before Halitov could answer, the Marine corporal threw off his straps and unclipped his particle rifle from the wall. In zero G, he floated around, leveling the rifle on Jing. "It's a goddamned shame these tubes don't have a self-destruct, 'cause I'm thinking I'd rather be dead than brainwiped. And I'm also thinking you people are too valuable to be in the wrong hands. So now we're all going to see Jesus."

I reached for my own strap.

The corporal swung his rifle, pointing it at his own men. He opened fire, spraying them before turning his bead toward Breckinridge, rounds flashing and flying in the bizarre ballet of zero G. Through a storm of floating blood, I saw Jing materialize in front of the corporal, drive his weapon up—but not before a pair of rounds punched Breckinridge in the shoulder. She flinched and swore, putting a hand on the wound as Halitov shouted her name and wrestled with his buckle.

I threw off my strap, pushed forward, even as a stinging cut across my thighs. Jing managed to pull the corporal's hand from the trigger. The firing ceased as I crossed behind him, took his head into my hands and, with a faint crunch, broke his neck. I yanked the rifle away from Jing and began batting the corporal until someone, I think it was Halitov, kept shouting for me to ease down while someone else, probably Jing, took back the rifle. I just hung there, groping for breath, the droplets of blood all over the cabin, the pain in Breckinridge's eyes screaming as loud as my own.

"What he did," Jing finally began, "is what we should've done."

"No. I don't give a fuck what the Alliance knows now," said Halitov. "Being a good soldier has nothing to do with suicide. Nothing at all." He looked at me, as though expecting my nod of approval. I winced.

They hoisted us onto gurneys, rolled us out of the life tube, then hauled us down to *Vanguard One*'s sick bay, where surgeons addressed Breckinridge's wounds while a special team worked to remove the bracelets that had kept us drugged. I heard someone call for synthskin repair as I lay back on the bed, not really caring what they did. I was feeling too damned sorry for myself to realize that I could still show people what it's like to be loyal and honorable. I just lay there as they worked on me, ignoring any question that wasn't related to my injuries.

I slept for several hours, then stirred to find Jing stroking my cheek. "How do you feel?" she asked softly.

"I don't want to feel," I said, pushing her hand away. "I don't want to feel anything, anymore."

"Scott, feeling it *is* remembering. And the worst thing we can do is forget." She looked up, across the room. "There's someone here to see you. I'll check back later." She headed for the hatch.

Paul Beauregard moved past the foot of my bed and strode to my side. He looked young, fit, wearing crisp utilities and Warden insignia on his breast. "Last time I saw you, I was the one who looked like shit. Finally, some symmetry, huh?"

"Yeah." I gave him the once-over for his benefit. "So everything they told me about you is true? You're a Warden?"

He bit his lip. "I know. I should've told the old man I wanted out. But I was facing a general court-martial. He got me the best defense attorney, and he took me to be reconditioned. I couldn't just leave him after all that."

"Is your transfer legal? Or did you have to go MIA?"

"It's legal. He got me reassigned. I know that they're doing everything they can to make your transfer legit, but if you don't put in a request, it'll never happen, and if you do want to join us, then you'll have to go MIA."

"I didn't know I still had a choice," I said. "Or is making me *think* I have a choice part of the plan?"

"Scott, I don't like any of this either: but my old man seems to think he can win this war, and he tends to get what he wants. He even promised to get me back to Exeter to recover Dina's body."

"How are you, uh, doing with that?"

"I've been talking to a couple of shrinks, but I'm

not sure it helps. You have to heal on your own. I don't know how long it'll take. Maybe never."

"You'll be okay."

"We both will. So, we're heading to Aire-Wu to get you reconditioned. That was one thing that made me feel better."

"Jing told me something—"

"About your brother?"

"She said—"

"I know what she said. And I can't confirm any of that. Only my father can."

"Then I want to talk to him."

"You'll get your chance. In a few hours we're all having dinner in the captain's quarters."

"Good. Let me ask you something else. Does your father know they scanned us?"

"He knows. The *Rhode Island*'s skipper tried tawting out a chip. We took out the probe."

"They could've sent a conventional signal."

"If they had, we would've intercepted."

"I'm sure the information reached somebody."

"That's not your problem, Scott. You got captured. I wouldn't have committed suicide either. There aren't enough people who would care that I did, you know? This war's about land and money. Get used to that, and you'll start feeling better." He crossed toward the hatch. "I'll come back for you in a little while."

"You see Rooslin?"

"He's over in the next bay with his new love. I think he's rubbing her feet."

I frowned a second before I conjured up an image of the big guy caressing Breckinridge's feet while fan-

ning her with a giant leaf as she plucked grapes from
a tray and told him, "A little lower, yes. Just a little
lower."

"Hey, Scott?" Paul called, tugging me away from
the image.

"What?"

"Don't tell anybody, but I think you're smiling."
He headed off.

The captain's quarters were huge and lavishly deco-
rated in a nautical motif that Jing explained represented Terran seafarers of the sixteenth century who
sailed in the Caribbean. She said they were the original pirates. I'm not sure what she meant by "original," but I assumed these pirates were famous for
their great feasts, since at the rear of the dining area
lay a half dozen tables arranged in rows and jammed
with more food than I had ever seen collected in one
place. I found Halitov and Breckinridge filling their
plates to capacity with meats and fresh vegetables
and fruit and whipped cream.

"Scott, man, how 'bout this spread?" asked Halitov. "Finally, some real food. No spaghetti and meatballs, but look at this!" He grabbed a piece of baked
chicken, stuffed it in his mouth, and chewed, then
narrowed his gaze in ecstasy.

Jing took a plate and drifted over to a tray filled
with steamed broccoli, corn, carrots, and what had to
be Tau Ceti asparagus. I joined her there. Beginning to
feel a bit giddy—and the feeling was good—I loaded
up my plate and crossed to the main dining table, a
rectangular affair that seated at least thirty. I took a
high-backed, ornately carved wooden chair between

Jing and Halitov. Well-dressed officers, mostly department heads who seemed quite used to the atmosphere of ostentation, slid casually into most of the remaining chairs.

Of course, Halitov was the only one who spoke with his mouth full, repeatedly commented on how good everything was, and asked twice why the colonel and the ship's captain still hadn't appeared.

"They're on their way," Paul replied, taking a chair opposite us and setting down a moderately filled tray. "There was a little action around Aire-Wu, but it's all been taken care of."

"What do you mean by 'a little action'?" I asked.

"Just that," he said curtly, then eyed the others. "So, is everyone enjoying the meal?"

"Are you kidding?" asked Halitov. "Best food I've eaten in my entire life."

"I wouldn't say that, but it's really good," said Jing.

"The best, as always," added Breckinridge.

Paul winked at us all, then waved a finger at me and Halitov. "You know, sitting here with you two reminds me of all those days back at the South Point, remember? We'd be sitting in the mess, studying for exams."

I nodded. "You want to talk politics?"

"Why not?"

"Oh, here we go," Halitov groaned. "Can't we just eat instead of turning this into a debate?" Then, noting Jing's and Breckinridge's confusion, Halitov explained how Beauregard and I had often engaged in some intellectual sparring during lunch while he would just watch, cringe, and feed his machine.

"I assume your father's going to lean hard on me to

join the Wardens," I told Paul. "But how does he justify breaking the code? Everything you're doing undermines the new colonial government, yet you people still maintain that you're not attempting to seize control?"

"I told you we're trying to give the new government a polite nudge," said Breckinridge. "Of course, there are some senators who will never listen to reason."

Paul nodded. "Scott, do you think if we were really organizing a coup that we could keep it a secret? If we were, the word would've gotten out, and we would've been disbanded a long time ago. We're just trying to navigate around the Colonial Congress, which, I have to say, is as corrupt as it is ineffectual."

"This 'navigating' as you put it. You don't believe you're breaking the code? Come on. By operating without the direct approval of the Colonial Congress you're ignoring the oath you swore to the Seventeen and the colonies we protect. You're breaking the code. More than that, we're talking treason."

His lip twisted. "In the end, Scott, the mission is still the same: protect the colonies. Eight have already fallen. Nine left. If something doesn't give soon, we're all going to be wiped. You can sit there and worry about whether you're being a good little soldier and whether all the warrants of your argument make sense, but in the end, like I said, the mission is still the same. And if you abandon us, you're abandoning the mission."

I snorted. "That help you sleep at night?"

"No, but it reminds me how much I hate this, how much I'd rather be home. But that's never going to happen if I don't wind up on the winning team. So good or bad, that's the bottom line. You can go back, work for the Seventeen, for Rebel ten-seven, but you'll do that knowing we can't be stopped . . . we won't be stopped . . . and we'll save all our lives. I know you, Scott. You can't sit by. You need to join us."

I glanced away from him, shook my head fiercely.

"I know," he went on. "You think we're breaking the code. What if breaking the code has to be done in order to save lives and complete the mission? The code was created to that end, and if it's no longer useful, then why follow it? Misplaced loyalty isn't any good. You're not giving up on the colonies, you're helping them. You're not doing what your mother did."

I tensed at the mention of my mother. "I don't want to be like you: people who swear oaths, then turn their backs on them."

"You turned your back on the alliances when you joined the Seventeen."

"You know I was rushed into that. But now I see how it is. There's nothing important anymore. Oh, excuse me, I forgot. There is one thing: winning the war, right? Who gives a fuck about anything else? People don't matter. Just win, win, win. Fuck the code."

"The code *must* be broken. And whether any of us likes it or not, the Wardens are going to keep us free. And you're right. That's what it's about. Winning. Because winning equals freedom. And it's going to happen our way, and eventually, the new colonial government will thank us."

"Or have you put to death for treason."

Someone hemmed at the head of the table, and all gazes turned as Colonel J.D. Beauregard arrived, bringing with him the ship's captain, a man named

Lindemann who looked much too young and nervous to hold that station. On the other hand, the colonel (looking for all the world like an older clone of his son) possessed the gait and sharp stare of man who had commanded respect for most of his life—even when he had been as youthful as the *Vanguard*'s skipper. I guess some people were born to command. And while my name seemed to be fading from that list, the colonel's blazed brilliantly at its top. He took a seat to the captain's right, where the XO should have been, but that man now sat to the captain's left, in deference to the legendary colonel.

Captain Lindemann stood. "Ladies and gentlemen, welcome. And I'd like to extend a special welcome to Captain Kristi Breckinridge, Lieutenant Katya Jing, Captain Rooslin Halitov, and Captain Scott St. Andrew. If there's anything any of you need during your stay aboard, don't hesitate to contact me directly. Now then, before I interrupt your dinner any further, I'd like to propose a toast. To Colonel J.D. Beauregard, a man whose vision has once again resulted in another resounding naval victory for the colonies."

The other officers snapped to their feet, raised their glasses. Breckinridge and Jing followed quickly, as did Halitov and Paul. Begrudgingly, I stood and held a glass—but refused to lift it.

"To the colonel!" the captain cried.

"To the colonel!" the others shouted, then swigged hard.

I set my glass down and returned to my seat.

"As you were," said the captain. "Eat. Enjoy. Because it never lasts long . . ."

Keeping my gaze on my plate, I ate in silence, listening to Breckinridge and Jing discuss the attack on the *Rhode Island* with one of *Vanguard*'s weapons officers. Paul left his seat to go discuss something with his father, and Halitov found great interest in two thick slices of something called New York cheesecake.

As I was about to rise and fetch my own dessert, a tap came hard on my shoulder, and I looked up to find Paul standing beside the colonel. I liked Paul and didn't have the heart to disrespect him or his father by not bolting up and saluting.

"At ease, son," said the colonel. Interesting how to all older officers, we are always "son." Even more interesting is how I now carry on this silly tradition by calling male cadets in my counsel "son," as I was called.

"Scott, this is my father."

The colonel offered his somewhat wizened hand, the grip solid and telling. "Mr. St. Andrew, I've been watching your career quite closely, ever since my son told me you were in his squad back at the academy. If you don't mind, I'd like to take you up to my quarters for a brandy."

"I'm sorry, sir, but I understand what it is you want from me, and I just . . . I just can't do it."

"Captain, I insist. I'd rather you hear me out before you make a final decision."

"Sir, with all due respect. I've been going along with this little game and actually pretending that I have a choice. But I know I don't. Let's get to it. You want me to join. If I don't, you wipe me. End of story. Question number one: why is it so important that you get me to join willingly?"

"Sir, I'm—"

Paul was about to apologize to his father for my outburst, but the colonel cut him off with the wave of a finger. "Captain, your real combat experience is much more valuable than you know. Yes, we've had to wipe many individuals, cerebro them, and put them back out with a set of memories that were processed for them, not forged through real experience. Of course, we've had difficulties, you know, the same doubt you feel about your own cerebroed data. We'd rather not wipe anyone, anymore. Someone like you has far too much to offer. As long as I'm alive, none of you will be wiped. Now, please. Come with me to my quarters."

I looked to Paul for some reassurance, something, but he just turned away. "All right, sir. Lead the way."

We strolled out of the dining hall, into the corridor, and picked up a lift. Inside, the colonel asked, "Captain, if we could change the subject a moment. Tell me, how is my son?"

"Sir?"

"He doesn't talk to me anymore, at least not the way we used to. Yes, he told me all about Dina and the machine on Exeter, but I'm getting the feeling that he doesn't want to be a soldier anymore. Funny, all his life he's dreamed of becoming an officer. That's all I ever heard. And I've tried so hard to set a good example for him."

"Sir, I think Paul is an excellent officer. I'd serve with him anytime, anywhere. But there's a side to him that scares me. Still, we've been through a lot together. And if there's anything wrong with him now, it's probably the same thing that's bothering me. There's no one you can trust anymore. All we have left is the war. We give, it takes. And I guess we're all starting to run dry."

"You're a poet, Mr. St. Andrew, if not a dour one."

The lift doors parted, and he led me three hatches down to his quarters. Once inside, he took a brief call in the bedroom, then showed me to a spacious sitting room with a faux fireplace. I took a seat in a well-padded antique chair. He went to a small dry bar, poured us brandies, lit up a pipe, then took the chair opposite me.

I'd never had a glass of brandy before and winced over the taste. "Thank you, sir."

We just sat there, him smoking and sipping his brandy, me nervously rubbing the chair's arms. I figured he'd begin the conversation, but after five minutes of nothing, I finally asked, "Uh, excuse me, sir. But you wanted to talk?"

"That's right."

I repressed my grin. "Uh, sir, would you care to initiate the conversation?"

"No."

"Sir, did I say something back there in the lift that—"

"No, you did not."

"Maybe I forgot to say that I know Paul cares for you very deeply. And I know he's very proud of you. When we were at the academy, he talked about you all the time."

"Some people think I'm an abomination created by the military. I think my son agrees with that assessment."

I met his pained gaze for a moment, and I couldn't help but snort ever so slightly over the irony of him calling me into his quarters—not in an attempt to persuade me to join the Wardens—but to seek advice from me on how to deal with his son, whom he believed I knew better than he did.

"What's wrong with your father?" he asked.

"Sir?"

"What's wrong with him? What bothers you about him?"

"I don't know, sir. Did you get a chance to meet him? I heard you sent a rescue force to Gatewood-Callista. My father's supposedly on Kennedy-Centauri."

"He's there, and he's being well taken care of. And no, I didn't get a chance to meet him."

"He's a geologist, sir. A rockhead. Not the most interesting guy, but he was good to me and my brother. And I guess the one thing that bothered me about him was that he usually put work before us."

The colonel nodded, gaze distant, gaze probably on moments when he, too, had done the same thing. "Oh, nonsense," he suddenly said. "I want you to join the Wardens."

"I'm sorry—"

"Bullshit!" he shouted. "The only thing you're sorry about is that it was my ship that took out the *Rhode Island*. But Mr. St. Andrew, we can find you wherever you are." He took a moment to study me, perhaps pity me, then his tone softened. "You can help us. And if you do, you help yourself. I'm willing to bet that working with us is what your father would want . . ."

I closed my eyes as the hatchcomm beeped. The colonel sighed, yanked himself to his feet, answered. Hushed whispers came from the hatch, then the colonel returned, towing in a familiar face, a woman whose presence shocked me.

"Captain, I think you know Security Chief Brooks," the colonel said.

I rose unsteadily to my feet. "Uh, yes, sir."

14> **Ms. Brooks proffered** her hand, and before I could finish shaking it, she pulled me toward her and hugged me fiercely. "I got your message," she said softly, pulling back and frowning at my aged face. "And I'm sorry that you wound up in the middle of that fiasco on Eri Three."

"Ma'am, I, uh, I'm confused . . ."

She gestured toward my chair, and I sat as she crossed to face me and the colonel went off to fetch her a drink. Was she working with the Wardens? She had to be. Why else would she be aboard?

"We've had a lot of trouble back on Rexi-Calhoon," she said. "The Colonial Congress is divided on nearly every issue concerning this war. Relief funds are being misallocated. Three senators have already resigned from their posts, and, against our wishes, four colonial presidents have agreed to unconditional surrender. It's a nightmare. And it gets worse. The Guard Corps is being fractured, not because of what the Wardens are doing but because the remaining senators are launching investigations into how we deploy our forces. Because of that, regimental commanders have been forced to operate independently."

"You listening to what she's saying?" the colonel asked me, then handed Ms. Brooks a snifter of brandy. "The Seventeen is already doing the same thing we've been doing because we don't have time for all this political posturing and rhetoric. Our worlds are falling."

"Scott, I've only recently been in contact with Colonel Beauregard, and we've come to agree that if we're going to win this war, we need to resort to extreme measures—meaning the Guard Corps as you know it will be restructured and fall under the command and auspices of the Wardens. It's true that we won't have a majority vote in congress, but most opposing senators are being paid off by Alliance lobbyists who know that if the Wardens take over the Corps, we'll have a fighting chance. Of course they don't want that to happen."

"And if we do take over the Guard Corps, military personnel will answer only to us and not the congress. We'll fund ourselves and serve as independent contractors, meaning our mission will be motivated by victory and profit, not political bias."

"So, I guess it is a coup, huh?"

"Not a coup," said Ms. Brooks. "Just a restructuring without full approval. Scott, this has to be done. It will be done."

"I'm sure it will," I said gravely. "The Wardens are nothing if not efficient."

She put a hand on my shoulder. "Assigning you to Rebel ten-seven was a mistake. My mistake. I know where you're needed now. And it's with the Wardens."

"You came all the way out here to tell me that?"

"No, I've moved my office here. And I'll keep doing what I've always done: advise the Colonial Congress on military matters. We're no longer keeping any secrets. In the next few days, the Wardens will issue an official statement about the restructuring of the

Seventeen, and believe it or not, we've already gained the support of five of the seven joint chiefs."

"The congress is going to view this as a coup, no matter how you try to sell it," I said. "And you're going to have people like me who don't even know whom to fight for anymore. You might have company commanders taking matters into their own hands. You'll have anarchy. Chaos. The Guard Corps will be divided. And the alliances will exploit that weakness to capture more worlds."

"Almost makes you wish you had stayed with the alliances," said the colonel. "I know. But while it sounds disorganized now, Ms. Brooks is working on a plan to make this transition happen smoothly."

"Scott, we're here because we believe—both of us—that someone with your experience, someone with your power, can provide the rallying cry we need."

"They used to call it a wahoo, a Rebel yell, and if there was ever a rebel, it's you." The colonel winked. "Got it in your blood. I can tell. And that mistrust you have for us? I like it."

Ms. Brooks pursed her lips. "Scott, we all want the same thing."

"No. You want me to break the code."

"I can reinterpret the code for you so you can say that technically you're not breaking it because you're not doing anything that endangers the colos. But I can't lie. By deceiving the congress and joining the Wardens, you *will* be breaking the code. But maybe it's time for a new code, one that allows us to do what's necessary in order to save our worlds."

She had been right. But I couldn't have known that.

I needed something else, something to make me feel better about selling off my honor, my dignity, my loyalty—something that reassured me that I was not making my mother's mistakes and becoming an opportunist like Breckinridge. "Jarrett . . . I want to know about him."

Ms. Brooks glanced to the colonel. "He has a right," she said sternly.

The colonel shrugged. "Tell him."

"Your brother's alive."

I gritted my teeth. "Don't lie."

"We'll arrange for a meeting, right after you're conditioned," she said. "Colonel, I'm sure you can make that happen."

The old legend nodded, and for the first time since hearing that my brother might be alive, I allowed myself to believe, to really believe, that I had not lost him. I stood there, shaking, trying to remember the last words we had said to each other but drawing a blank, despite my enhanced memory. I regarded the colonel with a hard stare. "So it's true, then? The Wardens staged that accident on Exeter and kidnapped all of those cadets?"

The colonel narrowed his gaze on me. "They weren't kidnapped. They were transferred."

"Illegally transferred. *Sir*. So why didn't you have Paul taken? Why did you leave him there when you knew the academy would be attacked?"

"For the same reason why we left you: you're both high profile cadets. And that decision was more difficult than you could ever know." The colonel finished his brandy, then stared absently at the glass.

"Scott, you've helped me, and I've helped you,"

said Ms. Brooks. "Now here we are again. What do you say?"

I tried to read her wide-eyed gaze, searched for something earnest and telling, for a whisper behind that look, something that said, "It's okay. I'm telling the truth. And you can trust me." I couldn't be sure.

"C'mon, Scott. You know what you have to do."

"I'd like some time," I told her.

"We'll reach Aire-Wu in a few hours. We'll get you down there and reconditioned," she said. "No matter what you decide, I trust the colonel will allow you that much." She cocked a brow at him.

After a resigned sigh, he nodded.

I pushed myself out of the chair. "Ma'am. Colonel." I saluted and left, realizing that I was practically running by the time I reached the hatch, not that I was desperate to get out of there, but I was so excited about my brother being alive that I couldn't wait to tell Halitov.

Something dawned on me as I opened the hatch. "My brother," I called back to them. "Was he brain-wiped?"

"Scott, just relax," Ms. Brooks said. "Don't worry about a thing."

"Was he wiped?"

"Your brother's fine," she assured me. "Just fine."

Still unnerved, I closed the hatch after me and raced down the corridor, raced all the way back to the captain's quarters, where a midshipman who was cleaning up told me that the others had left for the ship's bar.

I found all four of them at the long counter, sloppy drunk, with Paul wobbling on his stool and Halitov hanging on Breckinridge as though he were an attention-starved juvenile.

"My brother's alive," I announced.

Only Jing actually met my gaze. "The colonel tell you?"

"Yeah. And thank you."

"Rumors around here . . . they tend to be true more often than not," Jing said.

"Old Jarrett's alive?" asked Halitov. "Always liked him. One of the best guys in our old squad. Let's have another drink."

I marched up to Halitov, grabbed him by the collar. "Are you in?"

"What?"

"Are you in?"

His eyes bugged out. "In what?"

"You are, aren't you," I said. "You already told them yes."

He nodded in realization. "Of course I did. What the fuck was I supposed to do? I'm in, and so are you." He ripped my hands away, shoved me back. "No more of this I-can't-decide bullshit. We're in."

"Okay. We're in."

He looked at me. "What?"

"We're joining. We're breaking the code."

"You're doing the right thing," said Breckinridge.

"Then why does it feel so wrong?"

"I asked myself the same question when I left my brother behind. But I had to, Scott. He's mentally disabled, and he needs more than I can give him. I fought my way up the ranks to pay for the best care. You think I'm an opportunist. Maybe I am. But it's always been about my brother. Leaving him was the hardest thing I've ever done in my life." She closed her eyes, massaged them, lost her balance a moment. "Anyway, have a drink."

"No, I'm tired. And I guess I owe you—"

"Respect. That's all I'm asking."

"Deal. See you later."

I was halfway back to my quarters when Jing called to me.

"Hey," I said. "You following me?"

Her cheeks grew flushed. "Thought maybe you'd like a little company. I'm getting tired of being around those drunks back there."

"I was going to get some sleep. We're going to be at Aire-Wu soon."

"There's a really impressive observation dome at the stern. We can go up there, watch the approach. Have you ever seen Aire-Wu before?"

I shook my head.

"They say that of all the seventeen worlds, it's the most Earth-like. Once you visit, you never want to leave."

"All I know about the place is what they jammed in my head: second of three planets orbiting an M-five star that sits about nine-and-a-half light-years from Earth. Seventy-one percent forest biome, fourteen percent ocean, and the stats go on and on and on, right?"

She grinned knowingly. "Kind of takes the awe and magic out of it . . ."

"I don't know. Let's see."

I followed her through the corridor, and two lifts and a half dozen levels later, an MP cleared us onto the OBS deck, a circular room beneath a plexi hemisphere that afforded breathtaking views of the stars.

"It's right over there," Jing said, crossing the room and pointing to her left.

The planet grew swiftly into view, an orb whose massive, finger-shaped continents bore hundreds of shades of green and brown and alabaster, while her much smaller oceans shone a deep, dark blue. Long tendrils of powder white clouds pushed out from the south pole, working their way across the seas and landmasses and breaking off into small dimples and haze and creases like those you'd find in a piece of leather. I had never seen so many colors, and I found myself voicing that.

"Yeah, and wait until you see the forests down there. Just wait," she said, wriggling her brows.

We went to the glass, pressed our foreheads against it, and just watched as the ship brought us closer. From the corner of my eye, I caught Jing watching me and pretended I hadn't seen her. But then, a few seconds later, it was hard to ignore her hand reaching around my head, pulling me toward her. "Please," she whispered. "Please." And her eyes welled with tears.

I wasn't a fool. I knew she hadn't called me up to the OBS deck just to chat and take in the view. And I felt damned guilty that I had agreed to come. I tried rationalizing my behavior, told myself that Dina was gone, that life had to go on, that if I felt something for Jing, I should explore that or suffer the regret.

And after all, she was the only one who really knew what it was like to be me.

So I kissed her. Even as our lips touched, I felt a pang

of guilt, and my lips suddenly tightened. She sensed it, and drew slowly back. "I'm sorry." She swore under her breath and pushed away from the glass.

"Not your fault," I said. "This whole thing, you know, joining the Wardens, being in that cell all those days, I guess it's just—"

"Difficult. I know," she said softly, sadly, rubbing her eyes. "Yeah. Think I'll go get a little sleep myself."

I nodded, turned as she strode out. As she neared the exit, she muttered something angrily to herself. And seeing her do that, seeing her, perhaps, agonize over her feelings for me, made me realize that despite everything that had happened to her, despite that thick skin, she still had a very vulnerable heart. A good heart. And I found myself even more attracted to her. I knew the guilt would ease in time. I knew I'd be a fool if I didn't pursue a relationship with her. But I didn't want my feelings for her to be influenced by my memories of Dina. I wondered if I was asking too much of myself. In fact, I was.

I left the OBS deck, returned to the colonel's quarters, and woke him from a sound sleep. The door cycled open, and he stood there, boxers drooping below his sizable gut. "Mr. St. Andrew?"

"Sir. I'm in, sir."

He scrutinized me a moment, then said, "Very well." Suddenly, he snapped to and actually saluted me. "You'll be promoted to major. Welcome aboard."

I returned his salute and tried to repress my grin—not a grin of joy but one of irony that I was, yet again, being shoved up the ladder and would now wear the gold "Major's angle," a triangle with a ruby in its center. "Yes, sir. Sorry to disturb you, sir."

As I walked away, I thought, You're committed. No turning back. The code has been broken. Or maybe, just maybe, the code has been redefined.

Once *Vanguard One* reached Aire-Wu and settled into orbit, we climbed aboard an ATC. The colonel and Ms. Brooks had business at the Wardens' outpost near the city of Orokean, and Paul was coming along for the ride. Breckinridge and Jing had to attend a briefing there as well, and they were about to receive their next assignment. I assumed that Jing knew that, and maybe she had wanted to be with me back on the OBS deck because now we might never get that chance.

We launched with the usual rumble and thunder, streaking away from the big cruiser. Off at our three o'clock lay Aire-Wu's lone moon, Theta-Marcus, a rocky world of volcanic plains and basins whose thin, Mars-like atmosphere made it unattractive for civilian colonization but a sure bet for the corporate and industrial sectors. Once the former colonial headquarters of the Inte-Micro and Exxo-Tally corporations, Theta-Marcus had been abandoned several months after the war broke out, and the Wardens, Colonel Beauregard explained, had utilized many of the companies' warehouse facilities to create a shipping hub the likes of which the seventeen worlds had never seen. He gestured to the rectangular porthole, where we glimpsed literally hundreds of transports leaving or jetting toward the grayish brown orb.

"Sir, if I might ask, sir. How did you find the second conditioning facility? And where is it?"

"Mr. Halitov, the answers to your questions are classified. Before soldiers are conditioned, they're drugged, then transported. Only a handful of people are aware of the facility's coordinates. I'll say this much . . . they're subterranean and not easy to reach."

"So we'll never get to know, sir?" Halitov asked.

"No. And let's just say that finding such a remote place wasn't easy. We had a little help from the local lumberjacks. And we'll leave it there."

I grinned inwardly. No, it couldn't be. That would be far too coincidental. Sergeant Canada, a native of Aire-Wu, had told me how her father, a lumberjack, had allowed researchers to dig on their land. Could the conditioning facility lie beneath her father's property? If so, fate had tipped her cards, and I had been glancing her way.

"Okay, sir. No more questions about that," said Halitov. "Just one more thing. What happens when we get to Orokean?"

"I know you're a little nervous, Captain," said Ms. Brooks. "Don't worry. We'll take care of everything."

"Will we get to eat?" he asked.

"You're still hungry?" cried Breckinridge. "After that feast we had?"

"I didn't eat that much," he said.

"Oh, yeah you did," I countered.

He just snickered at me, then pressed his head back into his jumpseat and closed his eyes.

For the next few minutes, we rode in silence, and I noticed that Jing would not look my way. I wished there was something I could say to her. I wished we had met under different circumstances. I wished she would just look at me.

As we made our final approach toward the Wardens' Orokean Perimeter Command Post, I called out, "Hey, Jing?"

She lifted her chin. "What?"

"You, uh, you all right?"

"I'm good. Thanks." She looked quickly away.

And I sighed.

Five major cities had developed on Aire-Wu: Cynday, New Sky, Orokean, Butanee, and Zhou, with a combined population of nearly 898 million people. Sure, that number is small when compared to Earth's population, but it's large for a colo. In fact, Aire-Wu was the second-most-populous world, just behind Rexi-Calhoon. And because so many people had chosen the Earth-like globe for their home, and so much grain, timber, asbestos, and gypsum were exported from her fertile ground, she remained one of the most heavily defended worlds of the Seventeen. The fact that the Wardens had created a shipping hub on her moon and had established several command posts on the outskirts of all the major cities was of little surprise.

What did surprise us was the sudden particle fire that stitched ragged holes in the tarmac, just a few meters off the ATC's bow, even as our landing skids touched ground.

"Captain?" cried Colonel Beauregard, leaning forward to shoot a gaze into the cockpit.

"Sir, the scope indicates multiple alpha bogeys, sir. Looks like a squadron. Insignia and IDs coming through now. They're Eastern Alliance atmoattack jets, but DTR also indicates that these particular craft were captured by us."

"Tawt out," ordered the colonel.

"Negative, sir. Tawt computer has been infected with a virus."

"Then get us over to that hangar. Now!"

I threw up the jumpseat's safety bars and cupped hands around my eyes as I went to a porthole. The hangar, a huge silver dome rising at least five hundred meters, lay about a kilometer away, and I nearly fell over as the pilot got us off the ground and swept along the tarmac, banking suddenly toward the east. In the background lay rolling, tree-covered hills, and some of those trees rose even higher than the hangar, with diameters probably reaching several hundred meters. My gaze suddenly turned skyward as the squadron of atmoattack jets swooped down, firing mercilessly upon the hangar.

"It's some kind of commando operation," yelled Ms. Brooks, her own gaze darting wildly around the hold. "A complete inside job, with traitors rising all the way through the ranks—because there's no way they could've gotten fighters through planetary defenses."

"We'll analyze this later," barked the colonel. "Captain, get us to the goddamned hangar!"

"Sir, the hangar is gone, sir."

"Then get us to the south-side access hub. Now!"

Jing came up behind me, put a hand on my shoulder. "I'll be right back."

"Wait—"

She vanished.

"Oh, no," moaned Breckinridge. "Jing, what're you doing?"

"Yeah, what is she doing?" I asked.

Breckinridge explained that Jing would will herself

into the cramped cockpit of one of those atmoattack jets. She would kill the pilot, disengage the tactical computer, and get out of there before the fighter meteored its way down to explode in a billion pieces across the tarmac and surrounding field. I riveted my gaze on the sky, saw one fighter veer off from the others then turn erratically and begin to plummet.

"One down," Breckinridge said.

"What if she blacks out from the maximum G?" I asked. "She can't force the blood back into her brain. She won't make it out."

Breckinridge glanced soberly at me. "That's right. She won't."

"Okay, hatch down, Captain!" yelled the colonel. "Skins up. Let's move!"

Paul had unclipped particle rifles for us and began distributing them as the rear hatch dropped away, and the muffled booming from outside became an ear-shattering thunder. The stench of burning fuel and kicked-up dirt competed with a sweet scent I would later learn was similar to that produced by one of Earth's evergreen trees. And still more stimuli pounded our senses: the echoing report of cannons and subsequent ground explosions, the whine of our own turbines, and the residual explosions thundering inside the now heavily damaged hangar. I had a pair of seconds to hop down from the ramp, get my bearings, and see the smoke rising into a sky so pure and blue I could hardly believe the color.

"St. Andrew, right here!" called the colonel from behind me. He stood beside a rectangular hatch, an access hub leading down, into the ground, and probably used only by airfield maintenance personnel. Halitov rushed Ms. Brooks onto the ladder inside the hub. Meanwhile, Breckinridge and Paul fired ineffectually at an approaching airjeep manned by two Eastern Alliance Marines, a gunner and pilot who were skinned up and wearing dark green uniforms. The airjeep's big gun spewed a thick bead of fire that rose cobralike from the tarmac and whipped forward to strike the energy skin over the ATC's canopy. The pilot wasted no time dusting off, leaving us exposed.

I threw down my rifle, thought of how Jing was risking her ass up there. I sprinted toward the airjeep, and while I had forced the beads from particle rifles to bend back toward the Marines who had trigged them, I had never disrupted a weapon as large as an airjeep's cannon. I ran even faster, reached out, felt the bond between me, the ground, the airjeep, and the bead those Eastern Alliance Marines directed at us. But that bead felt too directed, too strong, and though I tried like a son of a bitch to bend it back, it wouldn't budge.

With its engines kicking up dust devils tipped on their sides, and with the screaming roar continuing from those atmoattack jets as they began a strategic bombing of the command post, I drove myself into the *gozt* and came at the two Marines. Twice their beam ricocheted across my skin, and a nanosecond later my tactical computer warned me of the drain even as I reached the gunner, forced my bare hands past his skin, and choked him. My momentum dragged him out of his seat, and we both collapsed behind the airjeep, hitting the field in a cloud of dust. He struggled frantically to free my hands from his throat. I released one. Thought of ripping off his tac, then reached for my Ka-Bar. Thrust to the heart. Withdraw. He gurgled . . . and . . . was gone.

The pilot wheeled around, using one hand to steer the ship, the other to operate the gun. He zeroed in on me. I stood there, taking the bead a moment before leaping straight up and rolling forward, timing his approach a little awkwardly but still managing to come out of the roll to drop squarely on the hood with a terrific thud. The pilot, a young blond man with remarkably large ears, gaped at my appearance and jammed his control stick hard to port, but not before I kicked him under his chin, kicked him so hard that he blew out of the jeep and thudded onto his back. I jumped off the hood, turned a moment to see the air-jeep nosedive and burrow a sizable ditch before the turbines overheated. I ran over to the pilot.

"No! Please!" he moaned. "I can help you."

I dropped to my knees behind him, held my Ka-Bar to his throat. I felt him shudder as it dawned on him that his combat skin could not protect him from me.

"How can you help me?" I asked.

"If you let me live, I'll tell you who we are."

"What do you mean, who you are? You're an Eastern Alliance Marine. And I want to know how you people got down here."

"I'm not working for the alliances. They just want you to think that."

"Then who are you?" I screamed.

"I'm Second Lieutenant Kayleb Addison, Seventeen System Guard Corps, Special Operations: Rebel ten-seven."

"Rebel ten-seven?" I asked incredulously.

"Yeah."

I jerked away my Ka-Bar and pulled him around. "If you're lying, you're dead. Let's go."

PART 4

‹ ›

Rebels in Arms

15 ▸ **Lieutenant Addison and** I were the last ones down the hatch. Distant thunder from the aerial bombing droned on in a timpani roll as I sealed the door after us.

"Who are you?" Halitov asked, as Addison hopped down from the ladder and de-skinned.

"Your new best friend." The guy raised his palms in surrender and fixed Halitov with a twisted grin.

We stood about ten meters below the surface, near five intersecting tunnels with placards marking different maintenance stations or travel ports or operations centers. Breckinridge, the colonel, Paul, and Ms. Brooks were at tablet terminal, trying to pull up defense status and make contact with the post's CO. I de-skinned and told Halitov to watch our new guest, then jogged over to the colonel. "Sir."

"We're little busy, Mr. St. Andrew."

"I can handle this," Ms. Brooks told the colonel, who reluctantly detached himself and came toward me.

"Sir, that guy over there says he's Kayleb Addison, says he works for Rebel ten-seven. They're responsible for the attack here, but they want it to look like an Alliance attack."

"Clever. The Guard Corps can't get rid of us publicly, so they bring in your former Special Ops group to pose as alliance Marines, then they can blame it all on the alliances so the Guard Corps's hands remain clean."

"You saying you believe him, sir?" I asked. "I was going to kill him, then he confessed. But he seems way too forthcoming. Maybe he really is working for the alliances. Maybe this is their way of making the Corps grow more divided."

"I refuse to believe that the Alliances got people down here—not with the defenses we have in place. We'll get this Mr. Addison over to the operations center, ID him, and I suspect we'll learn that he is who he says he is . . ."

"Colonel? Have a look at this," called Ms. Brooks.

He strode back to the tablet terminal, and I joined him, where on three different conventional screens we watched the last of the atmoattack jets break into a flat spin and disappear over a mountainside.

"Okay, sweetheart," muttered the colonel. "Now you come back to us."

And with that, Jing appeared on the other side of the hub. She clutched the wall, leaned over, and retched. I rushed over to her, put a hand on her shoulder.

"I'm okay," she said, rolling out of my grip. "Guess I pushed it a little too hard. But see, I told you I'd be right back."

"Lieutenant? Tell me," said the colonel.

"That squadron was only one of about ten or fifteen," Jing explained, still gathering her breath. "I can't take them all out. They're still bombing the western hangars. Triple A batteries are gone. Our own atmoattack jets have either been destroyed or infected with viruses. It's . . . bad."

"Got interior vids back up," said Ms. Brooks. "Oh my God."

Images of utter carnage played across the three screens. Colonial Wardens lay slumped across their operations center stations, their heads caved in by particle fire. More bodies lay on the floor and across more terminals. Bodies were everywhere, and Ms. Brooks switched to the cameras in the hall, where the same twisted and bloody carpet unfurled all the way to an intersection.

"Tacs indicate life signs remaining in about thirty-seven, but all have been critically wounded," she said, reading a databar on another screen. "This entire base . . . it's . . . gone."

"And they timed this attack pretty well, didn't they, knowing that the both of you would be on planet," I said.

"That's right," added Addison from across the hub, with Halitov keeping him under close watch. "You two are the primary target."

"Oh, man. We have to get the hell out of here," said Halitov warily. "And I mean now."

"Brooks, see if you can bring up our ATC pilot," suggested the colonel.

"Forget that, sir," said Jing. "He's already been taken out. Channels are jammed as expected, so we can't contact *Vanguard*. And they've pretty much destroyed every other ride out of here, except the subway. We might be able to take it back to Orokean, if they haven't cut the power."

The hub's ceiling hatch blew inward and dropped hard onto the deck.

"Go!" screamed Halitov, as he skinned up and started for the shaft of light piercing the smoke and falling debris. He directed his particle rifle up, toward that light, and cut loose with a savage stream of fire. "Come on! Come on!"

At any moment they'd drop in a smart schrap grenade, and I knew Halitov knew that, so I couldn't figure why he wanted to play hero by standing there and pumping out rounds. Did he really think his efforts would buy us that much time? "Rooslin!" I hollered. "Let's go!"

My words echoed as the grenade hit the floor.

He gaped at me. I gaped at him. And we reached into the bond. The world froze a second, then everything save us moved in that strange, submerged slowness:

The smart schrap erupted from the orb and, like a miniature supernova, the gleaming cloud swelled. The others had already started down a shaft leading to one of the subway entrances, but I realized we were now cut off from that shaft and would have to find another. We ran toward the nearest conduit, feeling the smart schrap's heat on our necks. I wouldn't dare chance a look back, but judging from the shadows on the wall, we beat the first wave by just a meter or two.

Sweat dropped into my left eye, blinded me for a second until I blinked it away, only to feel Halitov's hand latch on to my wrist and yank me suddenly down another corridor. He threw me around the corner, where we both shadowhugged the wall. We didn't move. We didn't breathe, just released ourselves from the bond as the wave burrowed into a far wall and kept going.

Faint thuds resounded from the hub, and Halitov chanced a look around the corner, recoiled, even as shimmering rounds drilled into the wall near his head. "Shit," he groaned, flinching against the salvo. "They're closing in."

I tipped my head toward the corridor, and we dashed off, passing the bodies of several MPs and six or seven administrative personnel who had fallen in a terrible little row, as though they had been lined up for execution.

"Want to go back and take them out?" Halitov asked, as we reached a second hub and found a placard directing us to a subway entrance. "Jing and Kristi can take care of the others."

"No, we meet up with them."

"Oh, really?" he asked, then dropped to the deck, pulling me with him as a salvo exploded overhead and tore the subway placard to ribbons. "Sounds easy. It ain't." He bolted to his feet and launched himself up, into a *chak*, turning in a wide arc while extending his right leg to form the *ai*, a deadly floating kick, counterkick. He neared the point man of a squadron of Eastern Alliance Marines (or at least a squadron of people wearing those uniforms), and before the guy could cut loose with a single round, he broke the man's jaw with his boot, then, with his other boot, drove the cartilage in the soldier's nose into his brain.

As Halitov came down from his vault, I charged the squadron myself—since my overzealous partner had already committed us to the bout. I opted for the somersault-and-kick combination of the *dirc*, and I ripped through the move as the five or six other Marines positioned near the walls tried getting a bead on me. One actually did, and several rounds pinged off my skin as I came down on her, driving her so hard into the deck that my boot snapped her neck. She made a weird noise before her eyes rolled back. Strangled cries came from a few of the others, and Halitov screwed his face up into that flushed, predatory mask and broke bones as though they were some light, delicate wood. Stray rounds ricocheted around us as I took on the last pair of grunts, and, trying to ignore the fact that they might be members of Rebel 10-7, that they could very well have served under me, I worked my Ka-Bar with smooth and chilling efficiency.

Halitov and I stood over the bodies. I turned to him and began laughing, a laugh that bordered on hysterical, on utter grief. He glanced oddly at me as I bared my teeth and panted, then glanced at the bodies. "It's not about sides anymore," I said, my voice coming in a growl. "It's about killing everyone, killing everything. I don't want to be this person, this person who says fuck it all and just kills. This is not being a soldier. It's not."

"We got a subway to catch," Halitov said, sliding a hand around the back of my neck and shoving me forward. "And if you think killing and being a soldier don't go together, then you got a real bad memory, 'cause you've killed at least as many as I have."

"Believe me, I know," I muttered, then broke into a jog toward the subway corridor.

We found a lift and dropped down to the loading platform. Breckinridge contacted us on a private channel and told us to meet the others at Gate 17, a number I found painfully ironic.

As Halitov and I neared Gate 15, a bullet-shaped maglev train blasted by us, its windows and doors splattered with ever-changing patterns of graffiti created by a local parasite that young thugs mixed into their paint. Though we kept close to the platform's rear walls, and I only paused for a second to glimpse the train, Marines positioned near the platform's edge, just a meter from the train itself, popped up like computer-generated avatars. Hell didn't just break loose; it exploded.

We dashed forward, held under as many as twenty beads, the dimly lit platform glowing in an eerie, fluctuating firelight that made it hard to see. I tripped over some kind of scanning device rising to about knee height, and fell into Halitov. We crumpled, swore, scrambled to our hands and knees. Then, the fire tapered off into a series of muffled cries.

I rolled over, watched Breckinridge, Paul, and Jing working through the Marine snipers in a smooth, graceful ballet of blood and death.

As Jing ripped the particle rifle from the last Marine and split open his skull with it, Breckinridge shouted for us. We clambered over the small scanner and joined her and Paul in a race to Gate 17, where the maglev train had pulled to a stop. We dashed through the doors.

And what we found inside should not have surprised us.

The colonel and Ms. Brooks were seated in two jumpseats, their palms raised. Lieutenant Kayleb Addison gripped a handrail and aimed a particle pistol at them.

"See, we're fucking stupid," Halitov told me. "You should've knifed this son of a bitch when you had the chance."

Paul and Jing shifted inside, and the doors slid automatically shut. We all stood there as the train's driver drone spoke in a friendly, even voice, warning us to belt in and stand by for departure. The train jolted forward.

"When we get to Orokean, we'll all be going to the transit police," said Addison.

"Where'd he get the pistol?" Paul asked.

"It's mine, I'm afraid," said Ms. Brooks. "I never did learn how to set the user specificity code, so he's quite capable of blowing our heads off."

"That's right," Addison said with a nod. "Quite capable."

Jing sighed tiredly, vanished, reappeared behind Addison, and ripped the gun from his grip.

Without warning, Halitov rushed forward, yanked the pistol away from Jing, then jammed it into Addison's head. He widened his eyes at me. "This is what we do!"

"No," shouted the colonel, a word echoed by Paul.

The pistol went off, and most of Addison's head sprayed across the car's windows before he slumped.

"We're fucking soldiers," said Halitov, tossing the pistol hard at me. I tried to catch it, failed.

"You idiot," shouted Ms. Brooks. "We could've used him to testify before congress."

"Sorry," Halitov said, grinding out the word. "Next time I'll do a less efficient job of saving your ass."

"I'll take credit for that," said Jing, leering at Halitov.

"All right, Captain," the colonel began, rising to bring himself to full height and stare down at Halitov. "You killed him, you clean him up. Now."

Halitov sighed in disgust, then went over and

seized Addison's body by the shirt collar and dragged him toward the back of the car, leaving a blood trail in his wake.

I shrank into a jumpseat. After a long moment, I finally asked Ms. Brooks if Satcomm, our main comm relay station, was still being jammed.

She nodded. "We've already missed our first check-in with *Vanguard*. I'm sure they've tried to contact us and discovered the jamming. Major Kuhns will probably launch a counterattack. Once our fighters are under the jamming blanket, they can track and contact us. All we have to do is get out of this fire zone, get to Orokean, and stay alive."

The train's brakes jammed on, throwing Halitov halfway across the car and sending my own jumpseat belts digging into my shoulders. Turbines cycled down.

"They've patched into the driver drone," said Ms. Brooks, frantically scanning her tablet's screen. "Maybe I can override."

"Scott? Rooslin? Outside with me and Jing," said Breckinridge, keying open a pair of doors. "Paul, you're insurance."

He winked. As usual, Breckinridge continued commanding us, and I found it interesting how none of us questioned her authority. I still had mixed feelings about her, but since she had shared her feelings about her brother, I had begun to realize that she and I weren't that different. I even admired how naturally she took lead, and I knew I could learn from her—if I continued being a soldier.

She and Jing hopped onto a narrow catwalk that

paralleled the maglev track. Per her instructions, Halitov and I mounted an exterior ladder leading to the car's top. Once up there, we stared down the gloomy tunnel as the strings of glowing lights began winking out.

"Stop the train, cut the power, take the prisoners," sang Halitov.

"You didn't have to kill him," I said, eyeing the blood splattered on his uniform.

He shrugged. "I didn't like his attitude."

"So he deserves to die for that?"

"He was an enemy soldier. That's reason enough. The attitude just made it easier."

"None of this bothers you? Switching sides, killing people we could've served with . . ."

"Hey, asshole. My own sister's fighting for the other side, and I haven't seen her since the war broke out. Yeah, it bothers me, but you know what? You think too much. You keep wanting this to be some noble profession, and maybe it is when we're not fighting. But when it comes to war, we're supposed to be machines. We eat, fuck, and kill. That's why we're still alive."

"You're wrong."

"How 'bout you guys shut up and pay attention," said Breckinridge. " 'Cause here they come." She and Jing mounted the ladder and joined us up top.

We skinned up as four narrow lights, like the eyes of some dark-skinned monstrosity, appeared from the gloom, accompanied by a familiar and characteristic whir. My tactical computer fed me a magnified, infrared view of four airjeeps, each manned by the usual pilot and gunner, with two more heavily armed privates sitting in the backseats. There had to be more of them at the end of tunnel, I assumed. They knew we were conditioned. They wouldn't send a small air cavalry.

"Well this is nice," said Jing. "Four of us . . . and four jeeps. Scott, which one you want?"

Before I could answer, the train lurched forward, knocking all of us off our feet. I slid on my back across the train top, and, hearing Jing call my name, plummeted off the edge as the train sped away. I reached into the bond, and, with a shiver, felt only a cold numbness as I crashed back-first onto the track. My skin eased the blow, but a coruscating sea of light flashed across my eyes as I sat up and heard the train's hum grow fainter.

The airjeep gunners opened fire as I scrambled to my feet and charged after the train, running at a pace far too slow to reach it. I needed the damned bond, and I screamed for the mnemosyne in my head to do something. The train vanished and the report of cannon fire grew more muffled until there was nothing but my own breathing and a very distant booming pressing against the darkness.

Run, I told myself. *Just run. It'll come. Just keep reaching for it.*

"Scott, you there?" Halitov called on our channel.

"On my way," I managed.

"Where the hell are you? Little help, you know!"

"Just give me a minute."

"Aw, shit!" he shouted, then, a second before he cut the channel, I heard the rat-a-tat of an airjeep's cannon, a sound way too close for comfort.

"Scott?" called Jing. "We need you."

"I'm coming," I said, reaching yet again for the bond, my mental hands grasping air.

"Better move your ass, St. Andrew!" yelled Breckinridge.

My eyes burned with tears. I couldn't help them unless the bond helped me. I was letting them down, letting myself down, and being painfully reminded that I needed to be reconditioned.

With my lungs ragged and a fire raging in my legs, I slowed into a jog, into a fast walk, a walk, and then . . . I just stopped in the darkness, while my friends were taking on four airjeeps with probably more en route.

I like to tell people that I'm not a quitter, that even in the worst situations, I always find something I can cling to, something that allows me to see the plausible within the impossible. And for most of my life, that's been the case, but standing there, back on that track, with no bond and just the gloom, I realize now that I surrendered to the universe. A welcome peace came over me, a sense of utter relief in the knowledge that the war raging within and around me would no longer be fought. I had nothing to prove to anyone. I knew I was honorable, loyal, and had done my duty to the best of my ability, despite all of the deception and corruption. I knew that! I wasn't a killer. I was a *soldier.*

So I remained there, feeling a tremendous weight lift off my shoulders, feeling the bond slide in and envelop me with an intimacy I hadn't felt before. And as my thoughts traveled back to my friends, so did I—

The wind whipped over me, trying to peel back my

utilities as I found myself once more atop the train. Linear turbines hummed along as a discharge of cannon fire from behind sent me craning my neck.

. There they were, all four airjeeps. Halitov hung over the side of one and was about to propel himself up, inside. Breckinridge wrestled with the gunner of another. Jing had killed her jeep's four occupants and was trying to gain access to the pilot's controls as her jeep arrowed forward on autopilot. The fourth airjeep had circled back and was laying down an unrelenting bead near the back of the train, where the linear turbine housing lay. Even as I ran across the train top, we emerged from the tunnel, and there we were, smack in the middle of Orokean's downtown district, a vast metropolis built within an even vaster forest of gigantic trees, some of which had been bored out and turned into skyscrapers. Rope bridges festooned the branches between smaller residences, and condominiums had been constructed on some of the more colossal limbs, creating cul-de-sacs hanging five, even six hundred meters above the moss-covered earth.

I had just a handful of seconds to appreciate the city before the fourth airjeep's continued firing drew me fast and hard. I sprang off the train, found my bullet thrust, and took out the pilot with a single blow. Before the grunts in the backseat could withdraw their pistols, I grabbed the first by the throat, threw him overboard. Then I twisted the second one's head, felt the snap, and dumped him over the side.

The gunner did manage to lift his automatic pistol and fire a continuous bead point-blank into my face. I seized his wrist, pulled him out of the chair, then spun him by that wrist as though I were turning a key

in an antique lock. I released him and let his own inertia carry him overboard.

A powerful droning from above descended, and
amid the fettered canopy of huge trees, another four
airjeeps zeroed in on us. I leapt from my jeep and back
onto the train, the jeep following mindlessly along.

Jing vanished from her ride, and I knew she'd reap-
pear aboard another. *I can do that*, I told myself. *And I
can deal with the drain. I can.*

As Halitov and Breckinridge continued battling
with the Marines in their airjeeps, I willed myself
from the train to one of the new ships. And there I
was, gripping the seats behind the two Marines in the
back. I tapped one's shoulder. He turned, gaped at
me, tried to swing around his pistol. I pulled him out
of the seat, dumped him overboard, felt his partner's
rifle jab my skin, felt the rebound, then grabbed the
back of his jumpsuit and dragged him out. Their cries
faded as they dropped a hundred or so meters, only
to rebound into bags of broken bones.

I hopped into the backseat, grabbed both the pilot
and gunner by the back of the neck. As I pulled them
out of their seats, the airjeep yawed sharply. The
damned pilot had failed to set the autocorrect in the
event his hands left the controls. The pilot and gunner
flew out of the jeep, with me right behind them, about
to plunge the full hundred meters to the surface. I
slapped a palm on one of the jeep's stubby wings,
clutched it with everything I had, until I managed to
look ahead and see the oncoming rope bridge, a narrow, low-tech affair constructed between two housing
projects nestled on wide limbs.

Three, two, one, I let go.

And the airjeep collided with the bridge, even as I reached for one of the rope railings, seized it, watched the jeep forge on, the ropes growing tangled around it.

Two middle-aged women who'd been carrying stacks of laundry across the bridge had already dropped their loads and were racing toward the west end—

When the pitons that held the ropes there pulled free from the wood, and the bridge suddenly dropped and swung through the air, driven wildly by the airjeep still tangled within it. The two women screamed and were tossed about. One of them lost her grip, shrieked, and fell away.

Shuddering off a wave of dizziness, I willed myself beside her, appearing suddenly to clutch her before she hit the ground. I slowed our descent until we struck the moss. Our landing was anything but gentle, though I doubted she had even sprained her ankles. She looked at me, then her eyelids fluttered, and she fainted.

The second woman continued wailing, and the bridge whipped around the tree like a fishing line with the airjeep caught on the hook. I thought of leaping into the air, but I wasn't sure I could span the entire hundred meters, so, as a crowd began gathering below, I ran to the tree and right up it, weaving my way past windows carved into its bark. Once I neared the still-swinging bridge, I threw myself into the air, reached the rope, then, fighting against the roaring airjeep, I reached the woman.

"Take my hand!" I screamed.

She winced, took one hand off the rope, clutched mine.

"Okay, now the other hand."

She shook her head fiercely.

"You have to trust me."

The bridge jerked hard to the left, and I exploited the jerk to yank her other hand free. People below screamed and gasped as we fell from the bridge. I knew that if I survived the drop, Halitov would give me hell for "wasting time on saving civilians," but I felt responsible for these women, and the look on the second woman's face as we slowed, then struck the ground made it all worthwhile. She burst into tears and hugged me harder than I have ever been hugged before.

"Rizma!" a man cried, pushing himself through the crowd. I assumed he was the woman's husband. He took her into his arms, then eyed me intently. "Thank you. Thank you."

I could only imagine the reactions of the crowd when the soldier who had just rescued two women simply winked out of their lives.

And a billionth of a second later, I collapsed on top of the train, which forged on through the city, now following a serpentine path between great tree trunks and suddenly gliding through a tunnel burrowed straight through one. When we emerged on the other side, I sat up and searched the skies for the other air-jeeps. Nothing. I crawled across the top, toward the ladder, mounted it, then keyed open the doors, where the colonel, Ms. Brooks, and Paul still waited.

"Where are they?" the colonel cried over the engine's din and rush of air.

"I don't know," I said, swinging myself inside.

"We're almost at Blue Forest Station," said Ms. Brooks. "We get off there."

An airjeep whipped by the open doors, and I turned back, remounted the ladder, and spotted Jing in the pilot's seat. She wheeled around, then brought the airjeep into a hover, near the open doors. I climbed aboard, asking, "Where's everyone else?"

"I don't know. But look . . ." Her gaze went skyward, where squadron after squadron of Alliance at-moattack jets streaked down toward the city, their wings sagging under the weight of missiles.

"They can't be from Rebel ten-seven," I said. "They wouldn't bomb the city."

"No, they wouldn't. My guess is the alliances have been monitoring the Seventeen's attack on us. They saw an opportunity and took it."

"I knew this would happen," I said. "I just knew it."

She lowered her head. "The battle for Aire-Wu has just begun."

16 ❯

Halitov and Breckinridge approached in an airjeep, zooming in above me and Jing. Halitov had his hand wrapped around the throat of a nervous-looking pilot.

"The city's under attack," Breckinridge said evenly. "I thought I spotted some of our fighters up there. Screen shows all planetary defenses coming on-line."

"And the screen better show our asses tawting out of here," said Halitov.

"Brooks says we're getting off at Blue Forest Station," I said, then pointed ahead toward a cluster of gargantuan trees between which hung a metallic web of architecture that was the busy station's east side.

We came within a half kilometer of the station when the maglev tracks ahead exploded under missile fire. I hadn't even heard the atmoattack jet's approach, but there it was, its shadow wiping over us as the train barreled toward the twisted and smoking wreckage ahead.

"We have to get them out," Breckinridge said.

"I say we get Paul and leave the other two," corrected Halitov with a wink.

Jing rolled her eyes and took our airjeep in close to the doors. I jumped out, clutched the ladder, worked the keypad. The doors slid apart, and Jing brought the airjeep in recklessly close, its left side banging hard against the train. Paul helped Ms. Brooks into the jeep, then spotted for the colonel, who made an impressive leap into the backseat.

"I'll get out with them," Paul hollered, lifting his chin to Halitov and Breckinridge.

With a nod, I jumped back into the gunner's seat, and Jing thrust up, jetting us away. As we circled back, I watched with horror as the pilot Halitov had been throttling suddenly bailed out and fell a dozen meters to the ground. As he tumbled away, the airjeep pitched hard, throwing Breckinridge across its hood as the craft jetted toward the ground at a forty-five-degree angle. Breckinridge clutched a seam in the jeep's hood, and Halitov reached for her, his hand almost there, almost . . .

"Bail!" she yelled, then let go.

As she dropped, Halitov gaped at the oncoming ground, then jumped straight up, exiting the craft a heartbeat before it slammed into the ground, blasting up hunks of moss and showers of dirt that fell a second before a terrific fireball engulfed the entire zone, including Halitov.

"Oh my God," Jing muttered, then jerked the airjeep's stick, taking us toward the scene. A terrific explosion just ahead stole my gaze: the maglev train derailed, flipped onto its side, then piled up on itself as smaller explosions resounded and metal crunched on metal. And from that chaos materialized Paul, skin glowing as he raced for his life.

Below us now, Breckinridge swung around toward the fireball, set her skin to maximum, then sprinted into the flames. We zoomed in to hover a meter off the ground, the flames just off to my left and warming my cheeks.

Halitov came running out of the dying fireball, spotted us, then whirled. "Where is she?" he cried.

"In there! Looking for you!" I shouted back.

As he turned, about to run back toward the shattered airjeep, a powerful whir of displaced air grew louder and turned my blood to ice. Incoming missile.

Paul slowed to the airjeep, struggled for breath, looked disoriented, his senses probably overloading.

"Get in!" I hollered.

As he complied, Jing turned the airjeep around, and the bomb struck, maybe forty meters away, turning day into a nightmare of heaved earth and fire and shrapnel. As the burst came toward us, I felt Jing reaching into the bond, as I did, and together we turned that wall of death back in on itself, forming a bubble of life around our jeep. The force of the blast would have instantly killed Ms. Brooks, and might very well have penetrated our skins. As the debris cleared, I strained to glimpse Halitov and Breckinridge, then looked to Jing, who was already knifing out of the airjeep.

"What?" I called.

She didn't answer and wove a path through the smoldering debris. I took off after her, and we came upon Halitov and Breckinridge lying near the airjeep, their skins glowing a dull green. A large piece of shrapnel jutted from Breckinridge's blood-soaked calf, while another protruded from her shoulder. Halitov appeared dazed but uninjured as I pulled him to his feet. He took one look at Breckinridge, jerked himself away from me, and dropped to his knees before his unconscious girlfriend. "Son of a bitch!" he shouted, then glanced skyward. "Son of a bitch!"

"C'mon, let's get her in," Jing told me, digging her hands beneath Breckinridge's arms. I went for the legs, and we carried her back toward the jeep, with an enraged Halitov swearing and following closely behind.

Another missile struck on the other side of the train as we laid Breckinridge across Ms. Brooks's and the colonel's laps. Thankfully, the blast wouldn't reach us, but as Jing, Halitov, and I squeezed into the front seats, and Paul sat on the airjeep's trunk and gripped the rear seats, a thunderclap rocked the ground. Jing got us out of there as the explosion tore up toward the airjeep's belly. My neck snapped back as she punched to full power, and we sailed over the demolished train, thundering toward the station, with that last blast riding our wake.

"What happens when we get there?" I called back to Ms. Brooks. "Can you get us a ride out?"

"There's a probe depot there. I thought we could send one to *Vanguard One*, bypass all this jamming, and let them know where we are."

"You think that probe'll make it through this air attack?" Halitov asked dubiously.

"Probably not, but right now, it's the only chance we've got."

Those words had barely left Ms. Brooks's mouth when a pair of atmoattack jets swooped down, past us, zeroing in on the station.

"No, no, no," yelled Halitov.

White-hot flashes erupted from below the wings of each fighter, and four missiles streaked toward the great station suspended between the trees. The fighters arced up, peeling away as the missiles penetrated the latticework of alloy and disappeared inside. A moment of silence, then literally hundreds of explosions erupted from within the station, some blasting up through the hemisphere's apex, others gnawing their way out the bottom. Great stanchions affixed to the trees and helping to support the structure broke away, and with a horrible creaking the station broke free from two of its tethers and swung sideways to crash against the two trees still supporting it. As the teetering structure continued to explode, it shed debris onto a narrow, rectangular structure below, the maglev terminal, which succumbed to the falling stanchions, its entire entrance conduit now crushed, buried in metal, and impassable. A dense cloud of brown smoke swelled to blanket the scene.

"Jing, get us out of the city," the colonel ordered.

"But, sir, we have to get her some help," Halitov said, staring wide-eyed at Breckinridge.

"Get us out of here!" the colonel boomed. "Head northeast, into the mountains, toward Butanee."

"Yes, sir," Jing said gravely. She banked hard right, and we left the continuing destruction behind, diving toward the forest floor, skimming across leaf beds and streaking through suburbs, with some homes no more than Quonset huts erected in the shadows of enormous limbs.

The bombing, though growing fainter, continued, and while you could ignore it, consider it white noise, I was keenly aware of just how much devastation the alliances were wreaking and shocked that they had chosen to bomb civilian targets. Maybe that was their way of further demoralizing us. I could not imagine how many innocent colonists were losing their lives.

Later I would read that the death count rose into the millions.

As we flew on, finally leaving the suburbs for Orokean's unsettled limits, Halitov patched his tac into Breckinridge's and reported that her skin was already addressing her wounds and compensating for her fever but that she'd still need a doc to remove the shrapnel. The colonel just nodded.

I stared out beyond the narrow windshield, the hills blurring into great shoulders of earth driving toward the horizon.

Nearly eight hours later, as Jing took us up a mountainside, she broke the silence. "Bug eyes for snipers," she reminded me.

I rubbed my eyes, forced away the drowsiness, and kept my hand squarely on the big particle gun's handles. Once more, I jockeyed for room against Halitov's big elbow, which had become more than a minor nuisance.

"When we get up near that ridge, you can stop," said the colonel. "We should see Butanee from there."

Though I wanted to ask him if the conditioning facility was, in fact, located in Butanee, I didn't. The rift between the Seventeen and the Wardens might now result in a major defeat, and that impending loss burned in the colonel's eyes.

Breckinridge had regained consciousness, though she could barely move against the shrapnel. She kept apologizing for getting hit, and, finally, the colonel told her not to worry about it and assured her that we'd get help.

Jing set us down amid a loose row of dark green

shrubs. Halitov, Paul, and I jogged up the ridgeline, toward the mountaintop, where from that vantage point we looked out, across a broad valley, toward a mottled and sprawling sea of treetops twinkling with the city's lights.

"Looks clear so far," said Halitov, reading databars in his HUV.

I read my own, then spotted dozens of Alliance air-jeeps parked near a cluster of buildings near an outlying road. "No. Check frame two-five-nine, see them?"

"Where?" asked Halitov.

"I got them," said Paul. "They moved in real quiet. No air strikes. They want to keep this place intact. They'll take it with a ground force."

"Probably. They didn't hit the strike base," I said, scanning the tarmac and accompanying buildings in the southeast. "The fighters are gone. Probably sent over to Orokean."

"They've sent in a small recon force, probably platoon size. They're looking for something," Paul said.

"For what?" I asked.

"What do you think?"

"Is it here?" I demanded.

He shrugged. "The old man won't tell me. But I think it is. Funny. Even though they drugged me, there's something familiar about this place. Maybe the smell. I took that in unconsciously, but somehow I remember."

"You guys talking about the conditioning facility?" asked Halitov.

Paul winked at me, tipped his head toward Halitov. "You should've cheated off this genius at the academy."

"What the hell's that mean?" the big guy asked.

"Nothing," said Paul. "Let's head back."

While he ordered up a link to his father on a private channel and made a report, we returned to the ridgeline. I lingered behind and ordered my computer to zoom in past the airjeeps, toward a placard on one of the buildings: MILL #17A CANADA LUMBER COMPANY. Canada. What were the odds of me serving with the daughter of a man whose property concealed an ancient alien device that could help save my life? My encounter with Sergeant (now Lieutenant) Canada could not have been coincidental. The universe was trying to tell me something, and I had better be listening.

The others at the airjeep were ready to leave when I joined them, and my quizzical look drew Halitov's explanation: "Colonel says we're going down into the city. We can get Kristi to Raga Five Hospital there. Maybe send off that comm probe."

I shifted over to the colonel, who was backhanding sweat off his brow. The humidity had increased, and the air felt thick and harder to breathe. "Sir, those airjeeps down there—"

"Paul told me all about them," he snapped.

"It is there. And they're looking for it."

"Speculate all you want, Mr. St. Andrew. But right now, we're getting Captain Breckinridge some medical attention and seeing what we can do about contacting *Vanguard*."

"Sir, if the facility is that important, I don't understand why it isn't better defended . . ."

"If you think I'm going to admit anything to you, Mr. St. Andrew, you're sadly mistaken. Now, saddle up, *Captain*."

I repressed a snort and wriggled into the cockpit as Jing fired up the engines and skinned up, using infrared so she could see through the enveloping gloom.

We dusted off, and when we reached the first string of private residences, Jing commented on how the place had become a ghost town. Martial law, with its accompanying curfew, had probably been declared. The only people we saw were MPs, Colonial Wardens who confirmed our suspicions and volunteered to escort us to the hospital.

There, Breckinridge was rushed into surgery, with Halitov remaining at her side. Ms. Brooks and the colonel rode off to the nearest HQ, about a kilometer away, while Jing, Paul, and I waited anxiously in the hospital's cafeteria.

"This is weird," said Jing. "This city could get attacked at any moment, and here we are, conditioned officers, sitting around, talking about how bad the coffee is."

"Don't jinx us, all right?" Paul asked. "All comm's still down. We're literally and figuratively in the dark."

Jing frowned. "You hear something?"

I pricked up my ears, heard a low and distant rumble coming from outside. We raced out of the cafeteria, through a pair of corridors, and into the street, where the night sky had come alive with fighters and dozens of crab carriers whose running lights flashed brilliantly, ominously.

"Well, they bombed Orokean back into the stone age, but for some reason, this place they want," said Jing.

"Looks like an invasion force," I sang gravely.

"Right on time," added Paul, who shook his head at Jing. He skinned up and contacted his father.

Jing and I rushed back into the hospital as the attack alarms blared across the city. We dodged fleeing nurses and patients alike, and finally located Breckinridge's doctor, who distractedly told us that the surgeons had removed the shrapnel, applied synthskin to her wounds, but still had her on two large-bore IVs. He ran off before we could ask any more questions.

"Oh, shit," Jing said as we entered Breckinridge's room. "Can we move her?"

"No choice," said Halitov, holding Breckinridge's hand.

The patient smiled stupidly at us. "These drugs . . . they're good."

"I'm sure they are," I said, searching frantically around the room for a hover chair. "Screw it. We'll roll her out on the gurney."

"No, I saw a chair down the hall," said Jing. "I'll go get it." With that, she blinked out.

"Scott, I'm sorry," Breckinridge said.

"It's okay."

"No, I mean about me and Halitov. He's good in bed."

I grinned, looked at my friend. "Impossible."

"Scott, I know you're lonely," said Breckinridge. "Why don't you be with Jing? Our lives are too short, too fragile. You guys are meant for each other."

I glanced away. "Maybe . . ."

Jing returned with the hover chair and was trying to steer the thing from its backseat control board. The little seat caromed off the door and buzzed straight toward me. I dodged out of its path while she struggled to hit the brakes.

"I thought you were a good pilot," I said.

"Me too." She finally got the thing to hover near Breckinridge's bed, and we gingerly transferred our wounded friend to the seat.

"Look at this little gown they gave me," said Breckinridge, clearly enjoying her drug-induced high. "I kinda like the way it fits."

"Great. You can show it to all the Alliance Marines who're going to be here any second," I said. "You can give them a little fashion show before they cut you down."

"Hey, Scott . . ." Halitov warned.

"Take it easy," Jing told me, then activated the chair's controls.

We followed the flood of humanity out the main doors and into the stairwell, where Jing haphazardly guided the chair down a flight of steps. On the main level, we spotted Paul, who told us his father had arranged for transfer back to *Vanguard One* via ATC. The colonel wanted us to meet him back at the HQ. We abandoned the hover chair, loaded Breckinridge into the airjeep, then piled inside. Jing fired up the thruster as a throng of nurses came running around one corner and spotted our jeep.

"Please," cried one. "Busses ain't running! You have to get us out of here!"

"Can't do it," Halitov said sharply, then turned to Jing. "Go."

I stared at those nurses as the airjeep's engine

kicked dust into their eyes. Above them, a thousand crab carriers descended upon the city like multicolored stars, carrying with them thousands of troops.

"You know what's going to happen here?" Paul asked. "It's going to be another Gatewood-Callista. These locals won't stand by and let Marines occupy their land. These people are going to fight."

"And they're going to lose," I said.

"Hope your dad's got a plan," Halitov told Paul. "I really do."

Paul returned a grave look. "Me too."

We only had to travel a single kilometer, one thousand meters, .62 miles. We streaked down a city street, lined on both sides by office buildings and small businesses. After a few turns and a few minutes, we'd be there.

Unfortunately, Alliance Marines were already on the ground, and at least one squad had staked out positions along our route. We learned of their presence the hard way.

A low-level grenade, thankfully not a smart schrap one, thumped from a hidden soldier's rifle and drilled into the airjeep's hood.

"Grenade!" Jing cried.

I found myself hurtling backward through the air, my ears ringing from the explosion, my tactical computer warning me of the skin level drop, my field of view spinning from night sky to dusty street . . . then I hit the ground, rolled, came up, saw the burning airjeep, its front end gone. Jing, Paul, and Halitov had also been blown clear, and Halitov got up and ran toward the shattered vehicle.

It dawned on me that Breckinridge had not skinned up, that she had been too weak and too well medicated.

Snipers fired relentlessly upon us, but neither I nor Halitov acknowledged them. He was too intent on Breckinridge, I too intent on him. I leapt over the air-jeep's burning front end and arrived beside my friend as he cupped Breckinridge's head in his hands. The blast had torn apart most of her left side, and she had quickly bled out. The sheen had faded from her eyes.

"Oh, no," said Jing, charging up. "Kristi . . ."

Halitov looked at me, hands trembling, his own eyes glossed with tears, then . . . it all came out in a scream. He gingerly set down Breckinridge's head, then spun and ran off toward the building behind us.

"This rifle squad is fucking dead," said Paul, jogging off after Halitov.

Jing gave me a fiery look, then sprinted for the building's stone wall. She darted up it, zeroing in on a sniper who stood near a fourth-story window. Halitov swore to the high heavens as he leapt straight up and into a second-story window, vanished a second, then blasted through that window and toward the street, only now he had an Alliance Marine in his grip and was choking the man to death. They hit the ground, tumbled, then Halitov swung the Marine by the neck, dragged him up, and crushed the soldier's larynx.

Still in shock, I stood there, trembling, just looking at Breckinridge. Yes, our lives were too short, too fragile. I felt guilty for the way I had treated her. And I told myself that she had not failed in her duty, that her loyalty never shifted from her brother.

Abruptly, I drew two beads from Marines on the roof of a three-story bank. I ran at them, launched into a *gozt*, and blasted the first woman off her perch. She tumbled to the ground, rebounding several times before her skin faded. In the meantime, the second woman spun and leveled her rifle on me as I rose and started for her.

"I don't have to kill you," she said.

"That's your job."

"Don't come any closer."

I did.

She fired.

The bead struck my skin, rebounded, and I was on her, knocking the rifle from her grip and withdrawing my Ka-Bar. "You should've killed me," I said, then closed my eyes and punched her with the blade.

Particle fire from the street suddenly blasted me away, the blade wrenching out of the woman. I staggered back, darted left, drove myself toward the edge of the bank's roof. The first woman I had knocked off lay in the street, one of her legs clearly broken, her right arm twisted, her left arm working the rifle. I jumped off the roof, coming down at her with one knee bent, the knee that would end her life. I caught her head, and it was over.

"Everybody?" Paul called on the channel. "I'm over here on twentieth, on top of the blue building. Looks like fourteen squads. We'll run it out, but we'll keep to the limbs and rooftops. Meet me here, copy?"

"Copy," I replied, then turned, spotted the building, and dashed off as Jing and Halitov checked in, and Halitov's voice came ragged and in a tone as familiar as it was chilling, a tone that summoned up the time I had found him in his hotel room after he had tried to kill himself. Later on, he would say, "They killed my fuckin' parents. They're all going to die." Now they had killed his girlfriend. I shuddered as I imagined the violence blazing within him.

Three beads of particle fire lashed out from somewhere behind and pummeled me to my stomach. I crawled forward, then found the bond and sprang toward the blue building, ascended the wall, and came up, over the top. I hopped down from the ledge and found Paul and Halitov hunkered down near a bundle of conduits. Above us hung the dense canopy, with still more businesses and residences affixed to the trunks, built within them, or perched on the limbs. The many shades of a green had deepened into hundreds of shadows. The distant thunder of crab carriers and grenades exploding and particle fire reverberating continued as the stench of our burning airjeep wafted up, across the roof.

"Where's Jing?" I asked.

"Right here," she said, shifting around the conduits and carrying Breckinridge's bloody body.

Halitov took Breckinridge into his arms, then regarded us, the skin protecting his face turning transparent to reveal tears streaming down his cheeks. "Mother*fuckers*." He fought for breath and bared his teeth. Tears stained my own cheeks, and when I glanced to Jing, she, too, was crying. Paul managed to hold back, but he was clearly on the brink.

"She was a bitch," Jing said. "A real bitch."

"Yeah," Paul agreed.

Jing closed her eyes. "Let's get the fuck out of here."

We all found the bond and leapt from rooftop to rooftop, occasionally drawing fire but darting so quickly from it that the Marines below saw only vague flashes of light.

A massive limb grew just over the roof of one building, and we bounded onto it, traveling quickly across the smooth, wide wood and onto a rope bridge similar to the one back at Orokean. As we hustled across the wooden planks, perhaps thirty or fifty streams of particle fire blasted from the darkness below and tore through the bridge. Five minutes prior we had opted to conserve our energy and release ourselves from the bond. We'd tap into it only as a last resort. The time had come much too quickly.

"Scott! Move it!" cried Paul as he reached the end of the bridge and whirled back.

I was bringing up the rear, shot a look over my shoulder, and saw the planks near the opposite end falling away. Halitov and Jing reached the edge, and I envisioned myself there, hoping the bond would comply. Nothing. I put my boot down, even as the plank dropped away. I reached for the rope railing, but it whipped too quickly away, and the darkness rushed up and morphed into the gray plain of the leaf bed below. I had already fallen about fifty meters, and if I couldn't slow myself, I'd rebound until my skin failed and my bones shattered. I swore at the bond, cursed my conditioning, and damned to hell my desire to become a soldier. I was a heartbeat away from smashing into the surface when I jerked in midair, froze, craned my neck.

Across from me stood an Alliance Marine, a sergeant brandishing a CZX Forty, its thick barrel emitting the wave that had captured me. I struggled to break free, but without the bond, I felt as though I were pushing against a bubble that yielded to my touch but would not pop. The sergeant thumbed a switch. I banged onto the ground, got on my hands and knees, and slowly raised my head.

"Don't move!" the sergeant boomed, as seven or eight of his troops surrounded me, the muzzles of their particle rifles held just above my combat skin, near my back and ribs. I doubted I could break free in time. One of their beads would weaken my skin and finish me.

"Scott," Paul called on my private channel. "Give me your eyes."

"You got them," I whispered, then quietly allowed him access to my HUV.

"Okay," he said. "Just stay there."

"Don't waste your time. Go meet your father," I said.

"On your feet!" ordered the sergeant. "Now!"

I slowly raised my hands, sat back on my haunches, and was about to stand when three shimmering phantoms dropped behind the circle of Marines.

A few grunts must have turned their heads, and in that second, Jing, Halitov, and Paul were on them, ripping away their rifles and pounding them to the ground. Two, maybe three other Marines opened fire on me, and I scrambled forward, even as they swung their beads around, toward the new attackers. I rolled, and there was the sergeant, about to hit the entire group with the CZX. I darted up, yanking free my Ka-Bar and charging toward him. His eyes bugged as

I dropkicked him down, then recovered, forced away the muzzle of a particle pistol he had drawn, and tingled with the bond as my blade penetrated his combat skin. He emitted a horrible gasp as I opened up his heart.

By the time I finished, the others had taken out the Marines, and the howl of turbines echoed overhead.

"Copy that," said Paul, in contact with his father. "You're right on top of us."

The ATC dropped in a vertical descent, weaving dangerously through clawlike clusters of tree limbs until it hovered just a meter off the ground. The rear hatch folded open, and the colonel waved us inside.

"Where's Jing?" I asked.

"She's up top, getting Kristi," answered Halitov.

I nodded and climbed wearily into the hold. I never thought a jumpseat could feel so good. The ATC rumbled up, toward the limb where Jing now stood, holding Breckinridge's body. The ship pivoted, lining up with the limb, and Jing carefully carried Breckinridge inside.

The colonel gazed soberly at Breckinridge, put a hand on her cheek, then closed his eyes. "Goddamn it."

"Goddamn it is right," yelled Halitov. "How the fuck could you let this happen? This entire planet is going to fall to the alliances. That part of your plan?"

"Shut up," Paul said. "You're way out of line. And it's not his fault."

"Oh, yeah?" Halitov asked. "Oh, yeah?"

I gave Halitov the look I used when I wanted him to be quiet. He knew that look, widened his eyes even more and, thankfully, said no more.

Surprisingly, the colonel said nothing in his own defense and returned to his jumpseat beside Ms. Brooks's. For a moment, my gaze met hers. "I'm sorry," she mouthed.

"What?" I mouthed back.

She just looked away.

Was she sorry for everything? For something in particular? I alone had made the choice to join the Wardens. She didn't need to apologize for anything.

Or so I had thought.

"Colonel, we're within transmission range," reported the pilot.

"Very well." The colonel leveled his gaze on me and Halitov. "Gentlemen, it's best you hear this from me. Intel indicates that Alliance Marines have penetrated the conditioning facility. We can no longer hold that position."

"So when the time is right, we come back. And we take it," said Halitov.

"Negative. We can't allow the alliances to use that facility. If they condition more soldiers and get them out on the front lines, we won't stand a chance."

"What are you saying, sir?" I asked.

"I think you know what I'm saying. And I think you know we've taken precautions against something like this ever happening."

"You're going to blow it up," I said, losing my breath.

"Ms. Brooks?" The colonel regarded her forcefully.

She lifted her tablet, touched a button.

"You fuck!" Halitov screamed. "You can't do this!" He shoved up his safety bars and went for the colonel, then he changed his mind and lunged for Ms. Brooks.

He ripped the tablet from her grasp and smashed it across her safety bars.

"It's already done," she yelled. "It's already done!"

I pried up my own bars, stood, went to the rectangular porthole, where below, a tremendous white light, as a brilliant as a sun, swelled violently.

"Tawting out," the pilot reported. "In three, two, one . . ."

17 **⊙** **The Colonial Wardens** had destroyed AQ Tower and the *Eri Flower* to prevent them from falling into enemy hands. Likewise, the colonel had chosen to destroy the second conditioning facility, and his decision would later be considered by military historians as a brilliant tactical maneuver, one that had saved many more lives than it had cost.

At the time, though, Halitov and I were livid, and understandably so, since our biological clocks were still misfiring without any hope of repair. Ms. Brooks's continued apologies and reassurances that Warden researchers were doing everything they could to address our accelerated aging hardly comforted us.

Instead of meeting up with *Vanguard One*, the colonel had our ATC pilot tawt us all the way back to Rexi-Calhoon, where Ms. Brooks, along with the joint chiefs, was going to make an impassioned plea to congress. She hoped that the senators would endorse the Seventeen System Guard Corps's reorganization under Colonial Warden leadership. If they didn't, the Wardens would take over the Corps anyway. In the meantime, Halitov, Jing, and I were taken to Rexicity Strikebase for debriefing, shown our bunkrooms, and told to report to the Lieutenant Colonel Diablo's office at thirty-one hundred local time. After we finished changing into fresh utilities, Colonel Beauregard and Paul arrived and escorted us to the chapel for Kristi Breckinridge's memorial service. Her remains would be jettisoned into space, as per her will's instructions. Halitov stood there bitterly, as the colonel, in a very practiced tone, discussed Breckinridge's unwavering commitment to the Wardens. I tried numbing myself to the whole affair, but all I could think about was that moment when Halitov had been holding her in his arms.

When we returned to our quarters, Halitov said, "You know, back on Exeter, I got the feeling from Paul that he wasn't buying what his daddy's selling. But did you see him at that service? He's bought into this so much he's already on credit. Then again, he's reconditioned. He ain't fucked—like us. Goddamn it, look at me." He went to the dressing mirror and stared long and hard at his graying hair and wrinkled forehead. "Jesus, God . . ."

I didn't look much better, but deep down, I welcomed the aging, welcomed the opportunity to retire before the military's absurdity drove me completely insane. And maybe I wanted to punish myself for the mistakes I had made and put an end to the guilt that turned my stomach. I think for a while there, I didn't want to live, so the aging didn't bother me all that much.

Jing sauntered up to Halitov and gave him the once-over. "You still look okay."

"You're not making me feel better," he growled.

She sighed. "Sorry."

I plopped down on the bunk, eyed the sparse quarters with more than a little disdain, then faced Jing. "What about me? How do I look?"

"You don't want me to answer that."

"That bad?"

She glanced away. "I didn't say that."

Halitov moved off from the mirror. "Hey, you guys, I got an idea."

"Every few years that happens to him," I told Jing, deadpan.

She almost smiled. "Really?"

Halitov crouched down opposite me. "Listen up. The Wardens . . . they need us more than we need them. And now they can't even recondition us. If we're going to die soon, then I want a hell of a lot more than what they're payin'."

"What do you want?" Jing asked.

"First thing is intel about my sister. Then I want a ton of money to be deposited into her accounts. If I ain't ever going to have kids, maybe she will. I want her kids to be set for life. Then, if I'm still alive, I want a nice place, waterfront. I want a lifetime supply of alcohol, and I want women. If the Wardens can't supply, then I go work for the highest bidder. I think it's high time we recognize our value and cash in on it. Look what happened to Kristi. They used her, and she died out there . . . like an animal."

"I already told Scott that I'm paid pretty well," said Jing. "Though I will take the booze. You can keep the women."

"What if the alliances would pay more? Does it really matter whom you work for?" Halitov asked. "Does it really?"

She sniggered, but only a little. "Guess not."

Halitov eyed me strangely. "No argument? You okay with screwing over the Wardens?"

"So what're you going to do? Give the alliances a call? Tell 'em you're available if the price is right?" I asked.

"Basically, yeah . . ."

I returned my deepest frown. "What happened to loyalty?"

"Nothing. I'm loyal to you, me, and maybe her," he said, tipping his head at Jing.

"Oh, thanks," she said sarcastically.

"I'm not loyal to any government or any organization," Halitov said. "We've already seen what that'll get us."

"So you think we oughta march into the lieutenant colonel's office and let him have it?" I asked.

He nodded. "Are you with me?"

I glanced to Jing, who half shrugged, then I faced Halitov. "No."

He snorted. Loudly. "What the hell's the matter with you?"

"The Wardens still have things I want: the truth about my brother and a chance to get back to Exeter. I'm not going to jeopardize them by making demands for money and whores—"

"Scott—"

"But that doesn't mean you can't go in there and do that. If you want to go off and fight for the alliances because you can cut a better deal with them, then do it. Don't let us stop you."

"You know I won't leave without you."

I stood, took a deep breath. "And all of this assuming they'll let you break the contract you signed when you were a cadet. That'll never happen. Come on. Forget about this. Let's get something to eat."

He boiled a moment more, then, resignedly, dragged himself toward the door. "I'll tell you something: if they don't have spaghetti and meatballs in that mess, I'm definitely joining the alliances."

Jing flicked a puzzled look my way. "Trust me," I told her. "It's not worth explaining."

After listening to Halitov bitch about how the spaghetti was undercooked, we killed some time by going up top and having an airjeep driver give us a grand tour of the base, which, from the air, appeared quite unremarkable—just a series of tarmacs with subterranean launch points surrounded by rather stubby-looking towers. Most of the base lay nearly a kilometer underground, and, not unlike the ancient aircraft carriers that sailed Earth's seas, the base was designed to service atmoattack jets within the caves, then send them up, through the tunnels, to rocket away and attack. We got a firsthand demonstration of that capability as, without warning, dozens of squadrons jetted up through the gaping dark orifices, fleeing like bats from a score of caves.

"What's going on?" Jing asked the driver, who had skinned up and was in contact with the base.

"Western Alliance fleet just tawted into the system," the young man said. "They got Aire-Wu. Guess we're next. And the lieutenant colonel wants you back."

My gaze locked on the skies, on all those fighters, until the driver dived toward the airjeep access tunnel that would return us to the billet and administrative offices.

We reached the drop-off gate and nervously

hopped out. Then, with alarms booming throughout the corridors, we jogged down to the lieutenant colonel's office, where we found him at his desk, skinned up and scanning multiple databars in his HUV.

"Sir, Major Scott St. Andrew reporting as ordered, sir!" I said, snapping to.

Halitov and Jing repeated the same, coming to attention alongside me.

Lieutenant Colonel Diablo, a dusky-skinned man with a thin mustache and narrow, dark eyes, saluted sharply, then came around his desk. "At ease."

"Sir, we're under attack, sir?" I asked.

"Not yet. Looks like a standoff so far." He thumbed the corner of a tablet on his desk, and a holo shimmered before us.

Seven Alliance capital ships and their battle groups sailed silently through space at a range 1.7 million kilometers. Squaring off with them was a joint fleet of Colonial Warden and Seventeen System Guard Corps ships, eleven in all, with the planet shining like a tiny piece of granite behind them.

Diablo switched off the holo. "If the attack does begin in earnest, and crab carriers do get through, we'll need everyone we have down here."

"Understood," I said.

"Sir, what about Captain Beauregard?" Jing asked.

"Ironically enough, he just tawted out with his father aboard *Vanguard One*. They're leading a strike team back to Exeter. I'm hoping I can get them back."

Halitov and I exchanged a look of disgust, then I said, "Sir, I respectfully request that we be reassigned to the colonel's unit, sir."

"Major, are you kidding? That fleet is poised to attack. You're not going anywhere. I'm giving you Fifth Battalion, with Halitov here as your XO. Lieutenant Jing? You'll be promoted to captain and assigned to Saturn Company."

Halitov stepped forward. "I'm afraid that's not satisfactory, sir."

"Excuse me?"

"Sir, this sounds like we're getting a raw deal, sir."

"A raw deal? You people are members of the Colonial Wardens. We assign. You go. Hell, at least you're all in the same battalion, thanks to your friend, Ms. Brooks."

Halitov's cheeks flushed. "With all due respect, sir, *fuck that!*"

I turned, grabbed my friend by the throat. "What're you doing?"

"You know, I would expect this kind of insubordination from raw recruits, but to find it in conditioned officers . . ."

"Sir, he didn't mean it, sir," I said. "We've just been through a lot."

Diablo considered that, then finally nodded. "Given the loss of Captain Breckinridge, I'll overlook that remark Mr. Halitov, but I should remind you that I have a very low tolerance level. Understood?"

I increased my grip on Halitov's throat. "Yes, sir," he gasped.

"We're a special operations group, and we like to believe we've recruited only the best. I'll expect nothing less from all of you."

"Yes, sir," Jing and I answered in unison.

"Yes, sir," Halitov muttered.

"Now then, I'll upload battalion data to your

tablets. You'd best get oriented—now. Although we outnumber them, I have a feeling Alliance Marines will make planetfall."

I lifted my chin. "Sir, one more thing. The colonel and Ms. Brooks said I'd be able to see my brother. Ms. Brooks was going to set up a meeting, but she never said anything before she left."

The lieutenant colonel stiffened. "I'm afraid I don't know anything about that."

"They fucked us over," Halitov gritted out.

"What was that, Captain?" asked Diablo.

"Sir, nothing, sir. Absolutely *nothing*."

"Very well. Now just remember we're on Gamma Alert. Total lockdown. Dismissed."

We saluted, left, and in the corridor outside, I leaned back against the wall and closed my eyes.

"Satisfied?" asked Halitov, hollering above the still-wailing alarms. "Now we really know what loyalty is, huh? No reconditioning. No meeting with your brother. And now we're stuck here. Our transfer's official."

"We don't have to accept this," said Jing.

"What? Go AWOL?" Halitov asked, beginning to chuckle.

"Yeah, then we do what you said. Maybe we contact the alliances and make them an offer."

"I'm ready to do that right now!"

"Both of you shut up," I said, wrenching myself from the wall. "We're not going AWOL, and we're not cutting any deals with the alliances. This is Rexi-Calhoon, the capital world of our new government. We will defend it."

"Scott, you're letting them walk all over you," Jing

said, grabbing my shoulders. "It's not right. We're soldiers. We don't lie down. We fight."

"That's right. So we stay here. And we fight. If my brother's alive, I'm going to find him myself. I still believe in something, and that's being a soldier. I have to believe."

"Oh, yeah? Believe in this: you can still be a good soldier without letting the machine take advantage of you." She got directly in my face. "Listen to me, Scott. You're going to contact Ms. Brooks, and you're going to make your demands."

"Why do you care?"

"I don't know. Let's go."

She actually dragged me by the hand, all the way down the hall, toward one of the communications hubs.

Once we reached a hub, an MP outside cleared us for entrance. Jing asked one of about twelve comm officers seated at stations to track down Ms. Brooks, who we assumed was inside the capitol building. While we waited, I watched a few of the video feeds, two of them piped in from civilian news stations. Though I expected citywide panic, citizens moved swiftly but orderly through the subways, toward evacuation zones. Rexicity, it seemed, had been preparing for attack since the very beginning of the war.

We learned from the comm officer that the capitol had, indeed, been evacuated, and that Ms. Brooks had been moved to a Guard Corps operations bunker not found on any map. Finally, the officer patched in to her tablet, and her face appeared on his screen.

"Ms. Brooks?" I began. "Sorry to bother you at a time like this."

"Let me talk to her," Halitov said, shoving me out of the way. "Ma'am, we have a problem."

"What is it, Captain?"

"I joined the Wardens because you promised me I would be reconditioned."

"We haven't broken our promise. You will be."

"How?"

"Trust us."

"That's not good enough."

"You need to be patient," she said slowly.

I elbowed my way past Halitov. "Ma'am. What about my brother?"

Her eyes widened. "The lieutenant colonel gave you Fifth Battalion, didn't he?"

"Yes, ma'am."

"Then if I were you, I'd go meet the man who's commanding Turbo Company. He might look familiar."

My jaw fell open. "He's here?"

"I had him transferred."

I bolted out of there, running like a madman down the hall. I grabbed MPs, privates, even another major to ask where I could find Fifth Battalion's billets. Eventually, I located the door marked Turbo Company and burst into the administrative offices.

A second lieutenant sprang up from her desk. "Sir!" She saluted me and stood, visibly trembling.

"Where's the company commander?" I demanded.

"Sir, he's with the company, sir. They're on the confidence course, sublevel eight."

"Thank you."

"Sir, we've been expecting you. Would you like to—"

I was out the door before she finished.

* * *

The confidence course, an urban combat environment replete with skyscrapers and small business lining a half dozen city blocks, reminded me of similar courses I'd trained on, some of them computer-generated but none of them as real or as elaborate. A squad corporal at the nearest rooftop monitoring post agreed to contact the commander, whose name, she said, was Captain Taris Markland. I shuddered at the name, suddenly thinking that Ms. Brooks had lied to me, that this Taris Markland was not my brother operating with a new identity.

But when an airjeep came whirring up, and the captain hopped out, onto the roof, my knees buckled.

I was about to shout my brother's real name, then thought better of it. "Captain!"

When his gaze met mine, his jaw went slack, and he stumbled toward me. "Scott?"

Jarrett's hair looked longer, his face a bit more rugged than I remembered. His dark gray utilities fit him well, and the way he carried himself . . . I couldn't believe it. One look at him, and you knew who was in charge. He was a captain. A commander. Nothing about him suggested otherwise.

We embraced right there, on top of that roof, in that faux city far below the surface. It seemed fitting for a couple of mining brothers to reunite in a place like that.

I pulled back and just stared at him. "You're a ghost."

"You too."

"And you're a captain."

"You're a major," he countered, glancing at my major's angle. "Guess I owe you a salute." He took a step back, raised his hand.

I gripped his wrist. "You didn't want this."

He slid out of my grip. "They never gave me a choice. They told me you were dead."

I nodded. "We both were." I wiped off a tear and grinned awkwardly. "You haven't changed."

"You're wrong. And look at you . . ." His gaze found my eyes, my hair.

"It's my conditioning."

"We all had that problem. They fixed ours. Why didn't they fix yours?"

I shrugged. "They wanted to. But it's just . . . I don't know . . . bad timing, I guess. There was a second facility on Aire-Wu. It's gone now."

"What about Exeter?"

"That facility is tommyed."

"So what's going to happen?"

"I don't know."

He bit his lip, began losing his breath.

"Hey, we're back together. Brothers in arms. That's all that matters."

"Yeah. I just can't believe I'm standing here, talking to you. I can't believe it."

"I wish we could talk to Dad," I said. "He thinks you're dead. He must think I'm dead by now, too."

"I thought Dad was—"

"No, they said he's on Kennedy-Centauri. They said he's okay."

"Do we believe them?"

"I don't know. Maybe. Ms. Brooks came through

this time, but they'll all lie to save their asses. Being a
soldier . . . it's nothing like I'd thought it'd be. Nothing at all."

He squeezed my shoulder. "You'd better not be
that way, because let me tell you something—I made
it all the way to captain because of you."

"Because of me?"

"I let myself buy into this honor crap. And you
know what? I actually believe it now. I actually think
that what the colos are doing is right. I want to fight
for 'em."

"But now the Wardens are trying to take over the
Seventeen. What do you think of that?"

"I think it's okay. The Seventeen is too disorganized. We're bringing order—and we're still fighting
for the same side. Why are you giving me that look?"

"I don't know what to say."

"Take the blame. You had to go and die. Make me
feel guilty, make me realize that I had to be a good soldier because that's what you would've wanted."

I shook my head. "Are you really my brother?"

"Yeah, and now that you're alive, I guess I can give
this all up, go AWOL like I wanted to in the first place,
head back home, maybe get a job in the mines, if the
alliances don't control them, right?"

"I guess you are my brother," I said. "They didn't
brainwipe you."

"They threatened us with that a few times, but I
just kept thinking that if you were dead and Dad was
dead, somebody had to remember you guys, and it
had to be me."

"So now I can't call you Jarrett anymore . . ."

"No. But I will always be your brother."

I gave him an exaggerated sigh. "Unfortunately."

My brother made a face, then tossed a look back to his airjeep. "Well, Scott. There's a fleet up there breathing down our necks. And we're supposed to be getting some new people, including a new battalion commander, so I have to get my ass and my new company's asses in gear before the CO arrives. You know, we have to put on a little show for him before he gives the usual pep talk. Then I bet we'll be topside, waiting for those crab carriers to show, if they show. What about you?"

"Yeah, I'm real busy, too."

"But you're not leaving now. You can't leave."

"No. I'm sure I'll see you again," I said.

He gave me sharp hug. "God, this is like a dream. I don't know how many times I've told people my kid brother's dead. And here you are."

"You too."

My brother strode off toward his airjeep. I could not have been more proud, could not have savored the moment any more than I had, though I looked forward to another moment when he learned that his kid brother wasn't just alive but was, in fact, his CO.

I found Halitov and Jing waiting for me outside Turbo Company's door, and to my surprise, they both seemed rather agreeable.

"What?" I asked.

Halitov shrugged. "Was it him?"

"Yeah, he's fine."

"Aren't you mad?" he asked. "They lied to you."

"I don't care anymore. I'm just glad he's okay."

"I'll have to go say hi," Halitov said. "Like I said, I've always liked him."

"You had a funny way of showing it."

"Yeah, well, that was then."

"So, what did Ms. Brooks say?"

"Whatever we want . . . she'll work it out," Jing said. "More money, nice homes . . . whatever."

Halitov sighed. "Whether she comes through, well, all we can do is wait and see. I still don't trust her, but what're we going to do?"

I steeled my gaze on him, on both of them. "Our duty."

"You're amazing," Jing said, more in disbelief than awe.

"No. I just won't let any of this make me forget who I am." They nodded slowly. "All right. What're we doing standing around? We have a lot of work to do. I want a meeting with company commanders and squad sergeants ASAP. And I want the entire battalion assembled and ready to move in twenty minutes."

"Yes, sir," Halitov said. "I'm on it."

"I'll go meet my people," said Jing.

They started off. "Oh, by the way," I added, drawing their gazes. "Thank you."

Jing brightened. "You're welcome."

"Yeah, you'd better say thank you," said Halitov. "You put me through a whole lot of bullshit. And I'm blaming it all on you." He grinned, then marched off.

My meeting with the company commanders and sergeants was all business, save for the first five minutes, when Jarrett AKA Taris, immediately raised his hand, then stood among the group crammed into the briefing room. "Sir, you're our new battalion commander, sir?"

"That's correct, Captain," I said, struggling to contain my grin. "You sound as though you don't believe that."

"Sir, I believe it, sir."

"Any other questions, Captain?"

Jarrett smiled, shook his head. "No, sir." As he sat, I caught him chuckling to himself. The squad sergeant next to him, an attractive brunette whom I would later learn was his lover, whispered something to him, but he just waved her off.

I gave my new people updates on the Alliance fleet's position, estimates of the invasion force aboard their ships, then relayed our plan of defense, as dictated to me by Lieutenant Colonel Diablo. We would be taken over to Columbia Colony, some nineteen thousand kilometers away. There, we would establish a perimeter around LockMar Randall, an Exxo-Tally defense contractor who designed navigation and targeting systems for extrasolar craft. It was imperative that the site, which encompassed nearly ten kilometers of hangars, test facilities, and tarmacs, neither be occupied nor damaged by alliance forces. Though it was no glamour or hero mission, there were still civilian engineers working within the plant whose efforts were so vital to the war that they were not being evacuated. Most of my commanders had a hard time accepting that, and I simply read to them my own briefing: "Your mission is to secure the facility and ensure that production does not cease under any circumstances." I further added that those civvies inside knew the risks and had all signed contracts regarding their responsibilities.

"But we should expect some fallout," Halitov added. "You couldn't pay me enough to stay there."

That drew a few chuckles.

I dismissed the group, and they went off to assemble their companies in sub hangar twenty-one, from where we would board ATCs bound for Columbia.

Jing, however, hung around, waiting for me. "Ready for the big speech?"

"I think you'll be surprised."

"Scott. I mean, Major—"

"Scott will do, Lieutenant. I mean, Katya."

She lowered her head, trying in vain to hide her smile. "I just wanted to . . . you know, talk."

"I wish we had more time."

"I know. I guess I don't want you to feel uncomfortable around me."

"That might be difficult."

"Really?"

"Yeah, because most of the time you're either making me realize what an idiot I am or you're kicking my ass."

"Sorry."

"No, it's okay. It's what I need."

She narrowed her gaze on me. "What else do you need?"

I smiled. "Hey, I, uh, I need you close."

"So I can save your ass."

"I'll take all the help I can get. Ready?"

"For the big speech? I can't wait."

* * *

Every member of Fifth Battalion stared up at me as I crossed onto a dais and glanced out across the hundreds of troops. I didn't bother to introduce myself; I felt certain the rumors of my taking command had already reached them all. "Who are you?" I boomed.

"Colonial Wardens, sir!"

The fervor and volume of their voices shocked the hell out of me. With a chill, I went on. "What do you do?"

"We fight! We win!"

"Very well, then. Speech over! Time to fight. Time to win. On the ready line! Move! Move! Move!"

Stunned by my brevity, the long lines of soldiers broke apart and scrambled for their boarding lines.

Halitov stepped over to me. "Your best speech yet," he said with a wink. "Loved it."

Later on I would regret not having said more to those soldiers. I guess I wanted to be regarded as a CO who was all business and unconcerned with pomp and circumstance, a characteristic I knew they would like. I had assumed that they were seasoned specialists, former guardsmen who had been handpicked by the Wardens because of their extraordinary capabilities. I had assumed that they had all heard more than their share of pep talks and had become, like me, experts at falling asleep with their eyes open. I had been right. But even those people, the best of the best, could not have anticipated what would happen once we reached Columbia Colony. No one saw that coming. And I wish I would've said something to them, even just a thank-you, or, perhaps, a more powerful rallying cry, something that would have allowed them to deal with the situation better, something that would've reminded them that I understood, really understood, that moment when you are certain you are going to die.

"How many did you lose at Columbia?" came a familiar voice from the front row of graduating cadets.

I froze, looked at the beautiful young woman—Joanna St. Andrew, my daughter—then stared off at the mesas beyond the academy grounds.

"How many?" she repeated.

"Nearly all of them."

"But not your XO. Not Halitov."

"That's right. I forgave him for that."

I had never told her the story. She frowned.

"Ladies and gentlemen, I'm afraid that's all the time I have. As you embark on your new careers, ask yourselves this—am I going to let the failures ruin me? Or am I going to accept and learn from them? Am I going to become stronger because of them? Finally, do I know, really know, where my loyalty should lie?" I sighed. "Now, I have to get the hell out of here. I have a war to prevent. Good luck to you all."

As I moved away from the lectern, the thunder of their applause sent a chill up my spine. I was reminded that if I failed in my new mission, my daughter and the rest would know pain, suffering, and death the way I knew them. I prayed for their naïveté. I prayed for peace.

We hope you've enjoyed this Eos book. As part of our mission to give readers the best science fiction and fantasy being written today, the following pages contain a glimpse into the fascinating worlds of a select group of Eos authors.

Join us as acclaimed sf great C.J. Cherryh unveils a brand new universe where two interstellar empires, scarred by nanotechnology, are poised for battle on a distant desert planet. As Ben Weaver takes us on an action-packed adventure into an intergalactic civil war, and James Alan Gardner visits the most dangerous and mysterious planet in the Expendable universe—Earth itself. As Anne McCaffrey and Elizabeth Ann Scarborough reveal the latest adventure of Acorna, the beloved unicorn girl, and her fight to save her homeworld. And as Stephen R. Lawhead concludes the sweeping historical saga of faith, magic, and mystery—Celtic Crusades.

FALL 2002 AT EOS.
OUT OF THIS WORLD.

HAMMERFALL

C.J. Cherryh

August 2002

Imagine first a web of stars. Imagine it spread wide and wider. Ships shuttle across it. Information flows.

A star lies at the heart of this web, its center, heart, and mind.

This is the Commonwealth.

Imagine then a single strand of stars in a vast darkness, a beckoning pathway away from the web, a path down which ships can travel.

Beyond lies a treasure, a small lake of G5 suns, a near circle of perfect stars all in reach of one another.

This way, that strand says. After so hard a voyage, reward. Wealth. Resources.

But a whisper comes back down that thread of stars, a ghost of a whisper, an illusion of a whisper.

The web of stars has heard the like before. Others are out there, very far, very faint, irrelevant to our affairs.

Should we have listened?
—The Book of the Landing.

Distance deceived the eye in the Lakht, that wide, red land of the First Descended, where legend said the ships had come down.

At high noon, with the sun reflecting off the plateau, the chimera of a city floated in the haze, appearing as a line of light just below the red, sawtoothed ridge of the Qarain, that upthrust that divided the Lakht from the Anlakht, the true land of death.

The city was both mirage and truth; it appeared always a day before its true self. Marak knew it, walking, walking endlessly beside the beshti, the beasts on which their guards rode.

The long-legged beasts were not deceived. They moved no faster. The guards likewise made no haste.

"The holy city," some of the damned shouted, some in relief, some in fear, knowing it was both the end of their torment and the end of their lives. "Oburan and the Ila's court!"

"Walk faster, walk faster," the guards taunted them lazily, sitting supreme over the column. The lank, curve-necked beasts that carried them plodded at an unchangeable rate. They were patient creatures, splay-footed, towering above most predators of the Lakht, enduring the long trek between wells with scant food and no water. A long, long line of them stretched behind, bringing the tents, the other appurtenances of their journey.

"Oburan!" the fools still cried. "The tower, the tower!"

"Run to it! Run!" the junior guards encouraged their prisoners. "You'll be there before the night, drinking and eating before us."

It was a lie, and some knew better, and warned the rest. The wife of a down-country farmer, walking among them, set up a wail when the word went out that the vision was only the shadow of a city, and that an end was a day and more away.

"It can't be!" she cried. "It's there! I see it! Don't the rest of you see it?"

But the rest had given up both hope and fear of an end to this journey, and walked in the rising sun at the same pace as they had walked all this journey.

Marak was different than the rest. He bore across his heart the tattoo of the abjori, the fighters from rocks and hills. His garments, the long shirt, the trousers, the aifad wrapped about his head against the hellish glare, were all the dye and the weave of Kais Tain, of his own mother's hand. Those patterns alone would have damned him in the days of the war. The tattoos on the backs of his fingers, six, were the number of the Ila's guards he had personally sent down to the shadows. The Ila's men knew it, and watched with special care for any look of rebellion. He had a reputation in the lowlands and on the Lakht itself, a fighter as elusive as the mirage and as fast-moving as the sunrise wind.

He had ridden with his father to this very plain, and for three years had seen the walls of the holy city as a prize for the taking. He and his father had laid their grandiose plans to end the Ila's reign: they had fought. They had had their victories.

Now he stumbled in the ruin of boots made for riding.

His life was thirty summers on this earth and not

likely to be longer. His own father had delivered him up to the Ila's men.

The others all had their stories. The caravan was full of the cursed, the doomed, the rejected. Villages had tolerated them as long as they dared. In Kais Tain long before this, Tain had issued a pogrom to cleanse his province of the mad, ten years ago; but the god laughed at him. Now his own son and heir proved tainted. Tain of Kais Tain had successfully rebelled against the Ila and the Lakht, undefeated for ten years, and had all the west under his hand. But his own son had a secret, and betrayed himself in increasing silences, in looks of abstraction, in crying out in his sleep. He had been mad all along. His father had begun to suspect, perhaps, years ago, and denied it; but lately, after their return from the war, the voices had grown too persistent, too consuming to keep the secret any longer. His father had found him out.

And when shortly afterward his father heard the Ila's men were looking for the mad, his father had sent to the Ila's men . . . had given him up, his defiance of the Ila's rule broken by the truth.

REBELS IN ARMS

Ben Weaver

September 2002

From my seat on the dais, I looked over the crowd of
cadets about to graduate from South Point Academy.
Could they really listen to a middle-aged soldier like
me drone on about the challenges of being an officer?
After all, the commandant, a war vet himself, was already at the lectern and boring them to death with
that speech. In fact, when the commandant had asked
me to speak, I had panicked because I knew those
kids needed something more than elevated diction
and fancy turns of phrase. But what?

The commandant glanced over his shoulder and
nodded at me. "And now ladies and gentlemen, at
this time I'd like to introduce a man whose Special
Ops Tactical Manual is required reading here at the
academy, a man whose treatise on Racinian conditioning transformed that entire program. Ladies and
gentlemen, I give you Colonel Scott St. Andrew, Chief
of the Alliance Security Council."

Applause I had expected, but a standing ovation?
Or maybe those cadets were just overjoyed that the
commandant was leaving the podium. I dragged myself up, wincing over all the metal surgeons had

jammed into me after the nanotech regeneration had failed. Unless you were really looking for it, you wouldn't notice my limp. I tugged at the hems of my dress tunic, raised my shoulders, and took a deep breath before starting forward. The kids continued with their applause, their eyes wide and brimming with naïveté.

"Thank you. Please . . ." I gestured for them to sit, then waited for the rumble to subside. "First, let me extend my gratitude to the commandant for allowing me to be here today." I tipped my head toward the man, who winked. "As all of you know, we are living in some very turbulent times. The treaties we signed at the end of the war are now being violated. Rumors of yet another civil war pervade. But let me assure you that we at the security council are doing everything we can to resolve these conflicts. Now then. I didn't come here to talk about current events. I came here to tell you what you want to hear—a war story— not because it's entertaining, but because it's something you *need* to hear . . ."

I lay in my quarters aboard the *SSGC Auspex*, cushioned tightly in my gelrack and in the middle of a disturbing dream. My name wasn't Scott St. Andrew; I wasn't an eighteen-year-old captain and company commander in the Seventeen System Guard Corps, in charge of one-hundred and sixty-two lives; and my cheek no longer bore the cross-shaped birthmark that revealed I had a genetic defect and came from poor colonial stock.

In the dream I was a real Terran, born in New York, and about to download my entire college education through a cerebro. I sat in a classroom with about fifty other privileged young people who would never need to join the military as a way to escape from their stratified society. I looked down at the c-shaped device sitting on the desk in front of me. I need only slide it onto my head and learn.

But I couldn't. I was afraid I might forget who I was, forget that my father, an overworked, underpaid company geologist had tried his best to raise me and my brother Jarrett, since my mother had left us when we were small. Jarrett and I had entered South Point Academy just when the war had begun, and Jarrett had died in an accident during a "conditioning process" developed by an ancient alien race we called the "Racinians." The conditioning, which involved the introduction into our brains of "mnemosyne"—a species of eidetic parasite found aboard Racinian spacecraft—enhanced our physical and mental capabilities *and* aged us at an accelerated rate.

No, I couldn't forget. I needed to remember what I had become, because I sensed even then that if just one person could learn something from my story, from my mistakes, then the universe might forgive me of my sins.

They were many.

TRAPPED

James Alan Gardner

October 2002

It was a creamy tube of light, glinting with colors like the Aurora Borealis. Green. Gold. Purple. As it shimmered in the darkness, I could see the stars behind: the tube was like glowing milky smoke. It stretched so high it disappeared into the blackness as if it soared beyond our planet's atmosphere—but that was just as terrifying as if the thing were simply a ghost. A ghost could only go, "Boo!" Mysteries from outer space could cause *real* trouble.

I couldn't help thinking of Opal's story. A Spark Lord. A Lucifer. An Explorer from the galaxy at large.

The upper body of the tube flapped and fluttered like a banner in a stiff wind, but the bottom seemed rooted in place. Though the trees blocked our view, I knew the spectral tube had attached itself to Death Hotel. I could imagine it like a phantom lamprey, mouth spread and locked onto the building's ugly dome; or perhaps the tube was a pipeline that fed ethereally into the sealed-up interior, and even as we watched, it was pumping down a horde of aliens. Or spirits. Or worse.

"Oh look," said Pelinor, pointing at the tube. "Isn't that pretty." Pause. "What is it?"

Nobody answered. The horses stopped one by one, either reined in by their riders or halting of their own accord as they saw the tube twinkling in the sky. The thing fluttered in silence—the whole world had hushed, as if even the horses were holding their breaths. Then, without a whisper, the ghostly tube snapped free of the mausoleum like a broken kite string, and in the blink of an eye it slithered up into the night.

Deep dark quiet. Then, beneath me, Ibn gave a snort that filled the cool air with horse steam. The other horses snorted too, perhaps trying to decide if they should worry or just shrug off what they'd seen. In front of me, Myoko cleared her throat . . . but before she could speak, an ear-shattering <BOOM> ripped the silence.

I had an instant to register that the noise came from the hotel: like a cannon being fired. Then there was no more time for thinking, as Ibn went wild with fear.

ACORNA'S SEARCH

Anne McCaffrey and
Elizabeth Ann Scarborough

December 2002

Acorna said, "I will take first watch."

"Watch?" Maati asked. "Watch *what*? This planet can't sustain sentient life. I thought we'd established that. Well, except for these jungly plants and that scuttling thing and—I guess I see your point."

"I will watch, also," Aari said. "It may be best to do so in pairs for now."

"I might as well watch with you also," Thariinye said, "because I cannot imagine that I will sleep a wink in this place." But he did, and almost immediately.

Acorna and Aari sat, relaxed, each with one knee drawn up to their chins, each with one leg dangling over the side of the largish rock on which they perched. They gazed toward the jungle growth slightly above them, instead of back in the direction from which they had flown. The leaves and fronds of the strange forest were not outlined black against the night, as they might have expected, but instead glowed in the darkness with a greenish iridescence. A small wind stirred the leaves. Otherwise all was silent.

Acorna almost expected to hear a birdcall, or the snuffle of some smaller creature in the woods around them. Neeva had told her once of the endearing furred creatures that lived in the forests of Vhiliinyar before the Khleevi came—but they were no longer here, and the jungle was nothing but mutated weeds and brush grown very tall. The creatures of old Vhiliinyar sang in lovely voices and delighted all who heard. Their beautiful forms entranced all who saw them. Acorna wondered—had *aagroni* Iirtye managed to save specimens of all those creatures, or even samples of their cells to clone them from later on? What a wrenching loss it must be to have known such creatures well, and to lose them, along with all of the other wonders this planet had held when it was beautiful and whole.

Absorbed in her thoughts, it took Acorna a moment to realize she was hearing a noise, a soft snuffling sound, from beside her. Trails of tears ran down Aari's face.

She took his hand. (Penny for your thoughts, or was I broadcasting, and you were responding to mine?)

He sniffed again and turned a chiseled manly countenance to her. (What is a penny?)

(A primitive coin used by one of the nations of humankind before it became so devaluated it was not worth the materials needed to create it.)

He gave a short laugh. (Ah, a coin worthy of my present thoughts, indeed. Which are that we would have a better chance of re-forming narhii-Vhiliinyar into a semblance of Vhiliinyar than we have to return Vhiliinyar to its former state, as the *aagroni* wishes.

Who would have thought even the Khleevi could so mutilate the landscape that its own people could not recognize it? I was wondering where the mountains were, where the lake was, and the waterfall. I see nothing here that resembles them.)

(And yet they are here. I sense the iron and granite of the mountain, and the plateau—the bones of that formation run beneath us and all through the area. Also the waters of the lake and cascade are here, though there are elements of sulfur and mercury and other contaminants in them. I do not think it will destroy our horns to purify that water. But there is something worrying about those plants . . .)

They heard something then: the thump of paws jumping down and a scattering of small stones beneath soft footpads, the movement of a dark plumed tail hovering at the edge of the plants. RK, Acorna realized, had to relieve himself and he wished to perform his duties unobserved, but he was not happy about the only available cover.

In a moment he disappeared from sight and the Linyaari couple concluded he had found what he was looking for.

Then an earsplitting yowl burst from the greenery several yards to the left of the campsite.

Acorna and Aari jumped to their feet, stumbling over the rocks in the dark. Acorna fell heavily and scraped the skin from her right arm and knee. Aari turned back to her, his horn lowered to help with the healing, but Acorna waved him on urgently.

(This will keep. See to RK. Help him!) she insisted above the cat's caterwauling as she climbed painfully to her feet. (That does not sound like a cat bellyache to me.) She brushed her wounded arm over her horn but the cat screamed before she could touch her leg. Her wound could wait. Something was very wrong with RK. She moved as fast as she could toward the noise. Sounds of thrashing and howling, snarling and more shrieks and screams rang through the night as she limped forward to see one of the tall plants whipping a furry tail back and forth in the air. Nothing remained evident of RK but his furious cries and his tail. A huge green bulbous protuberance on the plant concealed the rest of the cat.

Aari leapt for the lashing tail but it whipped out of his grasp.

They had no weapons handy, no implements or utensils that would be useful in destroying the plant. And RK's cries were growing weaker, strangled, more pitiful. They had to do something . . . now!

THE MYSTIC ROSE
Book 3 of the Celtic Crusades

Stephen R. Lawhead

December 2002

The younger man lowered himself to his seat, and Cait proceeded to the table, remaining behind de Bracineaux and out of his sight. She placed the tray on the table, and made to step away, her right hand reaching for the hilt of the slender dagger at her back.

As her fingers tightened on the braided grip, the Templar cast a hasty glance over his shoulder. She saw his lowered brow and the set of his jaw, and feared the worst.

Silently, she slipped the dagger from its sheath, ready to strike. But the light of recognition failed to illumine his eyes. "Well?" he demanded. "Get to your work, now. Light the lamps and leave us."

Cait hesitated, waiting for him to settle back in his chair. When she did not move, the Templar turned on her. "Do as I say, girl, and be quick about it!"

Startled, Cait stepped back a pace, almost losing her grip on the weapon.

"Peace, Renaud," said his companion. Reaching out, he took the Templar's sleeve and tugged him around. "Come, I have poured the wine." He raised his cup and took a long, deep draft.

De Bracineaux swung back to the table, picked up his cup and, tilting his head back, let the wine run down his gullet. *Now!* thought Cait, rising onto the balls of her feet. *Do it now!*

Her hand freed the knife and she moved forward. At that instant, without warning, the door burst open and a thick-set, bull-necked Templar strode into the room behind her. Cait whipped the dagger out of sight, and backed away.

"Ah, here is Gislebert now!" said d'Anjou loudly.

The Templar paused as he passed, regarding Cait with dull suspicion. She ducked her head humbly, and quickly retreated into the darkened room.

"Come, sergeant," called the fair-haired man, "raise a cup and give us the good news. Are we away to Jerusalem at last?"

"My lord, baron," said Gislebert, turning his attention to the others. "Good to see you, sir. You had a pleasant journey, I trust."

As the men began talking once more, Cait was forgotten—her chance ruined. She might cut one or even two men before they could react, but never three. And the sergeant was armed.

Still, she was close. The opportunity might never come again.

Reluctant to give up, she busied herself in the adjoining room, steeling herself for another attempt. Fetching some straw from the corner of the hearth, she stooped and lit it from the pile of embers. There was a lamp on the table, two candles in a double sconce on the wall by the bed, and a candletree in the corner. She lit the candles first, taking her time, hoping that Gislebert would leave.

She moved to the table and, as she touched the last of the straw to the lamp wick, became aware that someone was watching her from the doorway. Fearing she had been discovered at last, she took a deep breath, steadied herself and cast a furtive glance over her shoulder.

She did not see him at first. Her eyes went to the men who were still at the table on the balcony, cups in hand, their voices a murmur of intimate conversation. They were no longer heeding her. But, as she bent once more to the task at hand, she caught a movement in a darkened corner of the room and turned just as a man stepped from the shadows.

She stifled a gasp.

Dressed in the long white robe of a priest, he held up his hand, palm outward in an attitude of blessing—or to hold her in her place. Perhaps both, she thought. A man of youthful appearance, his hair and beard were black without a trace of gray and the curls clipped like the shorn pelt of a sheep. His eyes, though set deep beneath a dark and heavy brow, were bright and his glance was keen. He stepped forward into the doorway, placing himself between Cait and the men.

When he moved she felt a shudder in the air, as if a gust of wind had swept in through the open door; but the candles did not so much as quiver. At the same time, she smelled the fresh, clean scent of the heathered hills after a storm has passed.

"Do not be afraid," said the man, his voice calm and low. "I merely wish to speak to you."

Cait glanced nervously beyond him to where the

Templar and his companions sat at their wine.

"Blind guides," he said, indicating the men. "They have neither eyes nor ears to hear."

"Who are you?" As she asked the question, she glanced again at de Bracineaux and his companions; now laughing heartily, they appeared oblivious to both her and the stranger.

"Call me Brother Andrew," he said.

At the name, Cait felt her throat tighten. She gulped down a breath of air. "I know about you," she said, struggling to keep her voice steady. "My father told me."

"Your family has been in my service for a long time. That is why I have come—to ask if you will renew the vow of your father and grandfather."

"What vow is that?"

"I asked young Murdo to build me a kingdom where my sheep could safely graze . . ."

"Build it far, far away from the ambitions of small-souled men and their ceaseless striving," Cait said, repeating the words she had learned as a child on her grandfather's knee. "Make it a kingdom where the True Path can be followed in peace and the Holy Light can shine as a beacon flame in the night."

He smiled. "There, you see? You do know it."

"He did that. He built you a kingdom," she said bluntly, "and died an old man—waiting for you to come as you promised."

"Truly, his faith has been rewarded a thousand-fold," the White Priest told her. "But now it is your turn. In each generation the vow must be renewed. I ask you, sister, will you serve me?"